THE ETERNAL RETURN

A Wild Hunt Novel, Book 10

YASMINE GALENORN

D1362121

A Nightqueen Enterprises LLC Publication

Published by Yasmine Galenorn

PO Box 2037, Kirkland WA 98083-2037

THE ETERNAL RETURN

A Wild Hunt Novel

A Nightqueen Enterprises LLC Publication

Published in the United States of America

ACKNOWLEDGMENTS

Welcome back into the world of the Wild Hunt. We're at book ten, and this book wraps up the first story arc, before the second one begins. We're with Ember again, and I hope you're looking forward to her adventure in this episode. I love the world of the Wild Hunt, and am so grateful you do too. It's become a living, breathing entity in my thoughts and imagination.

Thanks to my usual crew: Samwise, my husband, Andria and Jennifer—without their help, I'd be swamped. To the women who have helped me find my way in indie, you're all great and thank you to everyone. To my wonderful cover artist, Ravven, for the beautiful work she's done.

Also, my love to my furbles, who keep me happy. My most reverent devotion to Mielikki, Tapio, Ukko, Rauni, and Brighid, my spiritual guardians and guides. My love and reverence to Herne, and Cernunnos, and to the Fae, who still rule the wild places of this world. And a nod to the Wild Hunt, which runs deep in my magick, as well as in my fiction.

If you wish to reach me, you can find me through my website at Galenorn.com and be sure to sign up for my newsletter to keep updated on all my latest releases! If you liked this book, I'd be grateful if you'd leave a review—it helps more than you can think.

Brightest Blessings,
~The Painted Panther~
~Yasmine Galenorn~

WELCOME TO THE ETERNAL RETURN

Sometimes, you have to exorcise ghosts from the past before you can move forward...

With the Tuathan Brotherhood taken care of, Ember and the Wild Hunt gear up for the coming darkness that threatens to plunge their lives into chaos. But first, they must take on the ancient liche who stole Talia's powers. Lazerous is living near Winter Hall Academy, located near Mount Rainier. Over the centuries, he's grown so strong that it seems futile to take him on. But with Lazerous stalking the students, stealing not only their magical powers but their lives, the Wild Hunt can't allow him to roam free. But before they can confront him, Talia attempts to take him on herself. Now, Ember and Herne must race against time before Lazerous finds her first.

Reading Order for the Wild Hunt Series (For Series Timeline, see Table of Contents).

- Book 1: The Silver Stag
- Book 2: Oak & Thorns

CHAPTER ONE

"*I*f you don't get your asses in gear and take care of my pixie problem, I'm going to spread the word to all of my friends that you're unreliable."

Macy Barnhart shifted in her chair and crossed her right leg over her left. Her legs were long and smooth, unmarred by any visible scars or stray hair. Willowy and tall, she was wearing a chiffon dress whose layers seemed to shift with every move. Her hair was perfectly smooth, the long blond strands gathered back into a loose chignon held in place by a cloisonné butterfly barrette, and her makeup was flawless.

In other words, she looked like a walking, talking mannequin. But Macy Barnhart had the personality of a viper.

I cleared my throat and glanced at Yutani. He was composed and congenial, but the light in his eyes told me he was suppressing his feelings. The IT specialist had little patience for whiners, and even less patience for members of the entitlement-set. And Macy Barnhart *obviously* felt she was entitled to star treatment. She was also Light Fae and had already tried to sideswipe me twice with poorly cloaked insults. I'd ignored them, but my temper was rapidly reaching overload, and I couldn't play nice-nice for much longer.

"I'm sorry, Macy, but we have other clients ahead of you, and we'll get to your pixies just as soon as we can," I said, gritting my teeth. "If our timetable won't work for you, then you're welcome to find someone else. We're the best there is, so we get *a lot* of clients." I smiled through my urge to tell the bitch to get out and stay out.

She held my gaze for a moment. When I didn't flinch, her eyes flickered to the side. Finally, her shoulders slumped. "I don't have the time to find anyone else."

Neither Yutani nor I said anything.

After an uncomfortable silence, she added, "Fine. Just get your asses over to my house as soon as you can."

I leaned back in Herne's chair, feeling a disconcerting satisfaction as I watched her ego deflate. *Schadenfreude.* "I think we'll be able to make it out there tomorrow. Expect us around sometime between nine and noon." The truth was, we could probably fit her pixie problem in today, but I didn't want to give her the satisfaction. "I think we have enough information."

"Will I need to be home?" she asked, tapping her stiletto-clad foot on the floor.

I shrugged. "That depends. If we can't find them, you'll just have to pay a rescheduling fee. If you're there, you can show us where they are."

"Fine. Tomorrow, between nine and noon." With that, Macy Barnhart was on her feet, and she flounced out of the office without another word, slamming the door behind her.

I glanced over at Yutani. "Man, she's a bitch."

"You got that one right." He snorted. "I'm tempted to cancel and just let her fend for herself."

"Well, we can't. We promised, so we'll be there. But I'm not looking forward to this job."

"Me either," he said. "I was amazed by how well you were able to keep your temper."

Laughing, I shook my head. "I was one step away from losing it, dude. However, I'm going to ask Herne to cross her off the list of clients once we wrap up her pixie problem. I have no desire to *ever* work with her again."

"Speaking of, when is he supposed to be back from the airport?" Yutani gathered up the papers and tapped the file folder on the desk to straighten it.

"Myrna was supposed to be in on a nine-thirty flight." I glanced at the clock. It was eleven-fifteen. "Depending on how much luggage she brought and how bad traffic is, they should be back here any time."

Yutani paused at the door, turning back to me. "You okay with her coming in?"

I considered the question. Was I okay with Herne's ex-girlfriend, who was also the mother of his child, coming into town to visit? Considering she was a first-class bitch, the answer was a resounding *No*, and considering she was also a lousy mother, again—a no. But I didn't want to sound jealous or petty, so I just shrugged.

"Eh, it's no skin off my nose. After all, they have a kid together and even though Danielle looks full-grown, she's not. There's no way you can have a child with someone and not cross paths now and then."

"You didn't answer my question," Yutani said as we exited the room. "Or maybe, by not answering, you already did." He ducked as I stuck my tongue out at him. "I'll be in my office. Talia's doing some research on Lazerous and I want to see what she's found so far."

I waved him off, then tossed the folder on Angel's desk. "Here, file this under 'B,' for 'Bitch.' "

She gave me a long look, half laughing, half serious. "You feeling okay?"

Pulling up a chair to the side of her U-shaped desk that faced the waiting room of the Wild Hunt Agency, I slumped down, leaning my head back.

"You could do me a favor and lose her file. Or accidentally delete her from the computer." At another look from her, I rubbed my forehead. "Macy Barnhart is an asshole and a snob. She epitomizes everything about my heritage that I hate. I wish we could turn her down, but Herne asked me to smooth things over with her, so that's what I did. At least, I did the best I could. Smoothing things over would require more ego massaging than I was willing to do."

"Well, she couldn't get out of here fast enough. I did manage to remind her that she had to pay the retainer before you and Yutani go out there tomorrow. She stopped long enough to hand me her credit card. I told her we didn't accept checks, because I don't trust her."

When Angel didn't trust someone, I knew enough to pay attention. "Did the charge go through?"

"Yeah, it did. Hopefully, she won't dispute it. I could tell by the look on her face when she stormed out that she wasn't happy." Angel tossed her pen on the counter, leaning back in her chair. "Has Herne texted you yet?"

I shook my head, then remembered that I had turned off my notifications while I was in the meeting. I pulled out my phone, unmuted it, then checked my messages. Sure enough, he had sent me a text message about twelve minutes ago. I opened up the message and read it.

MYRNA AND I ARE ON THE WAY BACK. TRAFFIC IS PRETTY BAD, BUT I HOPE TO BE THERE IN HALF AN HOUR. GO AHEAD AND HAVE ANGEL ORDER LUNCH FOR EVERYBODY SO IT WILL BE THERE WHEN WE ARRIVE. TRUST ME, THIS ISN'T GOING TO BE ANY PICNIC.

Myrna was Herne's ex-girlfriend, and the mother of his daughter. She was an Amazon, and she was a bitch on heels. The last time we had a run-in it hadn't gone very well, and I didn't expect any difference this time.

WE'LL SEE YOU WHEN YOU GET HERE, I texted back. Turning to Angel, I said, "Herne wants you to order lunch in now. They're on the way. He doesn't sound very happy."

"That's an understatement, isn't it?" Angel pulled out the takeout menus and began to skim through them.

"You might say that." I stood, moving the chair back to where it belonged. I glanced at the waiting room. "We don't have any more appointments right now, do we?"

"Nope. Not unless somebody else calls today."

"Good. This gives me a chance to catch up on my paperwork. Talia's researching whatever she can find out about Lazerous. Yutani's going to bone up on pixies, as well as help Talia. I'm not sure what Viktor is doing right now."

Angel nodded, shuffling the papers on her desk. "What do you want for lunch?"

I thought for a moment, but couldn't pinpoint

anything in particular that I was craving. "Whatever you order is fine with me. But I'm sure it won't be good enough for Myrna. Just make sure there's plenty of it, and that it's hearty. The guys don't go for salads, and honestly, neither do I."

I headed back to my office, hoping I'd have time to catch up on my paperwork before Herne and Myrna arrived. Although it was likely that Myrna wasn't coming in with a case. At any rate, why she was here wasn't any of my business, no matter how nosy I was.

Fingering the ring that Herne had given me—a promise ring formed out of his own antler tine—I realized that I really wasn't worried about Myrna. Herne was devoted to me and he had made that clear. I just didn't like her and didn't want to have to interact with her. But I wasn't worried about them getting back together.

For one thing, neither of them could agree on how to raise Danielle, their daughter. For another, whenever they talked on the phone it turned into an argument. I was grateful, mostly for Danielle's sake, that she was close to full-grown. Another ten or twelve years and she'd be ready to take her place as an adult, at least as far as the Amazons were concerned. In actuality, she was older than I was.

As I sat down at my desk, I brought up the Krown-4 news site, and clicked on the livestream video feed.

The newscaster was sitting in front of a picture of a cemetery, signs of disturbed graves in the background.

"Authorities have no idea who is responsible for the desecration of the Wild Thyme cemetery. Anyone with any information is urged to contact the police as soon as possible. Four bodies are missing, the caskets splintered, and the police have no leads at this time."

I set down my pen, staring at the screen. I pushed my laptop back and turned to my desktop computer, clicking over to another news site. There was the story again, with a little more detail.

On my second monitor—I had a two-monitor system now, like the rest of the office—I brought up *Earth Maps*, zeroing in on Seattle. I typed THE WILD THYME CEMETERY into the search engine, and waited.

When it brought up a map of the location, I saw that the cemetery rested on the outskirts of the Worchester district, the most haunted area of Seattle. The niggle of worry grew. After our meeting in Annwn with Cernunnos, Brighid, Morgana, and Lugh the Long Handed, anything concerning the dead or spirits or the undead made me nervous. I was about to call Yutani into my office when loud voices erupted from the waiting room. Even from my office, I could hear Herne and Myrna arguing.

"I still can't believe that you're letting her get away with this. I'm her mother, I should have some say in this matter." Myrna's voice echoed through the hallway. She wasn't a shrill woman, but her voice rose a good octave when she was angry.

"And *I'm* her father. I don't care whether or not this inconveniences *you*. Thantos is a sleazy, crappy excuse for a man. He's a lecher and the thought of him coming on to my daughter makes me sick. You know full well that she's not lying about it. I can't believe you're standing up for him! You call yourself an *Amazon*?"

"He did it *one* time, and I can't see what all the uproar is about. He didn't *hurt* her."

"How the hell can you be so blasé about this? Maybe he didn't hurt her physically, but he scared the hell out of her. You can let him back into your house after what he did to our daughter? I thought the Amazons frowned upon men like that? What did they have to say about you standing up for this creep?"

I decided somebody better get out there to diffuse the argument before it blew up into a full-fledged fistfight. Apparently I wasn't the only one who had that feeling, because Yutani, Talia, and Viktor were headed down the hallway as well. We all reached the main waiting room in a group, which felt rather awkward. There stood Myrna and Herne in front of Angel's desk, embroiled in their shouting match. Angel was trying to look busy, doing her best to ignore the spectacle going on in front of her.

I stepped forward, hands on my hips. "Obviously, you two are having some sort of beef with each other. Maybe you should take it into Herne's office instead of coming to blows out here in the waiting room. What if a client came in?" I glared at both of them.

Herne scowled, but gave me a nod. "Ember's right. Save the fighting for later. This is my place of business and it's no place to hash this out."

"So the tralaeth is running the show now? Not surprising, since she has your penis wrapped around her little finger." Myrna darted a sideways glance my way that—if it'd been an attack—would have left me flattened.

"Myrna!" Herne glowered at her, but I stepped in.

"Listen up. *I* work here, you don't." I turned to Myrna. "You can call me anything you want, but the fact remains this is a place of business." I wanted to tell her I agreed with Herne, that she was an unfit mother, but that would only lead to an even bigger blowup.

"Fine, I'll confine my comments to outside of your business establishment." She turned back to Herne. "We're not done with this yet, so don't get it into your head that this argument's over. I *know* you're trying to subvert Danielle's feelings toward me, so don't pretend you aren't. What time do you get off work? We're going to finish this, one way or another."

"All right, if you want to have it out, so be it. Meet me here tonight after six. Until then, I suggest you find yourself a hotel. I don't want to ever see you darken the doors of this building again." Herne looked like he'd swallowed a hornet's nest.

Myrna let out a string of curse words that would make a sailor blush, then whirled on her stilettos and marched back to the elevator. Her face was bright red, and it occurred to me that if she wasn't careful she might stroke out. Come to think of it, that wouldn't necessarily be a bad thing.

As the doors closed behind her, I turned back to Herne. He was standing there, arms crossed and feet braced firmly on the floor. The look on his face was somewhere between livid and apoplectic. I paused, not sure what to say. It would take him a while to calm down, and I knew better than to make a joke, even to break the tension.

"Ember, in my office, please." He turned, striding toward his office.

I wasn't sure whether he was also angry at me, but I

was about to find out. I glanced back at Angel, who flashed me a sympathetic look.

"Let us know when lunch is here. If you hear loud voices, text me when it arrives rather than knock on the door." And with that, I followed Herne into his office.

As I entered Herne's office and shut the door behind me, he turned and let out an enormous sigh. "I loathe that woman. I swear, on my father's throne, I hate her. She's an abomination. I can't seriously believe that she thinks she's a good mother."

The anger on his face was draining away, replaced by bewilderment and frustration. I moved toward him, unsure whether to offer him a hug. But he answered that himself, opening his arms to me, and I slid into his embrace. He squeezed me tight, holding me to him as he buried his nose in my hair. A moment later, he gently kissed me on the lips and stepped back, turning toward his desk to sit down. I pulled one of the wing chairs on the opposite side of the desk close, sliding into it and crossing my legs.

"So, tell me what's going on."

"Well, you knew I was picking her up, and that she flew into town because she wanted to talk to me about something."

"Right, that much I knew. So what did she have to say?"

"She wants Danielle to come stay with her during summer break. Danielle refused, because Thantos is back living with Myrna. You remember *that* whole mess?"

I nodded. "Thantos made passes at Danielle, and Myrna refused to believe it."

"Right. Well, Myrna insists that it only happened once, and that Danielle encouraged it. She's blaming our daughter for this jackass who's unable to keep his hands out of the kiddie aisle. He'll never change. I told Danielle she could come here during the summer if she wants, or I'd pay for her to travel around Europe or wherever she wants to go. As long as she takes someone with her who's a responsible adult."

"And I take it Myrna isn't too happy about this?"

"Myrna wants to parade Danielle around her friends and show her off. It's a coup having a daughter who's being trained by the Amazons. That's the *only* reason Myrna even wants Danielle to go home." Herne slammed his hand on the desk. "I have half a mind to drag her before the Triamvinate and gain full custody over Danielle. I could do it, you know."

I wasn't sure how much Herne wanted my advice or opinion on the subject. But I decided to give it to him anyway. "Honestly? I think you should. Thantos isn't going to change and in fact, if he's like most pedophiles, he'll try to make Danielle out to be a liar if she complained. Those creeps are uncannily good at that, you know."

Herne stared at me for a moment. "I'll call my father and ask if he can set up a hearing before the Triamvinate. Whatever they decide will stand, and not even Myrna can appeal it." He shook his head, a look of disgust on his face. "I hate men like Thantos. I'd like to break his nuts, and maybe someday I will. Thank you for backing me up."

11

"Hey, Myrna reminds me way too much of a few people I've known in my life."

"Okay, that's settled, then. So tell me what happened with Macy this morning. Fill me in."

I was about to give him the rundown when there was a tap on the door. I opened it, and there stood Angel, two bags of food in her hand from Fries With That, a new burger joint that had opened up in our neighborhood. They made excellent burgers, and the best fries I had ever tasted.

"Hey, Angel, thank you." Herne waved her in. She placed the bags on his desk. "Don't worry, the war is on hold for the moment. But if Myrna shows her face here, you let me know immediately."

"Will do," was all Angel said before she hurried back out to her desk again.

I shut the door behind her, then returned to the desk where I sat beside Herne, opening one of the bags. There were two cheeseburgers inside, a large order of fries, and a chocolate milkshake. As I tasted it, I realized it was actually mocha flavored. Angel knew me so very well. She'd better, given she was my best friend in the world.

"So, Macy McBraterson was here. Yutani and I agreed to go out and look at her place tomorrow—she's got a pixie infestation. But Herne, after this, write her off the books. She's one of the most obnoxious, snotty clients we've ever had. I wanted to wash the floor with her. It took everything I had to refrain from kicking her ass out the door."

"Maybe we should introduce her to Myrna. Maybe they'll fall in love and move away." He laughed, then set his own lunch out on the desk. As we ate, I also told him about what I had seen on the news.

"Do you think the missing bodies have anything to do with Typhon?" I asked.

We were headed into a dark period. An ancient evil was waking up, the father of all dragons whose name was Typhon. There was no way that we—the Wild Hunt— could take him on, but we had been warned by the gods that the dead would be walking, and there would be a lot of collateral damage to deal with.

"I don't know. The last timeline I heard placed him as almost awake. So this could have something to do with it, or maybe it's just some grisly grave robber at work. I'll look into it. While we're on the subject, Morgana asked me to meet with Saílle and Névé. We need to tell them about Typhon. I set up an appointment for next month at Ginty's. Right now, he's on vacation for some sort of holiday."

Just what I needed, an afternoon with the Fae Queens. But Herne was right, we had to warn them, because everybody would be affected by Typhon's rising.

I bit my lip, then asked, "So, are we to tell the rest of the United Coalition about this?"

Herne lowered his gaze to his food. After a moment, he said, "No. Morgana and Cernunnos were implicit about that. If the Cryptozoid Alliance gets wind of this, there's a chance Elatha will attempt to use it for his own gain. And the Shifter Association isn't going to be of much help, at least not as we see things now. As for the Human League, this would just terrify them. But the Ante-Fae know, and if they know the Fae community will soon know. Someone's going to let it slip. So if we can warn Saílle and Névé first, we're ahead of the game."

As we ate our lunch, I thought about the coming darkness. There wasn't much we could do to prepare for it, except have all our ducks in a row and enlist everyone we possibly think of to help us. Meanwhile, it was business as usual, and if that involved chasing down pixies in a snotnosed client's yard, then that was what we'd do. Trying to shake away my gloomy thoughts, I bit into my cheeseburger, and turned the subject to brighter topics.

CHAPTER TWO

*A*ngel unlocked the door, opening it to let me through. I was carrying the bulk of the groceries, and while they weren't terribly heavy for me, they were unwieldy. I staggered to the kitchen, trying not to trip over Mr. Rumblebutt, who had decided to plant himself in the middle of the hallway. I managed to reach the table with the bags intact.

"You know, if we'd make more than one trip we wouldn't have this problem," Angel said. She sat down the bag she was carrying, along with our purses.

"Yes, but it's raining like a son of a bitch out there, and I didn't want to get soaked. It's going to be bad enough tomorrow when Yutani and I have to go over to Macy's house and chase down pixies. The weatherman said we're due for a drenching. Speaking of rain, how's our garden doing? I haven't had a chance to look at it this week."

It was Friday night, and even though we had been short on clients, the entire week had flown by in a flurry of paperwork. Herne had decided we should clear out the file cabinets and spruce up the office, so we'd all been run ragged.

"The first seedlings are popping up. It's still early for anything like tomatoes, but the lettuce and carrots are starting to peek out of the ground. We should have planted winter vegetables, though given how rough this winter was, I don't think they would have done well."

I nodded. While Seattle had temperate weather, this winter had been rougher than usual. And the spring rains were proving unrelenting. "Maybe we can get out there tomorrow afternoon, after I come back from chasing down those pixies."

"I don't think it's fair you have to work on Saturday, especially since this isn't an important case." Angel began to unpack the bags, setting the cream and milk on the counter. I moved behind the counter and began putting things away as she handed them to me.

"It may not be fair, but it is what it is. I'd rather chase down pixies than spend an evening battling Myrna, which is what Herne's facing. I hope there's something good on TV. Are you staying in?"

Angel paused, staring at the floor for a moment. Then she glanced up at me and nodded. "Yeah, I'm staying in. Rafé decided he doesn't want company tonight." By the sound of her voice, I knew there was trouble brewing. I had suspected something was off, given the past two weeks Angel had barely spent any time with him at all, but I was still hoping I was wrong.

"Is he okay? I mean, I know he got the last of his casts off a couple weeks ago and he's still bound to be in some pain, but...how is he doing?"

"Rafé's stuck in a rough patch. I don't think he's

managed to shake the memories of what they did to him. He's never been involved in any sort of physical combat, and he wasn't prepared for what happened out on the peninsula. I'm afraid he's got PTSD. I think he needs to see a therapist."

"Have you told him that?" I suspected that she hadn't.

"No. I barely touched on the subject last week when we were out to dinner, and he blew up at me. We argued, and I finally left the restaurant because he couldn't calm down. I told him that I wasn't going to stick around if he was going to treat me like that. He apologized, of course, but he feels like a thundercloud, ready to break. I'm scared for him, Ember."

I nodded, silently putting away the vegetables and tucking the eggs and meat into their proper trays. Rafé had been severely hurt. We knew torture was involved, given the state Herne and I had found him in, but Rafé never told us how far it went. He wasn't part of the Wild Hunt, but Herne had accepted his offer to help, and Rafé ended up in way over his head.

I wondered if Angel blamed Herne for what happened Rafé.

"I'm sure Herne wouldn't have sent him out there if he really thought Rafé would be in danger—" I started to say, but she cut me off.

"Don't do that. Don't try to sidestep it. Herne knew perfectly well the situation could blow up at any time, but the stakes were so high he didn't have a choice. I understand that. Just like I know Rafé made the choice to go, even understanding what dangers he faced. Unfortunately, he ended up as so much collateral damage." Angel finished emptying another bag and folded up the canvas tote. "If anything, I blame *myself*. I'm the one who put the idea into Herne's head, it was me and my big mouth that caused the whole mess."

"Angel, stop. Just stop." I tucked the bags of sugar and chocolate chips in the cupboard and turned to her. "The truth is that nobody's to blame except for the asshats who actually hurt him. Rafé accepted the job because he wanted to help. Herne offered it to him after you mentioned the idea. We all were over there, and we still lost track of him. It just happened, and now, Rafé's bearing the brunt of everything that came tumbling down."

She finished unpacking the last bag and I began to put away the canned goods.

"I know," she said. "Logically, I know that. I'm just... I don't know what to do. Something has to change, though, or I'm going to have to break up with him. I promised Mama J. that I'd never stay in a relationship with a man who hurt me. Rafé's getting close, at least emotionally. I don't like the idea of bailing on someone who needs help, especially when it wasn't his fault. He didn't *ask* for the torture. But I can't keep putting myself through the emotional train wreck this relationship is quickly becoming. It's been almost been three months since the... Since they caught him." She paused. "I thought maybe we could talk to Ferosyn. That is, if Herne will put me in contact with him."

I realized she was asking for help.

"I can ask Herne. But maybe try one other avenue first? Talk to Raven about this. Rafé's close to her. He was Ulstair's brother, and I think he might listen to her. If anybody can reach him, she can. If that doesn't work, then we'll go to Ferosyn."

Angel slumped back in her chair. "You know, I never even thought about Raven. That might work. He thinks the world of her. I'll give her a call."

I pulled out a package of Oreos and opened them, fishing out one of the cookies and biting into it. "Good. Now, what do we want for dinner, and what's on TV?"

Since we were both tired, we opted to open a can of tomato soup and make grilled cheese sandwiches. The evening passed by in a pleasant blur of reruns, potato chips, and an early night to bed for both of us.

SINCE INTRODUCTIONS ARE IN ORDER, LET ME START. I'M Ember Kearney, and I'm half-Light Fae, and half-Dark Fae, which makes me an inkblot on a Rorschach test to most of my people, from either Court. Actually, I'm a smudge—to be ignored at best, wiped out at worst. I worked as a freelance bounty hunter/private investigator until Herne and I crossed paths not quite a year ago. He offered me a job with the Wild Hunt.

Actually, *drafted* might be a better choice of words, given neither Angel nor I had much of a choice. We both went to work for the agency at the same time, and our lives totally shifted directions. In exchange for a pretty lucrative salary, we agreed to join the organization and signed for it in ink—a tattoo emblazoned on the forearm of every member of the agency.

Until then, I'd pretty much been a loner, except for Angel—who's been my BFF since we were little girls.

Now? I have a number of friends, coworkers I genuinely like, and a greater purpose. I bought a house and Angel moved in, and for the most part, our lives are far more interesting, if also more dangerous.

I find it ironic that the Wild Hunt—and other agencies like it—was created to keep the petty squabbles between the Fae Courts from spilling over into the mortal world. I'm now policing the very people who loathe my existence. But life's like that. It hits us upside the head with a two-by-four every now and then.

As for Herne… Well, let's just say that I never expected to be dating a god, but there you go. Once again, life pushed me onto a winding route. Hell, I've ended up so far away from the life I led nine months ago that I feel like I fell into a movie.

If you had told me last March that within a couple months I'd be dating the Lord of the Hunt, that I'd be pledged to his mother—Morgana, a goddess of Fae—and that I'd be embroiled in situations that made my old job look like a walk in the park, I would have laughed you out of the room. But the nebulous "they" always say that staying in the same place only leads to stagnation. And for once, I agree with them.

ANGEL DIDN'T HAVE TO GO IN ON SATURDAY, SO I LEFT HER at home and drove down to the office to meet Yutani. She had still been sleeping when I left, so other than stopping to feed Mr. Rumblebutt, I was sans food or drink. Angel spoiled me by doing all the cooking.

I stopped along the way to buy a triple-shot mocha

and decided to add a sausage-muffin sandwich to the order. Then it occurred to me that we might get hungry on the job, so I added four slices of lemon pound cake, four chocolate chip cookies, and two brownies to the order. By the time the cashier handed me the sweets, I had eaten my sausage muffin and was ready for another, but I finally managed to get out the door before I'd spent every cent in my wallet.

The Wild Hunt Agency was on First Avenue in downtown Seattle. The streets were spacious, though marred by numerous potholes and cracks, and lined with trees that brought a suburban feel to the urban jungle. The buildings were brick and stone, old walkups sandwiched between tall stone high rises. The chrome and glass buildings were farther east, toward the Convention Center where a more genteel set of businesses made their home.

Our building was in downtown proper, and while it wasn't exactly a seedy part of the city, Old Town—as the Pioneer Square area was called—felt like one of the grande dames of the cinema, past its prime and yet still possessing an air of gentility. The streeps abounded—those who called the streets their home—and the Wild Hunt's building was nestled alongside neighborhood delis and boutique fetish brothels. There was also a pipe store, a marijuana store, and—inexplicably—an office supply store on the other side of the street. I pulled into the parking garage adjacent to our building. Luckily, the agency picked up the tab for our parking. We had to have our cars in case we needed to go out on a case.

As I pulled my coat tightly around me, zipping up my leather jacket, it occurred to me that I should carry a scarf to put over my head. My jacket didn't have a hood, and it was raining so hard that the water was beading up and bouncing on the sidewalks as it hit.

I stood by the door of the parking garage, holding the pastries, waiting to see if it would let up for a moment. But no such luck. So, shading my eyes, I dashed down the street, splashing through the puddles, grateful I had worn boots. I jogged up the front steps to the first floor of the building and darted inside. It was going to be miserable when we headed out to chase pixies.

The first floor of the building was given over to an urgent care clinic. There was a daycare and preschool on the second floor, both for low-income single mothers who needed an inexpensive but safe place to leave their children while they went to work. The third floor of the walkup housed a yoga and dance studio, and the entire fourth floor was ours—the Wild Hunt. The fifth floor was still empty and I was beginning to think the owner of the building would never manage to rent it out.

The elevator opened into our reception area, except when nobody was in the office. We'd lock it, so the car wouldn't stop on the fourth floor.

I usually took the stairs, but today the chill had already settled into my bones and I didn't feel like jogging up three flights of concrete steps. When I stepped into the reception area, I saw Talia manning Angel's desk. She was looking through a folder, a frown on her face.

She glanced up as I approached the desk. "Hey, happy Saturday. Yutani's waiting in the break room for you. I thought I would come in and do a little research on Lazerous." She stopped, staring at the ceiling as we heard thumping overhead.

"Somebody's upstairs?" I asked, surprised.

"Yes, didn't Herne mention it? The superintendent of the building dropped in yesterday and said that he's finally got a renter for the fifth floor."

"I just hope it's not a karate studio or anything loud." I yawned, shivering. The cold had gotten to me, and made me wish for a rainproof jacket. "I brought pastries." I held up the bag.

"So did I—I left some in the break room. Just put them on the plate with mine and we can pick and choose." She paused, glancing out one of the side windows. "Are you sure you want to go out in this today? It's absolutely pouring."

"Yutani and I promised. And the client's a first-class bitch who would have our heads if we didn't follow through." Even as I said the words, the thought of canceling still crossed my mind. I really didn't want to go play with pixies today. Not only were they pests, they were downright malicious at times.

As I headed toward the break room, I wondered how Herne had made out with Myrna. He hadn't called or texted, so I was left speculating whether either of them survived the meeting.

The door to the break room was open, and Yutani was sitting there, reading something on his laptop. He glanced up as I entered the room.

"You look like something the cat dragged in. Why didn't you wear a rain poncho?"

"Because you can't run in a rain poncho. I should have worn a windbreaker, though, instead of my leather jacket." It suddenly occurred to me that I had a spare set of clothing at the office. I couldn't remember if I'd left a jacket here or not, but it wouldn't hurt to look. "Here, I brought more pastries. I'll be right back. Maybe I left a warmer jacket here. I also need to dry my hair off."

"It's only going to get wet again," Yutani said with a laugh.

"Oh, hush." I headed back to my office and opened the narrow wardrobe that stood against the back wall. Sure enough, I not only had a pair of jeans, a turtleneck sweater, clean socks, and underwear, but I had also left a padded rain jacket. It would be a lot warmer than my leather one. I traded jackets then headed into the bathroom.

Complete with shower, should anybody return from a chase covered in mud and/or blood, the room was fairly spacious, with a linen closet filled with extra towels. I toweled off my hair, then braided it into a tight French braid. Even though my hair would get wet again, the braid would keep it out of my face and prevent the pixies from grabbing stray strands of my hair and pulling. Once done, I headed back to the break room.

"Give me a minute to finish my coffee," I said. I grabbed one of the brownies and leaned over Yutani's shoulder. "What are you looking at?"

He shrugged. "Actually, I'm house hunting on TriLow."

I blinked, startled. Yutani owned a good patch of land, although the trailer on it wasn't all that spacious. "You're thinking of moving?"

The coyote shifter nodded. "Yeah. The contractors who were going to start work on my house flaked out on me. They left me in the lurch, running off with a $4,000 deposit. Thank God I didn't give them any *more* money. Since I'm sick of the apartment I'm living in, and Aunt Celia needs a better place to stay when she comes up here to visit, I might as well just sell the place and buy something new."

Yutani's aunt was more like his mother. She came up to visit at least once or twice a year for several weeks, and even though they'd had a nasty argument the last time she was here, they had since resolved their issues. He had forgiven her for not telling him he was the Great Coyote's son, and she had forgiven him for being an ass about it.

"So, what are you looking for?"

"Oh, an acre or so, with a three- or four-bedroom house. I can do some fixing up, but it needs to be livable and not a dump." He pushed his laptop back, shutting the lid. "I suppose we better get a move on. Macy Barnhart isn't going to wait around for us, and the last thing we need is her haranguing Herne because she thinks we didn't do our job."

"I hear you on that one. Gods, she's such an asshole. She doesn't like me because I'm a tralaeth, but I have a feeling there's more to it than that." I paused, glancing at Yutani. He was good at reading people, and while I wasn't entirely sure I wanted to hear his take on the matter, he'd give me his honest opinion. "How about you?"

He paused for a moment, then shook his head. "No, I think it's pretty much superficial. Macy's too shallow to have ulterior motives and agendas. I think she just doesn't like many people. Period. She didn't cotton to me too much either." He took another cookie, biting into it, before he pushed his chair back. "Shall we go in one car?"

I nodded. "Sure. What equipment do we need? I don't know if I've ever gone pixie hunting before."

"You remember what knucklebones are like?"

I grimaced. Knucklebones—or nixienacks, as they

were also known—were nasty little creatures. They were part of the sub-Fae, and while they were pretty, they were also deadly, especially when they swarmed an enemy. They looked like six-inch tall winged creatures, feminine, but their mouths were circular and ringed with teeth. When they swarmed, they could strip a person down to the bone in minutes.

"Please don't tell me that pixies are like knucklebones!"

"No, they're not nearly as deadly. But they're malicious, and they take great delight in pulling nasty pranks on people. They also tend to swarm, so you'll seldom find one alone."

"Lovely. How big are they?"

"Oh, probably twelve inches tall. About double the size of a nixienack. One of the best ways to trap a pixie is to lure it into a cage filled with its favorite foods. One thing in our favor is they aren't too bright. If we drape a tarp over the cage, I'm thinking it shouldn't be too difficult."

I let out a sigh. I dreaded the thought of chasing a bunch of pixies around Macy's yard, but Yutani was right. Macy Barnhart would spread the word loud and clear at how we had flaked out on her if we didn't come through. Polishing off the last of my brownie, I picked up one of the doughnuts Talia had brought and stood.

"Okay, let's get going. We've got pixies to chase, though I have a bad feeling it could easily turn out to be the other way around."

CHAPTER THREE

Yutani said he'd drive, so we made a dash for the parking garage again. He had a Subaru, and he had already loaded the cages into the back, along with the tarps. As I fastened my seatbelt, I glanced at him.

"So, tell me, you said pixies can be nasty tempered. What kind of magic do they use? What should I be on the lookout for?"

"They're extremely good at leading people astray. Keep your eyes open, and if you think you hear me calling, make sure it's really me. They're excellent mimics. They breed like rabbits, so when there's an infestation, it doesn't take long to get out of hand." He snorted. "Can you tell I'm not fond of the buggers?"

"No kidding," I said. "You said they're not too bright?"

"Right. They aren't. I mean, they aren't animals—in terms of being on the same level intellectually. But I don't think they quite measure up to goblins in terms of intelligence. However, don't let that fool you. They're crafty and cunning, and they delight in making life miserable. Oddly enough, they do love cats and dogs. They torment cows and horses and birds, but they won't bother a cat or a dog. I'm not sure exactly why, because cats and dogs love to chase them around. Oh, and another thing—they can turn invisible."

I stared at the dashboard, my spirits spiraling lower with every word he said. "Is there *anything* positive about them? Besides the fact that they like cats and dogs?"

Yutani arched his eyebrows. "Not really. They aren't like garden devas, or flower spirits. They don't care about the environment. Consider them the mosquitoes of the sub-Fae world."

Wonderful. We were headed into a swamp filled with mosquitoes. The day just seemed to be getting better and better.

"Where does Macy Barnhart live?"

"Near the Green Lake district. She said she has a half-acre lot, and the pixies have taken up residence in the backyard." He paused, then added, "I have a feeling she's not telling us everything. But you know how it is, trying to pry information out of clients when they don't want to give it to you."

"That's for sure. All right, we go in and get this over with as soon as possible. Are you sure we can't trap Macy in a cage and just move her? Give the pixies her house?" I snickered. "I'd do it, if I had the chance."

"No, you wouldn't. I know you'd *like* to, but you wouldn't. Because Herne would have our heads. And I'm pretty sure you don't want lover boy pitching a fit."

"Eh, you've got me there." I leaned back against the

seat, remaining silent until we pulled into the driveway of a very tidy house on what looked to be a very tidy lot.

There were some houses where, the moment you saw them, you knew the owner was a control freak. The grass was mowed to a precise height, the house was neat and prim, and everything about it looked tightly controlled, without a single leaf out of place. Every window was spotless, there were no cracks in the sidewalk, the trees were ruthlessly pruned. All in all, it looked like a house directly out of a photo shoot for a weed control ad.

While I wasn't surprised to find it in good condition—the Fae generally kept their homes up—the lack of any sort of *wildness* struck me. Most of the Fae, both Light and Dark, tended to prefer their outdoor spaces with an edgy fierceness, a certain feral nature to the gardens. It was the way we were. Even the gardens in the great cities of TirNaNog and Navane felt undomesticated and untamed.

"Either she's been taking lessons from the soccer moms, or she's got a serious case of OCD." I glanced around as we stepped out of the car. There were no signs of any animals, no dog dishes, and I didn't even notice any birds in her yard, which made me even more suspicious. There were crows everywhere around Seattle, and grosbeaks. And since it was spring, we were starting to see the robins come in.

"I sincerely hope it's the former, or she's going to make our day even more miserable than I suspect," Yutani said. He straightened his jacket, then motioned to me and we headed up to the door.

When Macy answered, she looked just as pulled together as she had in our office. Not a hair was out of place, and she was wearing a tailored pantsuit with perfectly pressed creases. She flashed me a withering look.

"Why don't *you* meet me around back?" she said, barring the door.

"You've got to be kidding. You're refusing to ask me into your house?"

"I'm sorry, but the housekeeper just got done and my house is spotless. You're both dripping wet. Take the path around the side. I'll meet you out back." And with that, she shut the door on us.

I looked at Yutani. "You know this is because I'm a tralaeth."

"I suspect as much, but given she kept me outside as well, we can't exactly call her on it. Come on, let's get the cages and tarps and head out back. And remind me to tell Herne we're never working for this bitch again."

I felt irrationally happy. It was nice to have a comrade in arms. My spirits a little brighter, I helped Yutani gather the tarps and cages and headed around the side of the house.

AROUND BACK, MACY WAS STANDING JUST INSIDE THE door, the screen door shut. As soon as we walked through the gate, I could hear the whir of wings, and gleeful chattering. The trees were still bare of leaves—the buds were just blossoming—but there was plenty of space beneath the ferns and the juniper bushes for the pixies to hide. As Yutani began to set up the cages, a thought crossed my mind.

"Aren't they watching us set these up? Do you really

think they're going to stumble into a trap when they've seen us prepare it?"

He gave me a brief shake of the head. "Pixies are mad for their favorite foods. Their cravings for honey and cream are so strong that they'll chance darting into a trap. We just have to be quicker than they are. The traps are spring-loaded, which means that we stand a good chance of catching them when they remove the bait. Think of it like a mouse trap, only the door will slam shut, instead of a bar coming down to kill them."

I loved a lot of food, but I couldn't imagine walking into a trap I knew was there just for pizza and a latte. Then again, I wasn't a pixie. I wandered toward the door, where Macy was watching.

"How long have they been bothering you?"

"About two weeks," she said. "At first I hoped they go away on their own, because pixies are known to come and go like that. But they seem to have settled in."

"What do you think attracted them?" I watched her carefully. Something was off and I could feel it. She wasn't giving us the whole story.

She sidestepped my glance and mumbled, "I'm sure I don't know."

That was a lie. A blatant lie. I cleared my throat. "Macy, are you telling me the truth? We won't be able to help you if you don't tell us the entire story."

She pouted, her lips pressed together.

"You know, if Yutani and I don't have all the facts, it can make our job too dangerous. We retain the option to just walk away if we feel that there's anything…amiss."

She let out an exaggerated sigh, rolling her eyes. "Oh, all right. Don't leave."

"Then tell me everything." I leaned against the door-frame, watching her through the mesh screen.

After a pause, she mumbled, "All right, already. They might be angry at me."

"And *why* are they angry at you?"

By now Yutani had joined us on the porch.

She sputtered, tripping over her words. "If you must know, I trapped a pixie and stole her dust. But I didn't hurt her. I let her go afterward."

Yutani groaned. "Trapping a pixie and stealing its dust is about the worst thing you can do, in terms of a pixie. You do realize, don't you, that a pixie's dust is the only possession he—or she—owns? It's forbidden to sell on the open market, or to own it unless you can prove you've been given a vial from the pixie who made it. What the hell were you planning... *Wait.*" He narrowed his eyes. "You haven't been trying to catch them so you can steal their dust and sell it on the UnderWyre?"

The UnderWyre was a site on the Dark Web that offered up illicit items to collectors, and freaks who wanted to find illegal wares.

By the look on her face, he had hit the nail on the head.

I crossed my arms, shaking my head. "You've got to be kidding me. You've been trying to sell pixie dust on the Dark Web? What the *hell* for?" Now I was really pissed. No wonder the pixies were pissed at her. They had every right to be.

Macy shrugged, flouncing her shoulders. "It seemed like a good idea at the time. You can make good money that way, and anyway, what the hell do the little creeps do with it? It's like harvesting honey from bees, as far as I'm concerned. I didn't count on them getting their noses out of joint." She paused, then seemed to suddenly realize we weren't on her side. "You *promised* to help me. You're not going to leave, are you?"

"We should just leave you to them and let the pixies punish you for as long as they want. But we don't want you catching any more of them to steal their dust. We'll keep the bargain, as long as you hand over every bit of the remaining pixie dust, and as long as you never call us again." I glanced at Yutani, who nodded.

"Fine, just get rid of the creatures. I can't go out into my backyard without them divebombing me. One even peed on me the other day as he flew overhead."

I stifled a laugh. She deserved it, and far more. Stealing pixie dust from a pixie wasn't like harvesting honey at all. It was like grabbing a bumblebee and wiping the pollen off its legs.

"Go back inside, shut the door, and bring us your check. Actually, no. We want cash up front before we finish this job. I'm pretty sure you have enough around the house to pay for it. *In advance,*" Yutani said, folding his arms as he glared at her.

She stomped off cursing, and I turned to Yutani. "For half a doughnut I'd leave them here. But I don't want her to harm them and I wouldn't put it past her."

"Right. Pixies are annoying, but they don't deserve someone like Macy on their tail." He returned to the yard to finish setting up the cages. Macy returned, holding a wad of cash. She opened the screen door a few inches and I thrust my hand out, palm up.

"You paid us a retainer of three hundred. We need another nine hundred to finish the job." The figure was on the high side, but I figured she had it coming to her. She said nothing, just stared with piercing eyes at me as she slammed out the hundred-dollar bills onto my hand. When she finished paying me, I pulled out a receipt book from my bag and there, in the pouring rain, wrote her a receipt and stuffed it into her hand. "All right. Go inside and close the door and let us work. Don't come back out here until we call you."

I turned back to Yutani, who had set up the cages. They were large, about four-foot square, and their doors were open. He had placed bowls of honey inside of each and draped a tarp over three sides and the top of each cage. Then he motioned for me to join him on the porch. We sat on the wet deck, waiting.

The next moment, something hit the back of my head.

"Yowch! What the..." I turned, spying a pebble on the deck next to me. It was no bigger than a fifty-cent piece, sharp on one end, and it had been thrown with enough force to hurt. "Freaking hell, who threw this?" I said, scooping up the pebble.

"The pixies," Yutani said with a glance at the yard. "Ten to one, they think we're in cahoots with Sparkle-puss in there." He jerked his thumb toward the door.

I stood as someone laughed behind a nearby juniper bush. A shimmer of color shot by my head, and my hair flew into the air, jerking my head forward as the pixie grabbed hold of it and yanked, hard.

"Stop that!" I managed to steady myself, but that wasn't saying much, given how hard the pixie had pulled. I was surprised that he hadn't yanked the hair right out of my scalp.

More laughter, and then there was an explosion of

color from around the yard, with pixies emerging from bushes and behind trees. They swarmed us, poking, prodding, pulling hair, jabbing their bony little fingers into any tender spot they could find. It was like we'd suddenly been thrust into the movie *The Birds*, only sans the dangerous beaks or the attempt to pluck out our eyes.

I tried to beat them off, flailing my arms as they buzzed us again.

Yutani let out a shout and, as he whipped his hand up, one of the pixies went flying across the yard to slam into a tree. It slid down to the ground, looking dazed. I turned, trying to grab hold of one who was pinching my ear and managed to capture her in my palm. I held her by the waist, bringing her up to where I could stare at her. She was a pretty little thing, and her wings were fluttering madly. She kicked, trying to get away as she chattered away, sounding furious.

"Everybody stop, or I squeeze her in half." I held her up so the others could see her. I didn't mean it, of course. I wasn't about to kill her unless she managed to threaten my own life. But *they* didn't know that. There was a sudden cessation of activity as the pixies slowly backed away. So they *could* understand me. They might obey if they thought she was in danger.

"Everybody get in the cages, or your friend is toast. Come on now, we're not going to hurt you as long as you cooperate. Into the cages!" I nodded to Yutani, who walked over to stand between the two cages.

A crash of thunder lit up the sky, and rain began to pour down. Hail followed, the stones bouncing off of our shoulders and heads in a heavy shower of pea-sized ice bullets. I held the pixie out into the hailstorm. She flinched, trying to protect her head from the falling stones.

"Into the cages, now, or the hail will do my dirty work for me." I made my voice as menacing as possible.

It only took another moment before the pixies began flying into the cages, looking dejected. They looked like they had lost their last friend, and I realized they thought we were going to steal their pixie dust from them. As the last one entered the door, Yutani slammed the other cage shut. I leaned down and very carefully let go of the pixie I had been holding, pushing her gently into the cage. As Yutani locked the door, I leaned down to peer inside.

"We're not going to steal your pixie dust. We're going to take you somewhere you'll be safe and where people will be safe from you. So don't be afraid."

As I stood back, the hail began to subside. "Do you think we have them all?"

Yutani nodded. "I think so. This wasn't nearly as bad as I thought it would be. However, I'd like to kick Macy in the ass for what she did. Come on, help me get these pixies back to the car."

We made sure that the cages were shut, leaving the bowls of honey inside for them to eat. As we carried them back to the car, I thought about turning Macy in for stealing pixie dust. But I had no proof, and she would just say that we had misunderstood her. The pixies themselves wouldn't be any use in a court, they would just end up causing havoc.

"Yeah, so would I. But there's not much we can do. I suppose we could turn her into the local magic guild, or tell Névé about her. But either way, I imagine she'd only get a slap on the wrist. We're just going to have to let karma settle this one."

"Unfortunately, karma doesn't always work well. It's not at all what most people think it is." Yutani opened the back of his Subaru and we stashed the cages inside. With the back seat folded down, the hatchback was just big enough to handle both of them.

"Where to from here?"

"I'll call Quest Realto. She agreed to take the pixies through the portal for us if we could catch them. I'll drop you down at the agency and you can go home. I'll take care of the cleanup here."

"I owe you one." All I wanted to do was go home, take a hot shower, and call Herne to see what had gone down with Myrna.

CHAPTER FOUR

*A*ngel was waiting for me when I arrived home. I had called her from the agency, where Talia was still deep into her research. I considered staying to help, but I was tired and cold, and I wanted to get away from work for a little bit.

"Go take a bath. I'll make some hot cocoa. I was baking cookies when you called, and we can spend the afternoon on the sofa with the TV."

"Bless you," I said, dashing up the stairs. I had changed clothes back at the office, but I brought my wet things home to throw them in the washer. I stripped and climbed into the shower, turning it on as hot as I could stand it. As I lathered up, the water began to pound the knots out of my shoulders. I washed my hair again, since it had gotten soaked from the rain, and about half an hour later, my hair was dry, my makeup was fixed, and I was dressed in a comfortable pair of capri pants and a warm sweater. I slipped on ballet flats, and then headed downstairs for the promised cookies and hot cocoa. The doorbell rang, and I changed directions, heading over to open it. To my surprise, Rafé was standing there.

"Rafé! I didn't know you were coming over." I wondered if Angel had been expecting him.

"I wasn't sure myself," he said, looking uncertain. He was Dark Fae, with a shock of red hair down to his shoulders. Rafé was lithe and around Angel's height—she was five-ten—and he had alabaster skin that contrasted beautifully with her gleaming brown complexion.

I backed up, ushering him in. "Angel, we have company," I called out, shutting the door behind him.

She darted out of the kitchen to peek down the hall and froze when she saw Rafé. "I thought you weren't feeling up to coming over," she said, looking surprised.

"I wasn't, but then I thought I might as well. I don't have anything else to do, and I couldn't stand sitting in that cramped little shithole I call an apartment one moment longer than I had to." The harshness of his tone took me aback. He sounded angry, almost combative.

"I'm glad you're here, though," Angel said, leaning in for a kiss.

Rafé gave her a peck on the cheek, but it looked forced. Angel stared at him, and I could sense the tension between the two. I decided to do what I could to break the ice.

"Won't you come in? We were going to watch TV and eat popcorn and just hang out for the rest of the day." I motioned toward the living room, but Rafé didn't budge.

"I thought we might go over to Ginty's and grab a drink," he said, staring at Angel.

She frowned. "I'm not sure I feel up to going out today. And I don't feel like drinking this early."

"Meaning you think I'm a lush?" Rafé asked, immediately falling into defensive mode.

"I didn't say that—" Angel said, but he interrupted her before she could finish.

"No, you just *thought* it. You've been on my back about my drinking the past couple weeks, and I wish you would just knock it off. I'm not an alcoholic, I just want a drink. There's a game on, and I happen to like a beer with my game." He folded his arms, leaning back against the wall. "Are you coming or not?"

I turned back to stare at Angel, wondering if I should interfere.

"I told you that I don't feel like going out, and I'm not going to drink this early. If you want to watch the game and have a beer, that's your business. We're going to watch movies and eat popcorn. You're welcome to stay if you want, but not if you're going to keep needling me." Angel straightened her shoulders, hands on her hips. She reminded me of Mama J., fiercely independent, and not about to take crap from anybody.

Rafé stiffened, looking surprised. "I wasn't needling you," he said with a sullen downcast look. He sounded more disappointed than angry. "I guess I'll head out for Ginty's—some of the guys are going to be there." He paused, then added, "I'm sorry. I didn't mean to upset you. I'll call you later."

"Rafé, won't you stay and watch movies with us? We'll have fun, and I want to see you." Angel reached out for him, but he just grabbed one of her hands and brought it to his lips, kissing it before he turned back toward the door.

"I don't think I'm very good company right now," he

said. "If you'll excuse me, I'll just go. See you later, love. Bye, Ember," he said to me. He blew a kiss to Angel and then took off before we could say anything.

"You're right," I said. "He needs help. You should talk to Raven."

"Can we invite her over? She was there with us, she'll understand and maybe she'll be able to help." Angel was fighting back the tears. I bit my lip and held out my arms. She leaned against my shoulder, taller than me, but seeming very fragile at the moment. "Ember, I'm worried about him. I'm so very worried."

"I know," I said, rubbing her back. "I'll call Raven and see if she can make it over tonight."

I wrapped my arm around her shoulder as we headed toward the living room. I hoped that Raven would be able to make an impression on him, for both Rafé's sake and Angel's. Because I knew that Angel loved him, and I also knew she was getting ready to let him go.

RAVEN SHOWED UP AN HOUR LATER, RAJ IN TOW. ONE OF the Ante-Fae, she was a bone witch—a necromancer by any other name. She had started out as a client at the Wild Hunt, but now she was a good friend of ours. Her fiancé had been missing, and unfortunately by the time we found him, he was quite dead. Ulstair was Rafé's brother, and that's how we met him.

As Raven bustled through the door, I grinned. She was one of the most flamboyant people I knew, a grown-up Goth girl, and her style was as natural to her as breathing. She was wearing a black and purple tulle skirt, a black peasant blouse and a purple underbust jacquard corset, fishnet stockings, and a pair of Fluevog ankle boots with platform rubber soles, and laces up the front.

Raj was her pet gargoyle, although he was actually more of a companion than a pet. He lost his wings when he was young, and Raven adopted him and had a witch cast a Forget spell on him so that he wouldn't remember the pain of losing them.

I wasn't sure how Raven and the gargoyle communicated, but I knew they did, and he seemed to understand her. He was about the size of a large rottweiler, with gray leathery skin and puppy-dog eyes. He could be intimidating, but actually, he was a softy at heart. Angel and I had grown quite fond of him.

Mr. Rumblebutt took one look at Raj and headed upstairs. Raj had never bothered him, but Mr. Rumblebutt wasn't exactly delighted with large, smelly animals. And poor Raj really didn't have a bad smell, he was just a little too eager to be friends at times.

"Hey, what's up?" Raven said. "When you called, I could tell something's wrong." She held up a couple bottles of sparkling water. "I thought we could use one evening together where we weren't falling-on-our-ass drunk."

Raven and Angel and I had developed a noticeable pattern during our girls' nights. We had a blast, no matter what, but quite often we fueled that fun with several bottles of strong alcohol.

"Thanks," Angel said. "I'm really in no mood to get drunk tonight. Or even tipsy."

"You definitely look like you need some cheering up, though. What's wrong?" Raven set the bottles of sparkling water down on the coffee table, then sat down on the sofa and began to unlace her boots. "Raj, you behave yourself, and if you need to go out, you let me know."

Raj grunted, wandering over to one of the heating vents, where he curled up on it.

"Actually, we need to talk to you about Rafé," I said. "Angel, why don't you tell her?"

Angel hesitated for a moment, then said, "I don't know if you've noticed anything odd about Rafé lately. About his moods."

"Oh, good gods, I'm glad to know I'm not the only one." Raven set her boots to the side and crossed her legs on the sofa. "He's been an absolute ass to everybody. One of his aunts even called me to ask what the hell was going on."

"Here's the thing. You remember when we were all out on the peninsula, when we went hunting for the Tuathan brotherhood out there?"

Raven nodded.

"Well," Angel continued, "I think Rafé's suffering from PTSD. He needs help, but he won't listen to me. I'm…" She frowned, staring at the floor. "If he doesn't get his shit together and get into counseling, I'm going to have to break up with him. I can't deal with emotional abuse. And I sure as hell won't put up with anything worse."

"Has he ever hit you?" Raven said, her eyes flashing as she leaned her elbows on her knees.

Angel shook her head. "No, and he's never threatened me. But he's abrupt and boorish and downright rude. He apologizes, but I know that cycle well enough to know I'm not willing to play the game. I'm not going to go through repeated incidents of him lashing out and then apologizing. I want him healthy. I want him to ask for help. Do you think you could talk to him? He might listen to you, whereas he's *not* listening to me."

"I'll have a talk with him. If he blows me off, I may talk to his acting coach, or his agent. He does have an agent, you know. When he lost his job the other day, I thought about it, but wasn't quite sure—"

"*Lost his job?*" Angel said. "Rafé didn't say anything about that."

Raven let out a long sigh. "Yeah, he got fired from the restaurant a few days ago. Apparently, he was getting short tempered with customers and his supervisor warned him twice. He had just started back to work a few weeks ago, and he's already out of a job again. I'm not sure how he's going to manage to pay his rent, to be honest."

"When the Wild Hunt paid for his medical bills—well, we actually got him the best healer there is—we also gave him an lump-sum settlement to cover his needs for at least six months, since we weren't sure how long it would take for him to heal up. So unless he's run through the money, he should be okay for another few months. I know that Herne wouldn't object to covering the cost of a therapist for him as well. Or maybe we could talk to Ferosyn, and he could dig up a good counselor." I pulled out my phone, texting myself a reminder to talk to Herne.

"All right. I'll talk to him tomorrow. He's supposed to be coming over to help me put up some new shelves." Raven hesitated for a moment, then glanced at Angel. "I'd ask you not to give up on him yet, and I hope you won't, but I'm not going to press you. Rafé's a good-hearted man, and he's sweet, but even the best of men can falter when they face great trials. Maybe Kipa can talk to him, as well. They've become friends over the past couple of months, since Kipa and I started seeing one another. Kipa can be extremely persuasive," she said, laughing a little.

I snorted. "*Persuasive* is an understatement."

Kipa—or Kuippana—was the Lord of the Wolves. He was a wildcard, almost an elemental but yet, also a god. Basically, he was one of Herne's distant cousins, although I hadn't been able to figure out just *how* they were related. Kipa was a major player, although Raven seemed to have tamed him down a little. Or perhaps she was wild enough to challenge him. Either way, they were a flamboyant, colorful, and happy-go-lucky pair.

Raven grinned. "You're right about that."

Angel leaned back. "Thank you. I'm hoping that we can pull through. I really *do* love him, but I can't stay with someone who acts like an asshole. Okay, can we change the subject? I really don't want to keep talking about this."

"Let's crack the sparkling water and grab some cookies to go with the popcorn, and decide what we want to watch," I said, standing. Raven grabbed the bottles, and we all traipsed into the kitchen. As Raven poured the sparkling water, I turned to Angel. "I just hope you know your bottom line, because it's really easy to let behavior slide, especially when you care about someone. I don't want to see you fall into that trap. Rafé is a wonderful man, but…"

She nodded. "I know, and yes, I know what my deal breakers are. Love can't fix everything. Mama J. taught me that." And on that note, we headed back to the living room with our snacks.

WE WERE HALFWAY THROUGH OUR SECOND MOVIE WHEN MY phone rang. I glanced at the Caller ID. It was Herne. Slipping into the hall to keep from disturbing Raven and Angel, I answered, wondering what sort of mood he would be in. For that matter, was Myrna still around? I hoped she'd get tired of blaming Herne for her relationship with Danielle, and go back home.

"Hey," I said, suddenly missing him. "What's up?"

He hesitated for just long enough that I knew things weren't back to normal. Which meant the wicked Amazon of the West was probably still hanging around.

"What's up is that hag of a woman is out to make my life miserable. We tried having a civil dinner last night to hash out issues, but we both blew up and a lot was said, and the long and short of it is, I'm petitioning Cernunnos to ask the Triamvinate to oversee this matter."

"What is there to oversee?" I asked, a little confused. "I know Danielle isn't fully of age, but she's not a child. You guys were never married, so there's no divorce decree to deal with. Danielle lives with the Amazons now so it's not quite the same as a custody battle. Or did I miss something?"

"Since she's technically still a minor, Myrna is threatening to have me kicked out of her life until she comes of age." By the tone of his voice, I could tell he was pissed as hell. And he had every right to be. Myrna had surprised him with the news that he was her babydaddy only a few months back, and now she was changing her mind and wanted him out of their daughter's life?

"That's not fair. She's only mad because you won't let

her get away with exposing Danielle to a pedophile. What a bitch." I wanted to slap the woman silly. Any mother who put her child in danger like that didn't deserve to have children.

"That's about the shape of things. I'm going to talk to my parents today. They'll do what they can to intervene. My father's not like Zeus, who couldn't give a rat's ass about the rights of women and children." He let out a long sigh. "I'm sorry to drag you into this. It's not fair, I know."

"Fair, schmair. Who cares? I'm just worried about Danielle." After what was initially a bumpy ride, Herne's daughter and I had found a meeting place in the middle, and we got along now. She even sent me a birthday card and a present—a beautiful belt that she had made in leather class. "You do what you have to. I'll back you up all the way."

"Did I ever tell you what a wonderful girlfriend you are?" Herne said, relief washing through his voice.

"Yes, but that doesn't mean I'm tired of hearing it." I laughed. "Okay, Raven and Angel and I are binge-watching rom-coms, so I'll talk to you later."

"Before you go, how did you and Yutani fare with the pixies?"

I snorted. "Oh, just lovely. We managed to catch them, and Yutani took them over to Quest Rialto's place to send them through to Annwn, but I want your promise that we're never working for Macy Barnhart again. Did you know that she's been stealing pixie dust from the pixies and selling it on UnderWyre?"

"You're joking," Herne said. "That's disgusting!"

"No, I am *not* joking, and yes, it is. Macy admitted it when we forced her hand. I've a good mind to turn her into the authorities. Pixies may be obnoxious, but they don't deserve that." As I said it, I realized I really wanted to stick it to her. Yes, pixies were a pain in the ass, and yes, they were better off out in the wilds than in the city where they could rain havoc around, but still — pixie dust was a byproduct of their very essence, and stealing it was like stealing magic from a witch.

"You know, you're right. Let me talk to my father about it when I go talk to him about Myrna. We'll see what he has to say." And with that, he made kissing sounds into the phone and then hung up. I headed back to the living room, my thoughts churning. There were a lot of incredibly violent and vile men in the world, but Myrna and Macy were proof that women could be just as nasty and dangerous.

CHAPTER FIVE

he next morning, I woke up to the smell of fresh baked bread wafting up from downstairs. I moved a very sleepy Mr. Rumblebutt off my legs. He grumbled but curled back into a ball.

"Sorry dude. It's Sunday." I picked him up and carried him over to the cat tree in the corner. Usually, I left the bed unmade. My line of thought was that I was just going to mess it up again at night, so why bother making it? But today was Sunday, so I stripped the sheets and bundled them into the laundry, then smoothed clean ones on and fluffed up my pillows. Lastly, I pulled the comforter up and stood back, admiring my once-a-week handiwork.

Then, I slipped my robe on over my sleep shirt, slid my feet into my slippers, and padded down to see what Angel had concocted for breakfast.

She was in the kitchen, her apron dusted with flour, and three beautiful loaves of bread were cooling on the counter. My mouth salivating, I made a beeline for them but she held up her hand.

"Stop right there. I know how much you love fresh bread, but I have a batch of cinnamon rolls just about ready to come out and we'll have those for breakfast. The bacon and eggs will be ready in a few minutes, so why don't you go upstairs and dress, and I'll have food on the table when you get back." She brushed a stray curl away from her eyes, smudging her forehead with her flour-laden fingers.

I glanced around the kitchen. There were cookies cooling on racks, and I caught sight of a mound of apples in the sink. "You've been busy."

"Yeah, well I'm also making cookies and I thought I might throw together three or four pies while I'm at it. We can freeze what we don't eat and I won't have to bake again for a few weeks." But the flash in her eyes told me that she was therapy-baking.

Just like some women made use of retail therapy, and others exercised for stress release, Angel baked like a fiend when she was stressed. Her mother—Mama J.—had owned a diner, as well as reading tarot cards, and Angel inherited her mother's knack for cooking. It was an art with her, and her food never failed to offer a hug to those needing comfort.

"Good idea. While you bake, I'll tackle some of the housework and maybe get out there in the garden." I couldn't cook much more than a cheese sandwich, but I had a green thumb that wouldn't quit. I had always loved the outdoors. The ragtag side yard, which took up an entire lot, had once been a series of beautiful gardens. But when I bought the house, it had deteriorated into a ragged remnant of its former glory.

I had spent the past few months planning out a way to

revitalize the various flower gardens and herb patches. As I planned, I grew more excited, a deep longing to plunge my hands into the dirt growing with each passing week. I wanted to plant, to nurture the seedlings as they grew.

"How's the kitchen garden doing?" Angel asked as she scooped cookie dough onto a sheet pan using a small ice cream scoop.

"I saw some new seedlings peeking up yesterday when I checked on them. We'll have lettuce and carrots before you know it," I said, feeling proud as a mother hen. I had started a small kitchen garden in a raised bed, with lettuce and carrots shrouded under makeshift greenhouses of clear plastic. The seeds had germinated and the plants were starting to grow. It gave me no end of delight to see the tiny seedlings press their way through the dirt.

"It will be so nice this summer to have fresh vegetables from our own garden," Angel said, grinning at me.

"Yeah. I'll get starts for the tomatoes and cucumbers and the other plants at Beem's Nursery, where I got the roses. And I'm waiting on my order of summer bulbs to get here. I need to plant them this month. The spring flowers I planted last November should be showing their heads any day now."

I had taken to poring over seed and bulb catalogues for fun. During November, I had planted daffodils, hyacinths, crocus, and tulips. The trees had been pruned then, as well. I had hired an arborist to come in and check their health, and then a tree trimming company to prune them back and get them all spiffed up. Now, I was eagerly awaiting a shipment of begonias, dahlia, gladiolas, and calla lilies. If I planted them now, they'd bloom during the summer. And a week before, I had picked out twenty-four new rose bushes. They were secure in the ground, hibernating under a two-inch layer of mulch.

"Okay, I'm going up to get dressed. I took a shower last night so I won't be long." I headed down the hall to the staircase, dashing up to my bedroom where I traded my sleep shirt and robe for a comfortable pair of old jeans and a cobalt blue turtleneck sweater. I slid the belt Danielle had made me through the loops on my jeans, then spent five minutes putting on powder, mascara, and eyeshadow. Pulling my hair into a high ponytail, I wiggled my feet into a pair of old sneakers and clattered downstairs to the kitchen.

Angel was setting a plate of cinnamon rolls on the table.

I pulled myself a four-shot latte, adding milk, ice, and caramel syrup, and joined her.

"You've outdone yourself. This isn't just eggs and bacon, woman!"

Angel had made light and fluffy omelets filled with cheese, diced tomatoes, and ham, along with thick rashers of smoked bacon crisp from the oven.

"Cooking's my meditation," Angel said. But she looked pleased. I always remembered to praise her cooking—it made her feel good, and best, it was easy enough to do because everything I said was true. She was a whiz in the kitchen.

"I hope you know how much I love your cooking," I said, about to sit down. But then I heard a plaintive mew and stood up again. "Oh, wait. I need to feed Mr. Rumblebutt."

"Don't bother," she said, passing me the cinnamon rolls. "I already did. He's taken care of."

I glanced over at his dish, which was full of gooshie-food. "Liar," I said to him. He gazed at me with a look of disdain, then meandered over to the food and began to eat.

Mr. Rumblebutt had been with me for several years. A black Norwegian Forest cat, he weighed over sixteen pounds, and was basically a powder puff on legs. I adored him, and he adored both Angel and me. I had named him Mr. Rumblebutt because he purred like a freight train, and when he was happy he would do a little wiggle-butt dance.

"Thanks." I took one of the rolls, and set it on the bread-and-butter plate. "So, we actually managed an evening with Raven where we didn't wake up with a hangover."

Angel snorted. "Yeah, that's a miracle, isn't it?" She paused, then her eyes misted over a little and she said, "I hope Rafé listens to her."

"I hope so too, hon." I sighed, unsure whether I really believed he could manage to pull out of the depression into which he had plunged. *I* could get beat to hell and back and rebound, but I was used to it and it came part and parcel with my job. But Rafé was a sensitive soul, and he was an actor, not a fighter.

Angel cleared her throat. "I promised myself I wouldn't spend the day worrying. And I'm not. As soon as the cookies are done, I'll start on the pies. Then I'll come help you with the garden."

I smiled at her. "That's a good plan. There's nothing we can do to help Rafé unless he's willing to accept help, so you might as well focus on the positive for now. The only thing worry does is waste energy. Oh! I forgot to tell you.

When Herne called last night, he told me that he's going to seek sole custody of Danielle from the Triamvinate."

"Wow. That's a big step." Angel paused to fork up a bite of omelet. "What happened with the pixies yesterday? You never did tell me."

"We broke up Macy's attempted get-rich-quick scheme. She was trying to run pixie dust through the UnderWyre. But it backfired on her."

UnderWyre, along with UnderShot and UnderCast, were sites on the Dark Web where illegal traders dealt in goods, arms and ammunition, magical supplies, and slaves for both work and sex. Yutani had discovered information there that had helped us take down the Tuathan Brotherhood. It was a dangerous place to visit, though, and the fact that Macy had been selling pixie dust there made me wonder if she was connected to any gangs or organized crime, or even—perhaps—an illegal guild. She was Light Fae, but that didn't mean squat when it came to hanging around in the shadowed places of the world.

"So what are you going to do about her? It would seem that she should be punished."

"Herne's going to talk to Cernunnos about her. If we turn her in to the cops, they may just look the other way, given most of them are from the Fae community."

"True that." Angel offered me another cinnamon roll.

I held it under my nose, inhaling deeply before I bit into it. "You should enter a baking competition. Or go on one of the cooking show competitions. Maybe you should try out for *You've Been Diced?*" The show was a cooking reality competition where five home chefs from around the country were chosen to compete for a $10,000 prize over the course of four rounds—breakfast, lunch, dinner, and dessert.

"Right, and since I have *so much* free time, I might as well open a bakery." She laughed. "Seriously, it would be fun to do one of those shows, but I doubt I'd win. I'm good—no doubt about it—but the cooks they have on there are multi-talented."

"So are you, even if you don't think so. But yeah, time would be a factor. And going that high profile as a member of the Wild Hunt might not be a good thing." I polished off my omelet and bacon. "You'll just have to settle for lavish compliments from your friends, I guess."

Angel laughed and pushed back her chair. "Are you done?"

"Yes, though in an hour or two, I'm going to want some of those cookies. I'll head out to the garden now." I carried my dishes to the counter, then drained the last drops of my latte.

Angel nodded, pulling another batch of cookies out of the oven. She set the pans aside to cool, replacing them with fresh ones. As she began to rinse off our dishes and put them in the dishwasher, I headed for the foyer, to the coat rack, where I slid on a warm but light windbreaker and slipped out the sliding glass door in the living room.

The rain had held off, though the ground was still wet. But I could check on the roses and putter around with the area where I planned on planting the summer bulbs. I was also in the process of laying down a brick walkway that would lead through the various gardens. While the ground was too wet to work on that, I could begin to weed through some of the early spring growth that was coming up.

The side lot that was part of our property had been an added bonus to the house. It gave us a lot of privacy that we might not otherwise have. We had dug up quite a bit of the lot in preparation for the new gardens, but there were still patches of grass and undergrowth, and those areas were rife with weeds.

A butterfly bush had taken hold and was spreading. The plants were beautiful and they truly did appeal to bees and butterflies, but left unchecked they would choke off anything else that tried to gain a foothold in the ground. I ruthlessly began to dig out the tendrils that were rooting into the dirt. Some of them I would plant in large pots, but we didn't want the whole yard to become one giant butterfly bush.

The same went for a blackberry thicket at the edge of the yard. I wanted a thick stand of berries for eating, but brambles liked to spread and conquer. So after cutting away at the butterfly bush, I grabbed a set of heavy-duty pruning shears from the shed attached to the back of the house, pulled on a pair of soft leather gloves to keep my hands safe from the thorns, and started to work my way into the thicket.

As I worked away, pruning back the invaders, I began to sense that someone or something was watching me. I glanced over my shoulder to see a large crow hop onto a fist-sized rock. It wasn't a raven, but it was huge—its fat, glossy body thick and plump.

"Hey," I said softly. "What are you doing here?"

Crows talked to me a lot—although I seldom under-stood what they had to say. They were a symbol of Morgana, and they followed me around, showing up as omens. I wasn't that good at reading just what they had to tell me, but I was trying to learn. If I actually took the time, I thought I might be able to understand them.

I eased back, squatting on my heels as I stared at the bird.

It flapped its wings, then flew over to land in front of me. It eyed me cautiously as it stood there, less than an arm's reach away, and let out a shrill *caw* that echoed through the chilly morning air.

Startled, I almost fell back on my butt, though I pressed my hands on the ground to steady myself before that happened. The bird was staring at the house. I turned to look in the direction where its gaze was focused.

There, against the side of the house, I could see a shadow walking. It was dark and tall, and in the shape of a man, and it was walking toward the sliding glass door. But it halted. Another moment, and it turned its head, staring at me with deep red eyes. A wave of malignance washed over me. The shadow was angry, and it wanted to kill, whether me or someone else I didn't know, but it reeked of vengeance. I froze, not sure of what to do, but then, it suddenly vanished.

"What the fuck? What was that?" I launched myself to my feet as the crow flew up and circled my head once, then winged its way back to one of the nearby fir trees.

I glanced around. There was no sign of the shadow now, but that didn't mean it was gone. It could have just turned invisible, or disappeared from the spot where I had seen it. It could still be hanging around, though I could no longer sense it around. I hurried to search the yard, but could find nothing save for residue gunk where the shadow had paused. Turning back to the crow, I silently waved and headed inside to tell Angel about what I had seen.

"ANGEL—ANGEL!" I KICKED OFF MY MUDDY SNEAKERS AT the sliding glass door and yanked off my coat, dropping it on the floor. Then, slamming the slider shut, I hurried to the kitchen.

"What's going on? Are you all right?" Angel asked, looking up from where she was placing a top crust over one of the pies that were now resting on the counter.

"Is everything okay? I want you to tune in and see what you feel."

Angel was an empath, and she had a remarkable ability to tune in on both people and events. When I had bought the house, that had been problematic even though we had cleansed it, because it was a murder house and while we had cleared out the spirits and appeased the energy, there was always the lingering feeling that yes, two people had been murdered here. A young woman and her grandmother had been killed in a brutal axing by the girl's ex-boyfriend, who had then gone back to his apartment where he had shot himself. Every now and then, I could tell Angel was dwelling on it.

"What happened?" Angel asked, immediately turning to rinse off her hands. As she dried them on a tea towel, I glanced nervously toward the window behind the eat-in dining table. The window faced the front yard and the street, and while I had seen the shadow man in the side yard, he had obviously been able to move.

"I saw a shadow outside, lurking near the sliding doors in the living room. A crow warned me, and I got hit with a buttload of anger and antagonism. It made my skin crawl."

"Crap. Ghost?" Angel came swinging around the counter. "Show me where."

I led her out to the side yard, and pointed to the area where I had seen the shadowy figure. "There."

She slowly approached the side of the house, her arms raised, palms facing forward, in front of her. As she neared the place where the shadow had been, she shivered and let out a soft gasp. "There was something here, yes. I think it's gone, but whatever it was, it was nasty as hell." She turned toward me. "How up to date are the wards on the house?"

I bit my lip, trying to remember. We had cleansed it when we moved in, but there had been a fire recently—an old boyfriend had tried to burn us out of house and home —and while we had repaired the damage to the house, we hadn't strengthened the wards after that. Any disruption to a physical structure would disrupt the wards attached to it, that much I knew.

"Hell, we forgot to ward it after the contractors were here to fix the damage Ray caused. We need to get right on that. With your empathic abilities, my magical abilities, and the fact that we work for the Wild Hunt, we're prime beacons for all sorts of astral nasties."

Angel nodded. "I'm learning to ward myself—your mentor, Marilee, has been helping me. But I haven't learned how to effectively protect a house yet. Do you think Raven knows how?"

"If she doesn't, I'll guarantee she'll know someone who

can do it." I pulled out my phone and punched the call button. She answered on the first ring.

"Hey, didn't you get enough of me last night?" she asked with a laugh.

"We like having you around, all right?" I chuckled, then sobered. "Raven, we need to find someone who can ward the house. I saw a shadow man hanging around here earlier and he's trouble."

She didn't even hesitate. "Llew can do it."

"Lugh? *The god*? You know Lugh?" I had met Lugh the Long Handed when I took down the leader of the Tuathan Brotherhood, but I had no clue Raven knew him.

"No, Llew the owner of the Sun & Moon Apothecary. Llewellyn Roberts. You've met him, though I think it was in passing. Or at least, I think you met him. His husband Jordan runs A Taste of Latte, a coffee shop near Llew's store."

"Oh! *That* Llew! Okay, I know who you're talking about. Do you have his number? I need to get someone out here ASAP."

Raven gave me Llew's number. I thanked her and put in a call to him.

"The Sun & Moon Apothecary. Llewellyn Roberts speaking. How may I help you?" His voice was smooth and soothing.

"My name's Ember Kearney. I think we may have met at one point. Anyway, I got your number from Raven BoneTalker. She's a friend of mine. I need to make an appointment with someone to have our house warded. We recently had some work done on it, and that seems to have destroyed the warding we had. Also, I saw a shadow man in the yard today. Can you handle the job? Or do you know somebody who can?"

He laughed, sliding out of his salesman's voice. "Ember, yes, I know who you are. Raven talks about you a lot. I can come out…let's see, a week from Saturday, if you like. I'm booked until then. But I can be there at seven P.M., if that will work."

I frowned. I had hoped he could come out today, but I also knew that he was a busy man, and I was probably lucky to get him so quickly. "Thank you. That's fine. I'll jot you down on the calendar. Do you mind if I text you our address?"

"Text away."

We said good-bye, and I texted him. "He can't make it till a week from next Saturday. Until then, just keep your eyes open."

Angel nodded, shivering as the wind gusted, driving us back inside. As I shut the slider, I thought I saw the same crow out there, staring at me from the gate leading into the gardens. It let out one more shriek, then flew away.

CHAPTER SIX

I slept uneasily that night, and when the alarm went off on Monday morning, I wanted to smash it against the wall. But I managed to drag myself out of bed, shower and dress, and get my ass downstairs in time for breakfast. Angel had made Texas toast out of thick slices of homemade bread, and we had cold ham with the bread, and applesauce. She boxed up two of the four pies to take into work with us.

"How did you sleep?" I asked as I fed Mr. Rumblebutt.

"Not that well," she said. "I had vague nightmares that I can't quite remember."

"Me too. I don't know if it was the presence of that shadow creature yesterday, or whether it's just worrying about it that caused my insomnia, but I tossed and turned most of the night." I glanced around the kitchen. "One car or two? I expect Herne and I'll probably spend some time together tonight, so he can drop me off if that's okay with you."

"We'll take my car, then." Angel slid into her jacket,

handing me the sack containing the pies. "Can you carry this?"

I picked it up and followed her out the door. The morning was wet—it was raining again, a thin drizzle that cut through the mist rising from the ground. It was around forty-four degrees, and the wet chill cut deep into the bone. Maybe I had jumped the mark on planting the kitchen garden, I thought. But hopefully the mulch would keep the roots warm, and the plastic overlay would keep them from getting waterlogged.

The drive into work was slow. There were fender benders every step of the way. I stared at my Maps app and shook my head. "We might as well just hurry up and wait. We're not going to find a quick route into the office today. I'll text Herne that we might be late due to numerous collisions on the streets."

Angel snickered. "Mercury retrograde. Prime accident territory, you know."

I rolled my eyes. I believed astrology worked, though I didn't know much about it, but Angel was an ardent follower, and she had gone so far as to book a class with an astrologer who taught beginning western astrology. The classes would start in a few weeks. The longer we worked with the Wild Hunt, the more comfortable Angel seemed to be getting with her psychic side. She was still the soft-hearted woman I had known since our childhoods, but she was learning to utilize her gifts rather than fear them.

"Well, somebody tell Mercury to back off," I mumbled, staring at the red lines on the map.

"Sure thing, as soon as I take a spaceship in Mercury's general direction," she replied.

We fell into a comfortable silence, and I found myself very grateful that we had already had our caffeine this morning—me a triple-shot mocha, and Angel a double-bagged Earl Grey tea. As we eased along at a snail's pace, her phone jangled.

"Can you see who's texting me?" she asked. "It might be DJ."

I glanced at the phone. "Yep, it's DJ. Want me to read it to you and answer?"

"Please."

"He says that Cooper wants permission to take him to Canada. That there's a big wolf shifter get-together up there during spring break, and Cooper wants to take the whole family." I paused, giving Angel a sideways glance. I knew she felt like she was losing her little brother to Cooper's family with each passing day, and this would just be another reminder of that. But DJ was better off where he was, with a family who could teach him what it meant to be a wolf shifter. That was one thing Angel couldn't do, regardless of how hard she tried. And if DJ were to return to live with her, he'd be in danger from our enemies. Collateral damage dogged the friends and families of the members of the Wild Hunt.

She pressed her lips together, staring straight ahead at the crawling traffic. "Fine. Whatever. He can go. Will you tell him that I give Cooper permission to take him with them? He doesn't have a passport, though—"

I cleared my throat. Another text had just come through. DON'T WORRY ABOUT PASSPORTS. COOPER HAD THE DOCUMENTS TO GET ME ONE.

"Apparently, Cooper had the info he needed. DJ has a passport already."

We came to another jarring halt as the light turned. Angel clutched the steering wheel, hanging her head. "Damn it. Don't even tell me how lucky he is. I know it, okay? I know I should be grateful, but he's my little brother and I only get to see him every few months for a day or so. He's the only family I have left who matters— excluding you, of course. But blood? He's my only blood kin that I care about. And it feels like they've taken him away from me. I miss him. I know I can't offer him what he needs, but damn it, I miss my little brother." She burst into tears, her hands still firmly gripping the wheel. "I love him, Ember. I gave my promise on Mama's J.'s grave that I'd watch after him."

"You *are*. Don't you see? You're taking care of him by letting Cooper be his guardian and role model. You've given DJ something that a lot of orphans never get—a home and a family where he can grow up learning what he needs to learn. If he was with you, he wouldn't have half the chances he does now. And that *isn't* your fault. It's just the way things are." I wanted to make her feel better, but I wasn't going to encourage her to take DJ away from Cooper's home. DJ was thriving there, and he was reaching the age when puberty would soon hit and so would the full effects of his wolf-shifter heritage.

She grimaced, then finally shrugged. "I know. I just wish I could be a part of his life like I used to be. I'm afraid he'll forget me."

"He'll *never* forget you. You were there for the first ten years of his life, and you took care of him when Mama J. died. There's no way that little genius of a brother will *ever* forget you. So quit worrying your heart over it. Tell you what, see if he can come up here for a couple weeks during the summer. He can stay with us and maybe Herne can give you some time off."

"You wouldn't mind having him at the house?" The worry was rife in her voice.

"Of course not. I like DJ. He's a bright kid and he's good hearted. Ask Herne what he thinks. I'm sure he'll understand and I'm sure Cooper will, too."

By the time we reached the office, Angel was back to her smiling self. I could tell that the suggestion had done her a world of good.

As we stepped out of the elevator, Talia glanced up from Angel's desk. "I opened up since you texted you were going to be late." She glanced at the clock. "Only ten minutes—that's not bad, given the snarl traffic was today. I swear, if I hadn't glanced at the traffic app early enough, I would have been running late too. It's bad all over. There must be something going on."

"Mercury retrograde," Angel said, taking her place behind her desk. She motioned to me. "Would you take the pies in the break room and cut them into slices? We might as well have them for the morning meeting. Will you tell Herne that I'll be in there as soon as I listen to messages?"

I nodded, carrying the pies as I followed Talia. As I entered the break room, I saw Herne sitting there, arms crossed across his chest, scowling at the table. Yutani was reading something on his laptop, and Viktor was pouring coffee. As he saw me enter, he held the pot up.

"Cup of joe?"

I nodded, setting the pies on the counter. "Yeah, thanks. Angel baked. Both apple and cherry." I sliced them into six slices each, and then dished up a piece of apple pie for myself. No sense in waiting, really. Glancing around, I pointed to the pie. "Anybody else want a slice?"

"Cherry for me," Yutani said, still glued to his screen.

"Apple would be good," Viktor said.

Talia and Herne both asked for cherry, and as I finished handing the dessert plates around, Angel joined us. Viktor had made a cup of tea for her, and I cut her a slice of apple pie, carrying it to the table for her. When we were finally all settled, Herne called the meeting to order.

"All right, let's get started here. Angel, any pressing messages?"

She nodded. "One, someone who wanted to set up a meeting with you to discuss some problem with his neighbor. Let's see...his name's Thistle Browitch. He says he's a *vanlevitch?*"

Herne leaned forward, uncrossing his arms. "A vanlevitch? I haven't heard from one of the Fair Folk in a long time."

"Fair Folk?" I asked, cocking my head. "What do you mean? They're Fae? Isn't that a nickname for the Elves?"

"No, only in human lore. The vanlevitch are neither Elves, nor are they Sub-Fae. They're akin to the nature devas, somewhere between human kind and the devic world. They're attuned to the cycles of the seasons. Occasionally, you'll find one who has established his own hold rather than working with already established farmers. They tend to be smart but reclusive, and they're connected at the hip with the natural world. If he's truly a vanlevitch, then we'll do what we can to help him. They're always helpful to others, and they work to make the crops ripen on time."

"I put him down to meet with you tomorrow at eleven,

if that's all right." Angel ticked the note off her list. "Other than that, most of the messages were about cases that are closed—just clarifications on how much they owed, and the like."

"Good. Talia, you're next, what did you find out about Lazerous?" Herne glanced at her with an expectant look.

Talia pulled out her tablet and brought up a document. "I've done some deep digging. I think I found Lazerous's origins. If this is the same Lazerous who took my powers, he was born in Greece just short of four thousand years ago, during the Minoan civilization, near Phaistos. This was during the time when one of the finest palaces of the Minoan epoch was being constructed. Let's see, we're talking the Middle Bronze Age."

"He's ancient. That doesn't bode well," Herne said, a forkful of pie in his hand.

"You're right. Lazerous rose in power, becoming a sorcerer known for his abilities, and for his cruelty. No one trusted him, due to his thirst for power. He found out his life was forfeit—the king didn't trust him—and that seems to be when he set up the ritual to become a liche. He committed suicide before the king's assassins could get to him."

"Do you have any idea why he was in the crypt where you found him?" Herne asked.

Talia shook her head. "No, except that it's rumored that his family snuck him there before he took his own life, to prevent the king's henchmen from killing him before he could begin the ritual. There's not much more information," she added, "but it's enough to give us an idea of just how powerful he is."

"Why would he come over here?" Yutani asked.

"He probably got tired of hunting through Europe for magical energy. There's a freshness about the New World, so to speak. Even now, it feels vibrant and young here, and there aren't as many people who would know how to deal with a liche. Or even what one is, for that matter. Given the plethora of magical schools cropping up, well…think of it as 'good eats' for a creature like Lazerous." Talia pressed her lips together, shaking her head.

"So he's old as the hills, and has been accumulating power since the beginning," Viktor said.

"Yes, but remember that Lazerous *needs* to feed. He may accumulate magical power as he feeds, but he expends that power as well. To continue his existence, he has to utilize that power. So while his range of abilities increases with each kill, that doesn't mean that he never weakens or tires. If he were to go without feeding for a while, it would weaken him," she said.

"I get it. While each kill gives him more variety of attacks to choose from, it only renews him for so long. He needs to feed regularly to keep using *any* of his abilities, just like we need food to keep functioning," Angel said.

"That's the long and short of it," Talia said. "But we also need to discuss the headmistress of Winter Hall Academy. I've talked to her briefly. Her name is Nanette Leshan. Obviously, she's one of the magic-born, and she's tough as nails. She doesn't want to talk about the issue, but I think it's because she's frightened. I didn't tell her what's happening yet, but I can tell that she's petrified, and she has no clue what's preying on her students. If word gets out that something's killing her students, the school could be ruined. There have been six attacks so far, with seven students found dead. The one exception was Claudia Randell, who survived."

"I know you contacted her briefly, Talia, but I think we need to talk to Claudia. You talked to her on the phone, right?" Herne asked.

Talia nodded. "In January, after she was found wandering in a dazed, bloody state. She was expelled from school, given her magical powers were gone. Since she was an adult, she received a payoff from Winter Hall to keep quiet about the attacks. I'm pretty sure the school also paid the parents of the minors who died."

I grimaced. "Hush money, and they all took it."

"Right. As far as I can tell, Nanette Leshan has never reported any of the attacks to the cops. I managed to find a couple of the death certificates, and the cause is listed as 'unknown.' I think that Leshan wants to close her eyes and make it all go away."

"At the expense of her students. She hasn't instituted a curfew or anything?" Viktor asked.

Talia shook her head. "No, and I can see her reasoning, even though I don't agree with it. While she wasn't willing to talk to me, I could hear the fear in her voice." She shrugged. "I'm hoping that she'll talk to you, Herne. Your name carries a lot of weight around here."

"I'll give her a call later on this afternoon. It can't hurt, and you may be right. If she's as authoritarian as I think she is, she may only listen to someone else that she considers of equal status."

"You might want to call her sooner than that," Viktor said, looking up from his tablet. "I just got a breaking news alert. Another pair of students are missing—and this time it *was* reported to the police. They're from Winter

Hall Academy, and they were out hiking with friends from the University of Washington. The pair got separated from their friends, and when they didn't show up again, one of the UW students called the police."

"This could break everything wide open," Talia said. "I hate to say it, but I hope the cops don't look into it too deeply. Do you know what would happen if the public knew there was a liche on the loose?"

"Panic, for one thing," Herne said. "And for another, any wannabe hero will be heading into the hills after Lazerous. Angel, get me the mayor, if you would. Then I'm going to want to talk to Nanette—" he paused as the break room door slammed open.

Myrna was standing there, key to the elevator in hand. She tossed it on the table, or rather, she threw it as hard as she could. It bounced off and hit Viktor in the chest. He grabbed hold of it, glaring as he started to stand.

"I got your message, Herne. You really expect me to stop seeing Thantos, because you believe that he tried to feel up Danielle? I've been her mother far longer than you've been in her life. And I can tell you that Thantos has eyes *only* for me. If you think that he's after my little girl, when he has a grown woman ready and waiting for him, then you're a fool."

I groaned. Myrna's ego was as big as her muscles. "Danielle told *me* that Thantos was after her," I said. "How can you believe the word of an older man over a young girl who has no reason to lie?"

Myrna turned on me. Her voice razor-sharp, she leaned forward to yell in my face. "How dare you interfere! Danielle isn't your daughter. She's not even your concern. I warn you, Herne. If you try to prevent me from seeing Thantos, then I want Ember out of *your* life. I don't want her having any contact with my daughter! She's a bad influence."

"How the *hell* can you liken me to Thantos? I've never done anything to hurt your daughter, and he has!" I jumped up out of my chair, hands on my hips. "Don't push me, Myrna, or you may get more than you bargained for."

"Don't forget you're talking to an Amazon. I could bend you and break you like a twig." She started to shrug off her jacket, and I swallowed hard. I was good at fighting, but she was a lot stronger than I was.

"You might be able to break my arm, but I have other powers that I don't think you know about. Again, I warn you—don't push me or you'll regret it." I could feel my Leannan Sidhe side welling up and I tried to suppress her. The last thing I needed to do was seduce and kill Myrna in front of everybody else.

"Enough!" Herne stepped in between us, hands outstretched to keep us away from each other. Viktor quickly moved over to his side, taking Myrna by the arm to pull her away.

"Get your hands off me, you filthy ogre!" She whirled, turning on Viktor.

"Myrna, get the hell out of this office and stay out. I'll be in touch. But don't you *ever* come into this office again, and don't you *ever* talk to Ember like that again." Herne's eyes were blazing, his power rising around him.

I sat down in my chair, pressing my lips together.

Myrna turned, stomping off down the hall. Herne followed her, giving me a warning sign to stay put. He returned a couple moments later, leaning against the doorway, arms crossed.

"Well, it seems I'm going to *have* to talk to my father about her now. Ember, can we have a word in my office?" He turned to the others. "We'll pick this up in a bit. I need to make another phone call before I talk to the mayor."

And with that, he headed toward his office. I followed, wondering if I was going to get a lecture on proper behavior. But I didn't care. Myrna had just landed on my shit list. Trying to calm the anger seething below the surface, I took a deep breath and entered Herne's office.

CHAPTER SEVEN

*H*erne shut the door behind me. I waited, expecting him to blow up. After all, picking a fight with his babymama in the middle of the office wasn't good form. And it wouldn't do anything to help him deal with Myrna, either.

"First, I'm sorry about the way I acted. I know I shouldn't have gotten involved. But when she said she didn't want you to see me…"

"She's being an ass. I don't blame you for defending yourself, but Myrna's not acting rationally, and getting on her bad side will just make you a target like me. I'm going to ask Cernunnos to call the Triamvinate. What I wanted to say, though, is this. She won't ever drive you out of my life. She's trying to hurt us both, because she's angry at me. That won't happen. But please steer clear of her. The last thing you need is to have her as an enemy."

"I'm afraid that's a moot point. She doesn't like me and she's going to try to use me to get back at you and to get even with Danielle. That's what makes me so angry about this. She doesn't give a fuck about her daughter."

"I know. Go back to the break room, and I'll be there in a moment. I'm going to call my father about initiating a meeting of the Triamvinate and see if they will hand down a ruling. Whatever they decide, I'll have to accept. But I'm hoping that they'll have more common sense than Myrna."

A thought struck me. "Does she have to abide by it? After all, she's an Amazon, from the Greek pantheon. Will their ruling affect her?"

"She could appeal it to her own people, but I doubt if she'll try. For one thing, I'm a god and she's not. For another thing, most of the gods tend to respect these sorts of things as long as it's not something far-fetched. I doubt if the Greeks would see this as problematic. Especially if Danielle and I both testify about Thantos taking liberties with her. Regardless of Zeus's history, I think Artemis, who leads the Amazons, would take a dim view of Myrna's stance. And I happen to know Artemis, given she runs an agency like the Wild Hunt. Or rather, her priestesses do."

I nodded, heading for the door. "All right. I'll try to stay out of it."

"Before you go," Herne said, grabbing my wrist and drawing me to him. He drew me into his arms and pressed his lips to mine. Then, stroking my hair, he kissed my forehead and whispered, "No one is going to tell me who I can love. Ember, you're mine. Always remember that. Because I do."

Feeling somewhat pacified, though a layer of anger

still bubbled in my belly, I headed out the door, leaving him to call Cernunnos.

As I entered the break room, all eyes were on me. I waved them off.

"He's calling Cernunnos. He'll be back in a moment."

"All right, spill it. Would you *really* have taken on the Amazon? I can't see you winning, but it sure would have been worth watching," Yutani said, a sly smile on his face. "Better than mud wrestling!"

"Oh hush!" I paused, then flashed him a grin. "Yes, if she had pushed me, I would have probably punched her in the nose. No doubt I would have come out a bloody mess, but I'd give it my best try." I poured myself another cup of coffee. At least Yutani's joke had broken the tension in the room. By the time Herne returned, we were back to discussing Lazerous.

"Cernunnos promised to talk to the Triamvinate. Whatever they decide, I have to abide by, but I'm not all that worried. All right, Angel, get me the mayor."

They headed out to Angel's desk. Less than five minutes later they returned.

"Okay, that's taken care of. The mayor pulled the cops off the case really fast when I told him what we're up against. Now, let me call the headmistress—what was her name?"

"Nanette Leshan. Here's her number, texting it to you now." Talia texted the number to Herne. He put in a call immediately.

"Hello, is this Madame Leshan?... I'm not sure if you

know who I am, but my name is Herne. I run the Wild Hunt Agency… Yes, that one. Yes, I *am* the son of Cernunnos and Morgana… That's what I was calling you about. I was wondering if you would mind talking to my crew? We have important information regarding the dead students… No, I don't feel comfortable talking about this over the phone. I was wondering if we could drive out to the school and talk to you this afternoon… One-thirty? That's fine. We'll be there. If you could text me what building you're in… All right, thank you."

Herne leaned back, then tossed his phone on the table. "She's willing to talk to us. Yutani, Talia, Ember, and I will be heading out there."

"What should I do?" Viktor asked.

"I want you to stay here with Angel. We aren't going to be poking around in the hills today, just talking to the headmistress. Viktor, if anybody drops in to discuss a case, you take the appointment. Don't give them an okay, but just take all the information and tell them that we'll get back to them as soon as possible."

"Got it. You want me to polish up the weapons and make sure everything's ready to go?"

"Good idea. Okay, everybody else, we've got a drive ahead of us, so get ready. Angel, order an early lunch so we can take it on the road with us. Subs would probably be easiest. If anybody wants any pie, eat it now. I just got the interior of my Expedition cleaned and I don't want a mess. All right, everybody hop to it. It's ten o'clock now, and we need to leave by eleven. Given traffic, we still might be late."

As we scattered, I noticed that Talia was looking pensive. I joined her as she walked toward her office.

"Are you all right?"

She stared at the doorknob, her hand on it. "I don't know, to be honest. I'm not entirely sure about all of this. I know I said I wanted to take him down, but I keep remembering when he was draining my powers, and how terrified I felt, and how I thought I was going to die. Even after this long, it still haunts my dreams."

I patted her on the shoulder. "All the more reason to go after him. You were a full-fledged harpy, Talia. And even though you may not want all of those powers back, the fact remains, he stole them from you. And he's stealing lives right and left now. We can't let him continue."

"I know you're right," she said. "I guess I'm just afraid. For the first time in many years, I'm afraid. More for you —my friends—than me. He could drain you all dry."

"Don't worry about it, please. That's what we're here for." I tried to give her a reassuring smile, but it fell flat. I was as scared as she seemed to be.

Talia shrugged, smiling. "Thanks, Ember. You don't know how much I appreciate this."

As she ducked into her office, I watched her go, thinking she was right to be terrified. Liches were powerful. Anybody sane would be afraid of them. With a sigh, I headed back to my own office to get ready for the trip.

On a good traffic day, it would take a little over an hour to get from our office to the town of Buckley. On a bad traffic day? It could take two or three hours or more. Luckily, we started out at quarter to eleven. Lunchtime traffic hadn't really started, and the morning commute was well over. We took Herne's Expedition. It was raining again, typical for March, but the day felt a little warmer. It was nearing fifty-five degrees, a long shot better than the upper forties it had recently been. As the rain skittered off the road, Talia and Yutani scrambled into the back seat while I rode shotgun with Herne. We made sure we had all our equipment—tablets, notebooks, phones, and whatever else we thought we needed, and Talia carried the bag of subs and cookies.

"Can we stop for coffee on the way?" I asked as I fasten my seatbelt.

Herne laughed. "I suppose, but you're paying this time." He winked at me, and I waggled my credit card at him.

"Fine. I'm paying. I have no problem with that as long as I get my caffeine fix."

We stopped at Martini's Espresso Stand, a small independent espresso cart. They did a bang-up job, though, and I absolutely loved their caramel sauce, which was privately made. Once we were all outfitted with lattes, Herne headed onto the freeway.

We would take the I-90 bridge, then turn onto I-405. The stretch of freeway was a nightmare of gridlock during rush-hour traffic, but at this time of day it was relatively clear. Heading south on I-405, we would take Highway 164 to Enumclaw, then double back on Highway 410 down to Buckley. From there it was a short jaunt eastward to the Winter Hall Academy.

As we progressed along, the city thinned out, and once we were on Highway 164, the patches of city were interspersed with more rural neighborhoods. Here, the city was spread out, even though we were still in a dense population zone. For some reason, the road seemed wider to me, and everything felt less closed in. I could breathe easier.

As the rain splattered along the road, Herne kept a close eye on his driving. Highways 164 and 167 were both known for numerous accidents. A lot of semis barreled along the highways, not slowing to account for the rain, and they put themselves and everyone else in danger.

The trees along the side of the road were just starting to bud out. The leaves hadn't unfurled yet but they were there, green tips dotting the branches. The evergreens, firs, and cedars were—of course—still thick with their needles and greenery. Winter only saw them slow down, and the conifers were always thick with needles. The undergrowth had burgeoned out from the more desolate winter. The ferns were waking, the huckleberry starting to bud out, and the skunk cabbage was starting to make its yearly appearance.

After a while we passed the Muckleshoot tribal center, leading onto the Muckleshoot reservation. While I wasn't a fan of gambling, I appreciated that the tribes had managed to use the casinos to dig themselves out of the holes into which the treaties had dumped them. Shortly after we passed the tribal center, we passed the White River amphitheater.

The White River itself had a rocky history. Originating high on the glaciers that spun off Mount Rainier, the White River was wide, though not exceptionally deep except during whitewater season. It rolled along, eventually merging with the Puyallup River, and then poured into Puget Sound.

The water looked chalky, but that was from the minerals high in the glacial peaks, and only the Mud

Mountain Dam helped prevent flooding along the river's corridor. But the dam wasn't always successful. The Mud Mountain Dam also managed to block the passage of fish, threatening several species. In fact, fish were often carried by truck around the dam, and released so that they would be able to complete their migration.

At 196th Avenue, Highway 164 bent to the east. We passed a smokehouse and a dairy, and various stores that were spread out among the farmland. Before long, we entered Enumclaw, a small town northwest of Mount Rainier.

Herne turned on to Highway 410, and a few moments later, before we reached Buckley, he turned east onto southeast Mud Mountain Road. We followed the winding road through the trees, and a few miles later, we slowed when we came to the sign for Winter Hall Academy.

Pausing to let a car pass in the oncoming lane, Herne then turned left into the spacious driveway and we headed toward the main campus.

The drive up to the main campus was lined with trees —mostly giant maples, their leaf buds barely registering on the boughs. But in another few weeks, they'd be spreading out, growing like crazy in a cacophony of spring green.

The lawns were spacious, spreading wide and green, thick with patches of moss that gave a velveteen look to the groundcover. Along the drive, we saw tennis courts, and a track for track and field, as well as what looked like an obstacle course. A couple students were racing through it, leaping and jumping as they practiced parkour, smoothly gliding over benches and stairwells and tall stone railings. I wondered what kind of magic they practiced, or if they were just working on their physical fitness.

Up ahead, we could see a series of tall brick buildings, the bricks pristine white. A turnoff led to the closest one, which from the map that Yutani had handed me, I pinpointed as the library. Massive bay windows looked over the grounds, and lights twinkled from within. A parking lot hedged the side of the building, and walkways led to other parts of the campus. To the right, another turnoff led to the administration building. Herne turned in, slowing down to match the fifteen mile per hour speed limit posted along the way. The parking lot was full, although four visitor spots were still open. Herne eased into one of them, turning off the ignition.

"Here we are. The headmistress's office is in this building. We take the stairs over there, which lead up to the main entrance. There's also a ramp around to the side for disabled access." He unbuckled his seatbelt, stretching as he yawned. We'd been on the road about seventy-five minutes, but that's still a long time to sit in a car. "Let's have a bite to eat first. There's a bench over there, and the rain has let off enough to where we can sit outside."

"Come on, let us eat in your car. It's cold outside, and by the looks of the clouds, I don't trust it not to start up again soon." I made with the puppy-dog eyes. "It's not like your car is brand-new. You may have just had it cleaned, but it's seen a lot more mud and debris than a few sandwiches are going to cause." As he hesitated, I wheedled him. "Do you honestly think we're never going to be climbing in this car again, covered with mud from a fight?"

"Oh, all right," he said, laughing. "I just wanted to enjoy

a clean car for a little while. At least use your napkins, okay?"

Talia chuckled. "If we drop anything, we'll clean it." She began handing out the sandwiches that Angel had sent along with us, along with bottles of water and small bags of cookies.

I eagerly unwrapped mine, smacking my lips with satisfaction when I saw that it was turkey, Swiss, fat slices of tomato, and thick leaves of lettuce. I bit into the bread, moaning as the flavor hit my tongue.

"Mmm, this is so good. I'm hungrier than I thought."

"You're always hungry," Herne said with a laugh. But he didn't waste any time unwrapping his own sandwich and biting into it. As we finished our lunches, I glanced at the clock.

"It's one twenty-four. We should get in there if we're going to be on time." I slid out of my seat, brushing off the crumbs on the sidewalk. Then, slinging my purse over my shoulder, I shut the door and walked around front, waiting for the others. As Herne beeped his key fob to lock the Expedition, we jogged up the stairs, heading for the entrance of the administration building.

THE BUILDING ROSE TO AN IMPRESSIVE HEIGHT, REMINDING me of a combination between an old cathedral and a pristine village inn. It, too, was made of white brick, embellished with an edging of scrollwork. The scrollwork wasn't made out of iron, that much I could tell just by reaching up to place my hand near it. It looked to be some sort of metal, though I wasn't sure just what. Intricate, it reminded me of Celtic knot work.

The stairway up the slope from the parking lot was fashioned out of stone, with a sturdy stone railing. Once again, I noticed a ramp on the other side, also made out of stone, giving access for those who couldn't climb stairs or who were in wheelchairs.

"When was this academy founded? The buildings look fully up to code and relatively new. They're clean, I'll say that for them, and around here that takes some doing to keep the moss and mildew from growing amok."

Yutani consulted his tablet as he paused on the stair belong me. "It was founded in 2004, so it's relatively new. Winter Hall is based on several academies from the East Coast. No wonder they don't want any scandal. They're still too new to have a strong standing in the community. Although it says here that they get along well with the townsfolk in Buckley, and they've brought an economic revival to the area. That's not surprising, given almost seven hundred students attend school here, ranging from kindergarten through the first two years of college."

"What's the ratio of students to teachers?" Talia asked.

Yutani skimmed the article. "That depends on the grade, but no class will ever have more than fifteen students per teacher, according to this. That's a good ratio. I'll bet jobs here are prized." He tucked his tablet back in his messenger bag and dashed to catch up with us as we headed for the door.

I was in front, and I pushed open the doors in front of me, stepping into the tile-clad hallway. Nonskid rugs offered us a place to wipe our feet—no doubt a good idea considering how much it rained, and how slick tile could be. As we entered the foyer, the smell of learning overwhelmed me. It was a smell I associated with schools and children, and libraries. I inhaled deeply, holding the fragrance in my lungs for a moment before slowly exhaling.

"Let's see, here's a campus map," Talia said, stepping over to an interactive video display. It was a table, with a hologram spread across it, only the hologram was clear and showed a map of the buildings on campus, and a flickering red light read YOU ARE HERE. A keyboard offered a place to type in requests and Talia typed in *headmistress's office*. Within less than five seconds, the scene on the hologram changed to show the layout of the administration building, and a dotted line pointed us in the direction we wanted to go.

"I love technology," Yutani said. "I can't imagine living without it."

"Well, at some point you *did* live without it. You're over two hundred years old, aren't you?" I asked, poking him in the ribs.

He swatted my finger away, but grudgingly laughed. "Yes, I did live without it. Which is why I can say that the old days sucked. Count yourself lucky that you've never had to go without the Internet," he said.

I wasn't about to argue with that. "Come on, guys, the headmistress's office should be just around the corner. We're going to be just in time if we hurry."

We hustled around the corner, to find ourselves standing in front of an office that had Nanette's full name stenciled across it, with the word HEADMISTRESS underneath it. I cautiously opened the door and peeked in, to see a receptionist sitting there in front of yet another door. I waved to the others and they followed me in.

"We have an appointment to see Nanette Leshan. We're from the Wild Hunt Agency."

The receptionist, a sturdy and formidable-looking woman, glanced at a datebook in front of her. She nodded. "Let me ring for her." She picked up the phone, punched the button, and after a moment said, "The people from the Wild Hunt Agency are here to see you. Should I escort them in?" A second later, she replaced the phone on the receiver. "Go right in, Ms. Leshan is waiting for you." She motioned to the door behind her, buzzing us in.

We walked around her desk, and I cautiously peeked in.

"Come in, please make yourself comfortable." As Nanette Leshan stood behind her desk, I felt a tremor of recognition. There was something about her that seemed familiar. She looked me in the eye and gave me a broad smile. "I did not realize that one of my own people is working with the Wild Hunt." And with that she held out her hand to me. As I shook it, I realized that Nanette Leshan was not only magic-born, but she was Dark Fae as well. In other words: she was a tralaeth, like me.

CHAPTER EIGHT

$\mathcal{N}$anette Leshan was short and thin, and so bony she looked like she was carved out of marble. Her skin was a rich golden brown, and her gaze was so stern that it bespoke great punishment if you disobeyed her. But behind that rigid stature, I sensed a warmth that also promised to be fair and just. The fact that she was a tralaeth startled me. I seldom met other tralaeths, and all half-bloods, whether mixed Light and Dark, or mixed Fae and other races, were considered anathema.

She nodded to Herne but held her hand out to me.

"Welcome to Winter Hall Academy. Won't you all have a seat? Wilhelmina, if you could see to coffee and anything else our guests might prefer, I'd appreciate it."

The assistant—apparently Wilhelmina—nodded, pulling out a steno pad. "What may I bring you?"

"Coffee with cream and sugar is fine for me," I said.

Talia nodded. "I'll have the same, light on the sugar, please."

Yutani asked for a cup of tea, and Herne declined the offer. As Wilhelmina hurried out of the room and shut the door behind her, we turned to Nanette. The moment the door closed, her composure vanished and she slumped, looking glum.

"Thank you for coming. I know I resisted talking to you before, and I apologize. I didn't realize what a problem this was going to be, but it's obviously only getting worse. I can only explain so many times to the students' parents why their children died, especially when I don't even know myself. The truth is, I have no idea what I'm up against. What the *school* is up against. Do we have a serial killer? A deranged goblin out there in the woods? I don't know." She leaned back in her chair.

"Then allow us to enlighten you, because we know *exactly* what you're facing. I'm glad you agreed to talk to us, because I doubt if you have anyone here who can handle this problem," Herne said. He tended to be blunt and to the point.

Nanette stared at him as the door opened again and Wilhelmina brought in a tray of coffee cups. She handed Talia and me our drinks, then gave Yutani his tea. Without a word, she picked up the tray and left again, firmly shutting the door behind her.

Nanette leaned forward, resting her elbows on her desk. "You say you know what we're up against. Please, tell me. I need something to tell their parents."

"You aren't going to want to tell their parents about this, I guarantee you." Herne looked grim.

Talia leaned forward. "Have you ever heard of a liche?"

The color drained from Nanette's face and, with a gasp, she leaned back in her chair. "A *liche*? Are you certain? I've heard of them, of course, but they're rare. How did one come to be in the mountains here? I thought they were found mainly in the Old World."

Talia was the first to speak. "Not only is your serial killer a liche, he's an extremely powerful one. I know because long, long ago, I ran across him when he lived in Greece. That's where he originally underwent the ritual to change him into a liche. He drained me of my powers, but I managed to survive. I'm one of the few lucky ones."

Nanette slowly shook her head. "What powers did he steal from you?"

"I'm a harpy. He took almost every power I have—or had. Herne's mother, Morgana, granted me a great favor. She offered me a permanent glamour so that I could walk among humankind without being targeted."

"Tell me about him. Everything you know," Nanette said.

Talia licked her lips. "Well, his name is Lazerous. Almost four thousand years ago, he became an enemy of the court. He found out that the king was targeting him, so he set up the ritual of transformation and killed himself before the assassins could reach him. His family helped him. I met him centuries later, after he had time to gain power. I'm grateful to say I've never encountered him since then, but when I found out he had made the journey overseas and was living nearby, I knew I had to destroy him. I don't like unfinished business."

For the first time, Talia made me feel wary. The firmness in her voice—the absolute calm on her face—was daunting.

Nanette blanched. She just kept shaking her head as Talia spoke, looking more frightened by the minute. After a moment, she cleared her throat. "You're right. There's nothing I, or any professor on this campus, can do. None of us are powerful enough to take on a creature like that. I've tried to keep things quiet because the school is still so new it could fold over a business like this. And Winter Hall is too good to see it die. We help more students than you can imagine."

"You have to instill a curfew and you need to keep the students on campus until we can figure out how to defeat Lazerous," Herne said.

Nanette pressed her hand against her stomach, grimacing. "That's easier said than done. I'll set the curfew, of course, but though I can keep the minors on campus, I can't necessarily prevent the older students from sneaking out. I've learned the hard way. The children will listen, but teens and early adults? During those youthful years, they seem to think they're invincible. If you tell them it's dangerous, they want to prove you wrong. Yet if I come clean about what's actually happening, how long do you think this school will stay open? I guarantee within a week, it would be empty and it would never recover, even when you do kill the liche."

Herne shifted in his seat. "That's why we're here. We intend to destroy Lazerous. But it's not going to be an easy process."

"What do you need from me?" Nanette asked. "What can I do to help?"

"We need to talk to Claudia, the girl who survived Lazerous's attack," Herne said. "And we need to talk to the roommates of your missing students. Then we'll head out to see if we can find them before Lazerous does. Because unfortunately, if he finds them first, they're dead."

"Thank you so much," Nanette let out a sigh of relief. "I don't mind telling you how heavy this has all weighed on my heart and my conscience. I've had to lie to parents, to create *accidents* that would fit with the remains of their loved ones. I've had to pay hush money to keep people from talking. And if Winter Hall loses its reputation, it loses its funding and everything else that makes it the institution it is."

A cynical part of me wondered if she was just trying to save her own skin more than the school's rep, but I decided to let the thought go. Nanette seemed sincere. But a thought crossed my mind, and I wanted to know the answer. It would also affect how we talked to the students' parents, if we ended up doing so.

"How does your heritage affect your interaction with parents of your students? I mean…" I hesitated. While I had reclaimed the word *tralaeth* and wore like a badge, it was a nasty insult when used by someone who meant it that way.

Nanette seemed understand what I was trying to ask. "The fact that I'm a tralaeth doesn't bother most of the parents because almost all of them are from the magic-born. The Fae don't send their children to schools like this, at least not to Winter Hall. My mother was Dark Fae, my father was magic-born. I inherited my father's magical abilities rather than my mother's qualities. I grew up among the magic-born and encountered very little discrimination. So most of the students and their parents don't even blink an eye." She gave me a gracious smile.

I recognized the expression on her face. She knew what it was like to be ostracized, just like I did, and she had made her life work for her, even though the Fae had turned their backs on her.

"Did TirNaNog give your mother a hard time about her marriage?"

Nanette laughed, her harsh, angular features softening with her laughter. She looked almost pretty at that moment.

"Oh, make no mistake. My mother was excommunicated from her family and the city. Thrown out with the bathwater, you might say. I've never met any of my Fae relatives, but my father's parents doted on me. I've never once regretted my mixed bloodline."

"Regarding the students who are missing, we'll need information on them. Anything you can give us. And we'd like to talk to their friends, to see if we can figure out where they were planning to go hiking." Yutani pulled out his tablet, ready to take notes.

Nanette nodded, handing us two files that were on her desk. "Here are their student files. They're brothers, you know. I haven't notified their parents yet. I know that's wrong, but I just didn't know what to say. I didn't want to scare them, not before I knew the worst."

"For now, let us take care of this. Talia, call the parents and tell them that their sons went out on a hike and haven't returned. Tell them that's all we know, but ask them if there was any place in particular that their—" Herne paused, skimming over the files. "Ask them if there's any place in particular around here that Chaz and Branson talked about." He glanced at Nanette. "If you could ask your secretary to give us Claudia's information, I'd appreciate it. And also the names of the boys' roommates. We might as well start there, before we leave."

Nanette asked us to wait in her office while she went out to talk to Wilhelmina. A few moments later, she returned, a paper in hand. She handed it to Herne.

"Here's Claudia's information. And I've asked the roommates of the missing students to report to my office. They should be here in a few minutes, so you can question them. I'd rather not have you seen around campus at this point because I don't want to start off a panic. You are somewhat well known around the area. I'll instruct Wilhelmina to get the names of the victims for you, but be aware, if you talk to their parents, they all think their children died due to one accident or another, and none of them are aware of the other...*incidents*." She looked vaguely uncomfortable.

"We'll do our best to keep this quiet, but I warn you, we might not be able to keep it that way in the long run," Herne said.

"I know," Nanette said, looking pained. She glanced at Talia. "I'm surprised Lazerous hasn't come after you," she said, looking at her. "Creatures like that usually keep a list of those who managed to escape their plans. Do you know if he's ever made an attempt to trace you?"

Talia shrugged. "I don't know. In fact, I never even thought about it. What can you tell us about these brothers? The boys who are missing? How powerful are they?"

Nanette glanced through their files. "The twins? They're twins in looks only. Their powers are drastically different. Chaz has a knack for water magic, and in fact, he's gifted with healing magic. He's slated to enter into the medical arts next quarter. Branson is more rough-and-tumble, and while he doesn't have a knack for intricate detail, he's talented with earth-oriented magic. He's studying herbology and farming. But both of them are gifted, magically, and they emanate a strong aura. I can easily see how Lazerous would find them appealing." She winced, as though the words hurt her.

"Where can we talk to their roommates?" Herne asked, his voice soft.

"Let me check," she said. She walked to the door and peeked out, murmuring something to her secretary. Then she turned back to us. "Wilhelmina will escort them into one of the conference rooms down the hall. Are you going to tell them what's happened?" She turned a pleading gaze to Herne.

He paused, then shook his head. "No, I don't think it would be wise to let this information go public at this point. You said you haven't contacted their parents yet?"

"No," Nanette said. "but I have to soon, given their roommates called the police before they came to me. I guess they heard about the other missing students and didn't want to wait any longer than necessary. I'm also worried that some reporter is going to find out about the other missing students, and then everything will be lost. If that makes the news, Winter Hall will immediately be shut down."

"While I respect how much you care about the school, you should have spoken to us when Talia first contacted you. Surely you thought something was abnormal?" Herne said.

"Actually, no. We had no clue that the students who were found dead had been drained of the powers, not until Claudia escaped. You see, that's the thing. There wasn't more than a scratch or two on them. The medical examiner didn't even know what killed them and put it down to hypothermia. There was nothing in the toxi-cology reports, there were no marks on them, and there was absolutely nothing wrong with them except they were dead. I thought for a while that they were all just stupid kids getting lost in the woods during the winter."

"I can tell you how they died," Talia said. "Having your powers drained puts an incredible strain on the body. It can trigger heart failure or paralysis. Then if they're still alive but left for dead, they could easily freeze to death. What did the parents of the other students say?"

"There wasn't much they could blame us for. So there wasn't much to say. But we still offered them a settlement as long as they didn't discuss the deaths with the media. I told them I have an investigator on the case, and that we'd be in touch as soon as we found out anything."

"What about Claudia?"

"We had to discharge her from the school. There's not much someone without magical powers can gain from going to school here. But we also made a settlement with her as long as she didn't discuss the case. I'll contact her and tell her it's okay to talk to you."

Yutani let out a snicker. "Way to protect the school," he said, flashing Nanette a cynical look.

She bristled. "Look, all of you can scoff as much as you like. And you can tell me that I was wrong for trying to protect this academy. But the fact is, Winter Hall serves the needs of a number of students, and it does so with an impeccable record. But since we're relatively new, funding depends on individual donors as well as tuition. Imagine how that would dry up if people thought our students were being killed off." She met Yutani's gaze, her back stiffening. "You can imagine just how that would drain our reserves. I'm the headmistress of the school. I don't own it, but as long as I'm in this position I'm expected to do what I can to keep the school running smoothly, and that includes keeping it free from scandal."

Yutani shrugged, looking away.

Herne stood, sliding his hands into his pockets. "If you could lead us to the conference room where we can talk to the students, I'd appreciate it." He glanced at the rest of us. "Come on. Let's not bother Ms. Leshan any longer." To Nanette, he added, "We'll be in touch as soon as we find out anything. As I said, we'll make a trip out to the area where the students went to see if we can find them alive. And we'll do what we can regarding Lazerous."

"Thank you," she said. "I have to admit, this has been one of the most trying periods in my tenure as head-mistress here." She opened the door, motioning to Wilhelmina. "If you could take them into the conference room, then escort Chaz and Branson's roommates to me first."

As we headed out of her office, I glanced back at Nanette. She had a lot to prove, even though she might deny it. And dealing with any members of the law enforcement was going to be difficult, given she was half-Fae. It was like wearing an invisible bumper sticker that read, "Don't treat me with respect."

Wilhelmina led us down the hall to a conference room. A plaque by the door read CONFERENCE ROOM 102. She opened the door for us, standing back.

"I'll bring the students here as soon as they're ready. Meanwhile, there is a restroom down the hall and around the corner to your right. And I've made coffee, so help yourselves." She waited as we entered the room, then shut the door behind us.

I turned to Herne. "She may have made some mistakes, but I truly think that Nanette wants to do the best she can for both the students and the school. She's in a tenuous position at this point."

"You're right on that," Herne said. "Let's just hope when we talk to the boys' roommates that they have something for us to go on, because if the media finds out there's a liche in the area, a lot of people are going to be hurt. You know how vigilantes are."

With that thought, we took our seats, falling silent as we waited for Chaz's and Branson's roommates.

CHAPTER NINE

*C*haz's roommate, Triston, was a rather nerdy young man, and if he wasn't a genius, he gave a good impression of one. On the other hand, Jared, Branson's roommate, was congenial and laid-back, and I imagined when he wasn't being questioned, he would have a ready smile for anyone.

Unfortunately, neither one of them could tell us much to help. We questioned them as to why Branson and Chaz had chosen to go hiking, and the only thing either had to say was that the boys were athletic and liked to be out and about. Neither one knew the exact route the brothers had decided to take, but after talking to both Triston and Jared, we had a slightly better understanding of Branson and Chaz.

The twins were close—in fact, best friends, and they went everywhere together. They loved the outdoors, and regularly practiced rock climbing on the rock walls at the gym. Chaz was into parkour, while Bronson was hell on wheels when it came to free climbing. Both of them also did base jumping, which was highly frowned on at the school, and Chaz could swim like a pro. They routinely went off on camping trips and day hikes, so it was no surprise that they had taken off without much of a second thought.

It also seemed they were both handy in the wilderness and knew plenty of survival techniques. It wasn't likely that they had gotten lost, although that could happen in the blink of an eye, even for pros. Western Washington's forests were thick, and it was easy to get turned around. But given the skills the brothers had, I doubted they had run into that sort of trouble.

"Do you think they're okay?" Jared asked, concern filling his eyes. "If anybody can survive out there, Branson and Chaz can. But I don't know—I just have a bad feeling about this one. Even veteran hikers can tumble down a ravine and break a leg, or slip off a mossy rock."

"Are the boys risk-takers? Would they be likely to take chances?" Talia asked.

Triston bit his lip, then nodded. "That's one thing I would say about them. Branson and Chaz aren't afraid to take risks. They're *so* talented and *so* skilled that their egos can get ahead of them. I went camping with them once and swore I'd never do that again. By the time I got home, every muscle in my body hurt. They aren't the best hiking partners for lightweights."

"Thank you for being so helpful. Anything you can tell us means that we have that much more ammunition to find the boys. You're right. Even the best of climbers can make stupid mistakes if their ego outmatches their skill. And accidents can happen to the best of us." Herne stood, indicating the interview was over. "If you'd be so good as to say nothing about this meeting until we find out what happened, we'd appreciate it."

"Sure," Triston said. He paused, then added, "They *have* to be okay. Chaz has to be all right." His voice was strained and I suddenly put two and two together.

"You're Chaz's boyfriend, aren't you?" I blurted out.

Triston blinked, flushing a deep red, but the look in his eyes told me I had hit the nail on the head. After a moment, he nodded.

"Please don't say anything. His parents don't know he's gay. Branson knows, and he helps cover up for him because their parents are so conservative. They claim to love their sons, but if they knew about Chaz, they'd kick him out. We've talked about that before."

"Parents can surprise you," Talia said, but Triston shook his head.

"Not Chaz's and Branson's parents. They disowned Willow—the boys' sister—because she married a black man. They'd go ballistic if they knew about Chaz. They expect them both to continue the family dynasty."

Herne snorted. "Yeah, they really love their boys, all right. Okay, we won't say a word about that, and we'll let you know what we find out, since it's doubtful their parents would."

I glanced at Jared. "You know about this?"

"Of course. The four of us hang out together a lot, so there was no hiding it. And Triston's right. Chaz's parents would disown him. Chaz keeps hoping to do something so spectacular that his father will overlook his sexuality, but I don't think that's going to happen. Their old man is a piece of work. He's never been overtly hostile, but he's made it clear that either his sons do things his way, or they're out of the family."

As Jared and Triston left the room, I let out a long sigh and rested my elbows on the table. Life was hard enough in this world without feeling like your own family was acting against you. I knew that all too well. My parents were different and had paid for it with their lives, and I had almost died at the hands of my grandfather, just for being who I was.

Herne leaned over to kiss me on the forehead. "Don't dwell," he said. "We'd better head back to Seattle. We'll stop in to talk to Claudia when we get there. Talia, give her a call and ask if she can be free this afternoon or evening. It's two-thirty now, and we'll be heading into rush-hour traffic on the way home."

After bidding Nanette good-bye, we left the school.

As Winter Hall Academy faded behind us, Mount Rainer peeked out of the clouds to the southeast. She loomed over the land, a dangerously beautiful sentinel, and the White River tumbled off of her glaciers. I whispered a silent prayer to the mountain, asking her to show us the way to find Lazerous and the boys. After all, to the local tribes Mount Rainier—or Mount Tahoma, as her original name had been—had been a goddess. But I had no clue if she could hear me. Or if she even cared.

As expected, rush-hour traffic was bad. We finally made it back to Seattle by four-thirty, passing at least two car crashes on the way. Luckily, it looked like they had only been fender benders and not full-on wrecks. Claudia lived in the Seward Park district, in an area where bars on the windows were standard, and bulletproof doors were a wise investment.

Of course, in a number of the flop houses where the slumlords rented beds to the streeps in shifts, renters were lucky just to have a place to stay for the night—or the day, depending on which shifts they were assigned. It was common to see the streeps out on the corners, begging for money. While there were some grifters and conmen among them, all too many were so beaten down by the system that even the social welfare organizations offering a hand up found it hard to reach them. It was hard to accept help when you thought you were beyond hope.

Claudia lived in a weathered duplex on Brandon Street. The paint was peeling off the siding, and there were bars on the door and the windows. What little front lawn the duplex had was covered in beauty bark, one side edged with a squarish patch of hedge, while the other side had a fern that was as tall as the bottom of the windows. Neither of the plants looked healthy and there was generally an air of abandonment to the place.

Herne pulled over in front of the duplex. There was a small beat-up hatchback in front of us, and I assumed that was Claudia's car. We had called ahead and she said she'd be waiting for us. As we got out of the Expedition, I looked around, feeling slightly nervous. This was one of the areas where drive-bys were common, and there was an underbelly of gang warfare in the area that the police couldn't seem to control.

We followed Herne up the short sidewalk to the door, where he gave one loud rap and waited. A moment later, the door opened, and I could see it was still latched by a chain.

"Yes?" came the cautious query.

"We're from the Wild Hunt," Herne said.

There was a jangling as she removed the chain from the latch and opened the door, then unlocked the barred screen door and invited us in.

The inside of the duplex was just as rundown as the outside, and the furniture looked like it had been new about thirty years ago. The sofa was sagging, there were scratches on the armchair, and the dinette table and chairs seem to hail from the fifties. The duplex was small, with a kitchenette just off of the living room. Two other doors led to a bedroom and a bathroom, from what I could see.

"Won't you have a seat?" Claudia said, extending her hand to the sofa. "It's a little touchy, so be cautious as you sit down. It has a few loose springs, I'm afraid."

Since there was only room for three of us on the sofa, Yutani carried over one of the dinette chairs as Claudia took her seat in the armchair. She looked worn out. She had long brown hair, pulled back in a ponytail, and beautiful blue eyes, but they held a sadness that was palpable. She was wearing a pair of jeans and a T-shirt. An apron hung over one of the other dinette chairs that read POP UP JONES, which was a chicken fast-food joint popular in Seattle.

She must have noticed what I was looking at because she said, "Yes, I work for Pop Up Jones. Even though Winter Hall Academy paid me hush money, I don't want to waste it before I figure out what to do with the rest of my life." Her voice was bitter, and I couldn't blame her.

From what we had read, Claudia had been at the top of her class before Lazerous drained her powers and she was forced to leave the academy.

"Did Ms. Leshan contact you and tell you it was okay to talk with us?" I asked.

Claudia nodded. "She did, about two hours ago." She paused, then added, "Do you know what attacked me? Whatever it was, it killed my boyfriend and stole my powers. I'd like to know what it was that ruined my life."

I glanced over at Talia, who cleared her throat.

"Claudia, the creature that attacked you is called a liche. It attacked me many years ago—actually centuries ago. It stole my powers, too. I managed to get away like you did."

Claudia settled her gaze on Talia, then asked, "So what were you before this liche attacked you? One of the magic-born?"

"No," Talia said. "I was a harpy."

"A *harpy*? You don't look it," Claudia said.

Talia paused for a moment, her expression veiled. Finally, she spoke again.

"I'm under a glamour. It helped me forge a new life for myself. Lazerous took everything from me, or so I thought. He left me broken and in pain. It took me forever to reach my home and I don't know how I managed it. One of my wings was broken. I remember nothing from the time he drained my powers until I arrived home."

"What did your parents say?"

Talia shrugged. "My mother turned me out the moment I had healed up. I was useless in her eyes. I couldn't even hunt. I survived by scavenging until Herne found me and gave me a new life." She held Claudia's gaze. "I'm going to be blunt. You need to move out of this hellhole, and you need to decide to change your life. I know the hell you're going through right now because I went through it, but in the long run your anger won't sustain you."

Claudia blinked. She hesitated for a moment, then said, "I don't know how. I lost the love of my life. I was on my way to becoming a powerful sorceress. I was training with the best. And then…nothing. How do you do it? How do you let go when you're no longer who you were?"

The meeting felt oddly intimate, as though Talia and Claudia were the only ones in the room. I slipped my hands in my pockets, unsure whether or not to look away.

"You mourn your old self, and then you accept that you are living in a *new normal*. You *decide* to move on. You make a choice to accept the cards life has handed you, and fashion them into a winning combination. It won't look the way that you thought it would, but who knows? It might end up being better."

Claudia stared at her, a sullen look on her face. She started to shake her head, but Talia held up her hand.

"Oh, you can be stubborn. You can kick and scream and let bitterness consume you. Or you can accept that life doesn't play favorites, and you can decide that you aren't going to let Lazerous win. If you let him break you, if you go through life feeling cheated, then he truly *is* the winner." Talia leaned forward. She took Claudia's hands in hers. "Promise me you won't let him win. Because you're *alive*. You survived what was almost an unsurvivable situation. Don't let him take your life away from you twice."

Claudia seemed to be thinking over everything Talia

had said. After a moment, she let out a soft breath. "I'll try. Can I please call you when I need to talk to someone? Nobody's gone through this before, no one I know."

I broke in. "Actually, Claudia, when you think about it, a great many people go through having to rearrange their lives. Someone walking down the street gets hit by a bus, and *boom*, they go from fully mobile to disabled in the blink of an eye. Or someone who was living paycheck to paycheck loses their job, and all of a sudden they're home-less, with no idea of where to go or what to do. Everybody in this world is one step away from major change. All it takes is for one thread to unwind and we can all slide into what feels like catastrophe."

The anger seemed to vanish from her eyes. "I suppose you're right. I guess it's just when it happens to you, it feels like nobody else in the world understands. My parents didn't understand. All they knew was their bril-liant daughter was no longer the darling of Winter Hall Academy. When I told them what I could remember, all they said was that I was stupid for spending time on hiking and I should have been in my room studying."

So she hadn't just lost her powers. She had lost her family's support.

"Of course you can call me if you need to," Talia said, pulling out a card from her purse. "I'll give you my private number. Meanwhile, do you mind if we ask you some questions? We're looking for a couple missing boys right now, and we want to destroy Lazerous so that he can never do this to anyone again."

"Of course I'll help." Claudia paused, then the blood drained from her face. "Missing boys?"

"Yes, two boys," I said. "Twins. They went hiking and

vanished. We're hoping to find them alive, but we need as much information as we can so we can get out there and hunt for them."

"Whatever I can tell you, I most certainly will."

"Tell us exactly what happened that day—as much as you can remember it."

"Joachim and I decided to go for a hike. The academy had warned us against going into a certain area near the old White Peak Copper Mine, but nobody ever said why. We didn't know that several students had already died in that particular area. If they had said that it was dangerous—"

"You weren't told that it was dangerous? I thought a schoolwide warning had been sent out to avoid that area," Yutani said.

Claudia shook her head. "There are several school messaging systems. The EB—emergency broadcast—protocol is considered high alert, and that's when—for example—if Mount Rainier were to have a lahar or start erupting, that would be a high-alert warning. Then there are the standard WHGA text alerts that come through every morning on our phones."

"WHGA? What's that?" I asked.

"Winter Hall General Announcement. The announcements range from everything from classes being cancelled to reminders that the school would be closed for a few days during break. That sort of thing. This memo was sent through the standard WHGA protocol."

"Oh, for fuck's sake," I muttered. "They didn't want to cause a panic. You can bet that's why so many students actually ignored the warning. They didn't consider it an actual emergency."

"I'm guessing you're spot-on with that assessment," Herne said. "Before we leave here, remind me to call Ms. Leshan and tell her that she damn well better send out a high-alert memo. An EB? Whatever you call it." His face grim, he pulled out his phone and set it on his knee.

"All right, what happened next?" Yutani asked.

"Well, we went hiking up around the old mine. I thought I heard a little girl crying somewhere around the entrance. I was worried that someone had gotten trapped in there. I told Joachim, but he couldn't hear it. But I kept hearing her voice. I convinced him to go in with me," Claudia said, casting her gaze down.

"What happened?"

Her voice choked up. "He finally agreed. We went inside the mine, and it felt like… I don't know how to explain it, but it's as though we were compelled to go in. Or rather, I was. At first Joachim refused to go any farther, but then he caught up with me. The next thing we knew, a hideous creature appeared out of the tunnel."

"Did you get a look at him?"

Claudia nodded. "A light blazed around him, and he looked like a desiccated mummy, without the wrappings. Joachim pushed me behind him. He told me to run. I managed to break free of whatever spell was holding me and I turned to go, but then Joachim screamed."

She paused again, biting her lip as she fought back the tears. We gave her time and she finally said, "The creature was hovering over him, its bony fingers wrapped around his head. There was a mist rising around them, and the— you said it's a liche? The liche was drinking his energy. I don't know how I knew it, but I did."

"What did you do then?" Herne asked.

"I ran. I turned and ran, leaving him there." She burst into tears. "I ran because there wasn't anything else I could do. I was almost to the entrance when I heard a noise behind me. Then he got hold of me. He was hideous and he began draining my powers, like he had Joachim's. I fought back as hard as I could. I know one of the Unmaking spells, even though I'm not supposed to. I summoned up the last bit of my energy and cast it on him. Then everything went black and the next thing I knew, I opened my eyes and I was staggering through the woods, alone and bruised and bloodied."

She closed her eyes, pressing her lips together. After a moment, Talia gently prompted her to continue.

"I vaguely remembered what had happened, and I was terrified he'd come after me. I hid off trail for a while, but after a while, I realized I was alone. I staggered down the trail to the nearest building I could find. There are a couple of food stands along the way. Anyway, the barista at an espresso stand called the school for me. They came and got me. I don't remember a lot after that until I woke up in the infirmary. They found Joachim's body, dumped on the trail. And I realized, very quickly, that I no longer had any of my powers."

Claudia finished her story, looking sickened. "Will you tell me what a liche *is*? I think I've heard the word, but I have no clue as to what the creature actually is. Is it a demon?"

I shook my head. "No, a demon's from the astral plane and has never been human. A liche was once one of the magic-born. While they were alive, liches were powerful sorcerers. Some had curses cast on them, while others voluntarily performed a ritual that would turn them into a liche after they died. They feed on magical energy, and they're able to drain both powers and the actual life force out of their victims."

"Are they like a vampire?" Claudia asked.

Herne shook his head. "No, not really. Most vampires, at least now, are reasonable to a point. But liches are greedy. Their thirst for power takes over. The more they feed, the more their hunger grows. They not only crave the power of others, they need it to continue their existence. A liche who goes without feeding for too long will fade away and eventually become a form of ghoul, without sense or reason."

"And you say this Lazerous has been alive for thousands of years?" Claudia bit her lip.

"Yes, and he's extremely powerful. Which is why we have to keep him from ever doing this to anyone again. Every kill makes him stronger, every victim who loses their powers adds to his own. We're lucky that there are so few of them in existence." Herne glanced at Talia, who gave him a slight shrug. "You say you were out at the White Peak Copper Mine?"

Claudia nodded. "Yes. Here, I have a map. Let me show you where we were." She jumped up and ran over to a ratty old dresser serving as a sideboard, where she pulled out a map from the top drawer. She spread it out on the dinette table and motioned for us to join her.

"I'm sorry I don't have more room, but let me pencil it in for you." She drew a line from the Winter Hall Academy along to Highway 410, the Chinook Pass Highway. She frowned, then placed a hasty X on the map. "I think we were around there, if I remember right. There should be a trailhead to the White Peak Copper Mine trail around there. And there's a small campground, the White Peak Campground, where you can make camp and stay. From there the trailhead is only about a quarter of a mile."

Herne nodded. "Well, we have a place to look. Thank you, Claudia. We'll let you know when—*if*—we manage to take down Lazerous. You deserve to know."

She guided us to the door, and as we left, Talia turned to her.

"You remember what I said, all right?"

"I will," Claudia promised, and then, with a little wave, she locked the door behind us.

CHAPTER TEN

We reached the office by five-thirty. Angel and Viktor were waiting for us. Herne motioned us all into the break room.

"All right, we have a starting place to look for the missing boys. Which means that we're going camping. Viktor, Yutani, Ember, and me, that is. Talia—don't even bother. You're *not* coming. We're not hunting for Lazerous this time around—just the missing students." He gave her a serious look. "No arguments."

She didn't look happy but answered, "Yes, boss."

"When do we leave?" I asked. "If we want any chance of finding Chaz and Branson alive, we'd better get our asses in gear."

"Tonight. It means driving in the dark, but the sooner we get there, the sooner we can start hunting for them." Herne glanced at the clock. "I'd like to leave by seven so we can arrive at the campground around nine o'clock." He paused, then asked, "Ember, do you have spare clothes here that you can just pack? Or do you need to go home?"

"Damn it, no. I forgot to bring in new spare gear after rounding up the pixies. I'll have to go home and grab warmer clothing. It's going to be damned cold out there." I stood. "Can you swing by and pick me up? That will give me about half an hour to pack. I assume we're taking your Expedition?"

He nodded. "It's big enough to hold everything. Viktor, start assembling gear for the trip. Two tents, food, LED floodlights, water, sleeping bags. It's all in the storeroom. Yutani, download GPS directions for the White Peak Copper Mine—and the nearby campground. In the meantime, I'm going to make a few calls. Angel, find out what you can about the campground and order us some takeout to bring with us. Talia...cross your fingers and hope."

"I'll do you one better," Talia said. "I'm going to see if I can find a better job for Claudia. Your mother played Faerie-godmother for me, maybe I can do the same for her." She leaned against the doorframe. "You sure I can't come along?"

"Not a good idea at this point. But I like the idea of helping Claudia. She didn't ask for this, and it sounds as though she has no support now—at least not emotional." He stood, gathering his files. "Okay, everybody get moving. Ember, we'll pick you up in around an hour. Try to be ready on time. I feel like we're really pressed up against the wall on this."

As he clapped his hands, we darted to our respective tasks.

"Herne, can you give Angel a ride home when you come to pick me up? We brought her car today and I need to head home." I turned to Angel. "Keys?"

She dropped them in my hand.

"Sure," Herne said. "See you in an hour."

I hurried out to the parking garage, where I eased out onto the street and sped off for home. The gridlock was so heavy that my "speeding" was actually at a snail's pace. But half an hour later, I pulled into the driveway and ran inside. Angel could take care of Mr. Rumblebutt, so I wouldn't need to call Ronnie to pet sit. He was lying on the staircase and I scooped him up and pressed my forehead against his.

"Hey dude, I have to go out of town for a day or so. But Angel will be here and she'll make sure you get fed and get tummy rubs and all that good stuff."

I kissed him on the head, then set him down on the bed as I entered my room. Camping meant a backpack. I found my *serious-business* backpack. I had a lightweight one to run around town with, and then there was this one, that had full gear and could take a rough trip.

I opened my dresser and tossed three pairs of jeans on the bed, along with two lightweight sweaters and an insulated vest. On top of that pile, I added four pair of underwear, a second bra, and six pair of heavy socks. I didn't need to worry about my sleeping bag or a tent—those were down at the office and Viktor would get them. But I'd need weapons.

I eyed Brighid's Flame, my sword. Brighid had let me keep it after I had defeated Nuanda, but running around the woods with a sword seemed like a tad overkill. Then again, if we ran across Lazerous, it might come in handy, though if a sword were able to destroy a liche, somebody, somewhere, would have already killed him. He had probably racked up more enemies than a boozehound racked up hangovers.

Replacing the sword in my closet, I opted to take Serafina—my bow. I'd been practicing with her, and we were bonding more and more. Herne had made her, a long time ago, and she had come to belong to my great-grandmother. Now, the bow was mine. A pistol-grip crossbow, Serafina was small enough for me to easily carry through the forest.

In addition to the bow, I strapped sheaths around both thighs and slid wicked-sharp daggers into them. The daggers were a gift from Herne because I had lost my own. The hilts were carved from antlers, and the blades were a good nine inches long and fashioned from some magical metal. He had told me the name of it, but I couldn't remember it off the top of my head. Anyway, they glowed when enemies were near, and they held their edge longer than most daggers.

As I snapped the peace-binding into place, I suddenly felt light-headed. I sat down on my bed, staring at the daggers on my thighs and the bow sitting on the bed. So much had changed over the past ten months, and my old life seemed so far away.

I had been a freelance agent until Herne had recruited both Angel and me. While my work had been dangerous, now the stakes were so much higher, and the danger so much more daunting. I'd gone from dispatching the odd goblin here and there to chasing ancient undead sorcerers. I'd discovered my heritage, and while embracing both my Leannan Sidhe side and my Autumn Stalker side had made me stronger, it had also made me more ruthless.

And then, there was *Herne*. I was in love with a god,

and he was in love with me, but all the baggage that came with the relationship overwhelmed me at times. I was pledged to his mother, which entwined our lives even more, and I worked for him. Walking away wasn't an option should something happen to us.

I fell back across the bed, staring at the ceiling as Mr. Rumblebutt settled on my chest, all sixteen pounds of fur and razorblades.

"Dude, I have to pack," I said, ruffling my fingers through his long fur. But I didn't move and he just purred.

"What's wrong, you ask? Nothing, in particular. I'm just...having a moment." I lowered my voice. "You know, Mr. R., when I think about how much has changed over the past year, it makes me reel."

He let out a *purp.*

"No, no, it's good," I whispered. "Most of it."

But there had been some events that left me with flashbacks and nightmares. My grandfather trying to kill me, for one. And killing him in return, for another.

"Mr. Rumblebutt, do you ever feel like you don't quite know who you are? Like, you woke up one morning and everything looks the same and sounds the same, but you know...things are different? Sometimes, it feels like the past months have been one long blurry dream. And yet...I know they haven't."

"Mrrr," Mr. Rumblebutt said, starting to purr.

I rolled back to a sitting position, holding him against my chest. I buried my face in his fur. "I think I need a little vacation, off on my own. Or maybe just me and Angel. But I'd better take it soon, because when Typhon rises, there won't be any time to rest. Not if what Cernunnos and Morgana are saying is true."

Maybe *that* was the problem. Maybe I was just dreading the start of what promised to be a disaster. The waking of the father of dragons, who would bring the rise of the dead with him, had to be far worse than anything we had faced.

"I'll bet that's what's bothering me. I'm apprehensive and it's directly related to the coming...well, *apocalypse* isn't the word, exactly. Disaster? Chain of regrettable events?"

It seemed clear now. My anxiety was connected to anticipating Typhon's rise.

I let out a sigh and set Mr. Rumblebutt to the side, rubbing his head. "Thanks, little dude, for the talk. It always helps talking things over with you. Now, I'd better get my ass in gear."

I began to jam the clothes into my pack, adding a pair of old sneakers that were still good enough to wear but that I wouldn't be upset over if they got beat up.

Then, stripping out of my corset top, I pulled on a purple V-neck sweater. I clipped a sleek flashlight to my belt, along with a holster for a water bottle. Digging out my hiking boots, I changed my socks and then laced up the boots. Hoisting my pack over one shoulder, I headed for the door.

Downstairs, I tossed a box of protein bars in my pack, along with a half-dozen candy bars, a bag of trail mix, and a bag of Angel's thick, gooey chocolate chip cookies. I added a couple bottles of water, as well as sticking one in my belt holster. Then I added a roll of toilet paper to my pack, a half-used roll of paper towels, and my travel kit.

As ready as I could get in such a short time, I texted Herne. I'M READY. LET ME KNOW WHEN YOU'RE OUT FRONT.

Ten minutes later, he pulled up, with Viktor and Yutani in the back seat. As Angel gave me a hug and headed into the house, I tossed my pack in the back and climbed in to ride shotgun. And, just like that, we were off.

INSTEAD OF TAKING MUD MOUNTAIN ROAD AND PASSING the Winter Hall Academy, we turned off on Highway 410 —the SE Enumclaw Chinook Pass Road. It would save us some time, and we'd be able to turn onto White Peak Campground Road from there, which was past one of the state access roads.

By now, it was dark, and the unending woodlands on either side were thick patches of gloom, silhouettes of the trees rising into the night. The clouds had backed off, and overhead the moon shone down on the roadway and forest, full and silver as she cast her eerie radiance across the land. I leaned my head against the window and stared at the mistress of tides.

I had grown up loving the moon. The night felt like a comforting blanket, and the moon, my silent companion. When I was young, I used to climb outside my bedroom window and sit on the roof, watching the sky. On nights when Angel stayed over, she joined me. My parents never stopped us, and we knew better than talk about it in front of Mama J., because she would have had a fit. There was a flat space outside my window, where we'd spread a blanket and sit there, with our sodas and potato chips, and talk about the future. We talked about our dreams and hopes, about boys, of course, and during the summer we'd watch for meteors, making wishes on every shooting star.

After a moment, Herne said, "What are you thinking about?"

I glanced over at him. His eyes were glued to the road, but somehow, he had known I was a long ways off. "Oh, when I was younger. Angel and I used to go stargazing on the roof of my parents' house."

"How long have you two known each other? You told me, but I can't remember."

I looked back out the window. "Since we were eight. She's always been there for me. She and her mother. And I'll always be there for her."

I fell silent, remembering something that Herne had pointed out at one time. He hadn't meant to be unkind, but rather to prepare me for the inevitability that while my aging process had drastically slowed with the Cruharach, Angel—because she was human—would age out of my life eventually. I had brushed the thought aside, but now, on this moonswept night, it loomed large in my thoughts, leaving me melancholy and incredibly sad.

"Herne, are there any longevity potions or spells? Ones that can extend a human's life?" I had refused to allow my thoughts drift in this direction earlier, but now, on this dark night when we were hunting down potential victims of an undead sorcerer, it seemed fitting.

He paused before answering. "I know of a few. Yes." But he didn't ask me why I asked, for which I was grateful. I didn't feel like telling him, though he could easily figure it out.

Another curve around the darkening bend of the road and we were nearing the turnoff to White Peak Campground. As Herne slowed, gently making a rightward bend into the turn lane, the night seemed to deepen. I glanced at the car clock. It was nearly eight forty-five.

"How much farther until we reach the campground?" Viktor asked.

I glanced over my shoulder. Yutani was reading on his tablet, and Viktor was staring out of the window.

"Another ten minutes, I'd say. The copper mine is about half an hour's hike from the campground, but there are potential sinkholes and other dangers. We're going to get set up tonight, go to bed early, and start our search at dawn." Herne slowed down as a deer came racing out of the woods, leaping across the road. "She looked spooked."

Herne could read animals better than any human— especially given the fact that when he shifted form, it was into a giant silver stag.

"Do you want to track her down to ask what's wrong?" There was enough of a roadside edge that we could pull off onto the shoulder if we needed to.

He paused for a moment, then shook his head. "No, I think it's best we just head on to the campground." Accelerating again, he drove on. "Keep an eye out for the entrance to the campground. It will be on the right side. I'm trying to make sure we don't hit any potholes."

The road leading to the campground was paved but rutted with potholes, and the SUV bounced along over the broken asphalt. There wasn't a lot of money for road upkeep in the government lately, and with the short-sighted attempts to slash taxes, it was only going to get worse. After a while, the pavement gave way to dirt and pebbles, and before long, we were at the entrance of the campground. Herne slowed as we entered the White Peak

Campground. He stopped at the entrance to pay our fee and grab maps of the campground.

We drove through the campground until Herne found a campsite he liked, not far from restrooms or the public showers. As we set up for the night, Viktor and Yutani tackled the tents while Herne built the fire in the firepit. The campground required that we bring in our own wood, and Viktor had thrown several good-sized bundles in the back of the SUV, along with all the other supplies.

After the tents were up—one for Yutani and Viktor, the other for Herne and me—I unrolled our sleeping bags and shook them out. Fifteen minutes later, we were sorted out for the night except for dinner. But Angel had ordered sandwiches and salads for us, as well as several thermoses of hot soup. For dessert there were cookies, snack cakes, and apples.

I spread out a waterproof tarp, then sat on the ground, leaning back against a log. Herne sat on the log beside me, while Viktor and Yutani broke out the camp chairs, unfolding them on the other side of the fire. We ate in a comfortable silence, enjoying the fact that the rain had backed off. I glanced up at the sky. There were still patches of clouds, but for the most part, the night was clear, the stars glimmering down from the black canopy overhead.

"It's going to be cold tonight. Did you remember to bring the thermal blankets? The sleeping bags are good down to thirty-five degrees, but I wouldn't mind a little extra warmth," Herne asked Viktor.

"Yeah, I remembered. I also have a bundle of hand-warmers that you can tuck near your feet, as well as in your pockets." Viktor stared at his sandwich for a moment. "We're really on a recovery mission rather than a rescue mission, aren't we?"

Herne hesitated.

I was gazing into the fire, but I knew what he was going to say. The fact was, if Lazerous had run across Chaz and Branson, they were already dead. Unless somehow they had managed to be as lucky as Claudia, but that wasn't likely.

"Yeah, I think we are," Herne finally answered. "I don't have a sense that they're still alive. I mean, there's always hope, but seriously, I don't think this is going to turn out with a good end."

"I have a question, too," Yutani spoke up. "Do you really think we can defeat Lazerous? I know we need to take him out, but how? We've fought demons, yes, but this is a liche and they're in a class of their own. I know you're a god, Herne, but do you really think this is going to be all easy-peasy?"

Herne swallowed the mouthful of sandwich he was chewing on before answering. "No. It's going to be damned hard and I think we're going to need help. To tell the truth, I'm worried enough about this that I've asked Kipa if he'll join us on this. His culture is filled with powerful bards and sorcerers and so forth. He might actually have some helpful ideas. But first, we need to find these two students—or their bodies, if I'm right. At least Nanette's going to enact a firm curfew now that she knows what's going on."

"Do you really think she will?" I asked. "The school could be facing some pretty stiff lawsuits by parents, if any of the victims were underaged. She knows this. She also knows that the moment the news gets out that there's a liche near the academy, parents will be yanking their kids out right and left. She's not going to want that information to surface. She said as much."

"What are you saying?" Herne asked. "Surely she wants her students to be safe—"

"*Of course* she cares about her students' safety. I'm not disputing that. What I am questioning is how much her loyalty to the academy will factor into whether she informs the parents of the dangers." I shook my head. "Nanette Leshan is dedicated to preserving Winter Hall's reputation. My guess is she's going to wait, hoping we can take care of the situation before she has to say anything."

Herne picked up a stray twig and tossed it into the fire. "I can't force her to do what's right, but I hope you're wrong. She needs to be honest with her students."

"Well, she *should* be, but I'll be surprised if she goes through with it." I finished off my sandwich and ate a couple cookies, then stood to stretch.

The night air was bracing, and I closed my eyes, listening to the woodland around us. There weren't many campers at this time of year, and the night wore its solitude like a shroud. The only things I could hear were the sounds of frogs croaking—a sign we were nearing Ostara —and the buzzing of insects. Spring equinox was in the offing, and the earth was waking up and stretching her muscles.

I yawned. "I think I'll go for a short walk before bed. I won't go far, but I've needed to get outdoors for a while, and this seems like a good chance. According to the map, there's a shower facility down the road about a quarter mile. I don't need a shower, but I'm going to scope it out."

There were restrooms across the road from our campsite—close enough to use during the night—but I felt like being alone for a little bit. I seldom got much time to myself anymore. While I was thrilled that Angel was my roommate and that Herne was my boyfriend, sometimes the hunger to be on my own hit me like a sledgehammer.

"Keep alert," Herne warned. "I doubt if Lazerous would come this far into the campground, but you never know. Plus, the bears are waking up for the season and likely to be out and about."

I nodded, patting the daggers on my thighs. "I'm armed. I'm not taking Serafina, but I have some defense." I tossed my paper plate into the campfire, then stopped by the Expedition to grab my walking stick and headed down the road.

It was dark, but the moon shimmered through the thin streaks of clouds overhead, her light a cool silver against the night. I zipped up my jacket, grateful I'd changed clothes and worn a warmer sweater. As I hiked my way down the road, which was barely wide enough for two cars, I stopped every few feet to just breathe in the scent of wet cedar and tall fir.

There was an undeniable smell to the forest, a wild, bracing scent that came after a rain. According to scientists, *geosim* was the odor a certain bacteria in the earth released only after a rainstorm hit the woods. But for me, it was magical. The forest smelled heady and intoxicating and made me want to run off into the undergrowth and lose myself in it. And the more my Autumn Stalker side came out, the more I embraced the wild and the more I longed for it.

I was out of sight of the camp now, and ahead, about two hundred yards, I caught sight of the shower building.

There was some creature standing next to it, illuminated by the flood lights on the structure. I slowed, thinking at first it might be a small bear. If it *was* a cub, then Mama Bear would be close by, and nobody wanted to mess with a protective mother bear. But as I slowly closed in on the creature, I realized it was a cougar.

I froze. I knew enough not to turn my back on it, but I didn't want to challenge it, either. The mountain lion gazed at me, its eyes sparkling with a rich, brown light. And then, before I could edge my way backward, it began to move toward me.

Oh crap, what the hell am I going to do now?

I had no desire to hurt the cougar, and even if I managed to land a good blow, tangling with it would leave me torn to shreds. I slowly lowered my hands to my thighs, flipping open the snaps that held my daggers in place. I placed my right hand on the hilt, wishing that I had brought Serafina after all, and withdrew one of the daggers. I wasn't skilled enough to fight with both weapons at once yet, and though I was left handed, I tended to fight with my right.

I knew better than to run. If I ran, the cat would chase me. It was a cat thing and the chase would indicate I was prey. I also knew enough not to crouch. Frantically, I searched for what all the guidebooks said to do and landed on the advice.

I straightened my shoulders, trying to look more intimidating.

"Go away!" I raised my arms along with my voice, not shouting but speaking as firmly and loudly as I could. "Go away, big kitty! You go back to your den." It sounded ridiculous, but the advice said to speak firmly and to try to appear bigger than I was.

The cougar paused, just shy of being near enough to leap on me, and the air began to shift, shimmering as the mountain lion began to phase in and out. I held my breath as the mist swirled up, spiraling around the cat till I couldn't see it. Then, as the clouds of sparkling light vanished, a naked man walked out of the shimmering clouds, and I realized that I was facing a puma shifter.

CHAPTER ELEVEN

"Y ou scared the hell out of me!" I blurted out, so relieved that I wasn't going to be a bowl of gooshie food for a very big cat that I didn't even think about being polite.

The man was around five-nine, and sturdy, though not stocky. He had longish black hair, down to mid-shoulder and pulled back in a ponytail, and his eyes shimmered with a gray light. His skin was darker toned, as though he had been in the tanning booth a little too long, and a long scar marred his left thigh. I tried to keep my gaze above his waist, but it was obvious the man wouldn't be sporting any inferiority complexes.

"You *do* realize that you're naked?" I asked, unable to focus on anything else for the moment. Naked bodies didn't offend me, but he seemed so nonchalant that it felt weird.

"Sorry about that," he said in a smooth, low voice. "I left my clothes in a locker in the shower room. I forgot I wouldn't be able to open the door when I returned in my puma form. If you'll excuse me, I'll just go and get dressed now."

The adrenaline rush from thinking I was going to be cat food collided with the sheer awkwardness of standing there talking to a naked man. I snorted, trying to suppress a laugh, but I failed miserably, laughing so hard that I sounded like a demented hyena.

The shifter gave me a long look, then shook his head and hurried into the men's side of the shower building. I thought about returning to the campsite while he was gone, but something urged me to stick around and talk to him. I decided to follow my instinct.

Five minutes later, he returned, clad in jeans, a T-shirt with an open flannel shirt over it, and a peacoat. He looked surprised to still see me standing there.

"So, you stuck around. Liked what you saw?" There was just a hint of arrogance behind his words—not enough to irk me, but I still frowned.

"If I say no, you'll be insulted, and if I say yes, I'll sound like a pervert. Let's just say my instinct told me to stay put for the moment." I paused, then added, "I'm Ember Kearney. I'm camping with my boyfriend and a couple other friends just down the road." I decided to buck propriety and add, "Who are you, and what are you doing out here? This isn't a great time of year for camping."

He blinked. "I might add the same goes for you. But the weather aside, my name's George Shipman. As to what I'm doing here, I live in the area, and I come out here to run under the moon." He paused, seeming uncertain for a moment, then added, "You want to be careful out here. There are dangers out in these woods."

"No, *really?*" I wasn't sure why, but he brought out the

smartass in me. I took a deep breath, letting it out slowly. "I'm sorry, I'm not usually so rude. You just startled me. As to the dangers, that's why my friends and I are out here. Do you come out here often to this campground? And do you know the surrounding area very well?"

It occurred to me that if he was well-acquainted with the area, he might be of some help with finding Lazerous's lair. Or he might have encountered signs of the liche in the area. And just because I sometimes played the good Samaritan, I felt we should warn him. If he hadn't encountered Lazerous yet, I wanted to make sure he didn't accidentally stumble into trouble.

George studied me for a moment. "Yeah, I'm out here a lot. What say I walk you back to your campsite and we can talk? It's dangerous out here at night, especially lately. Also, the bears and pumas are out, and you don't want to run across one that might actually think you'd make a good meal."

He sounded sincere. Since my alarm bells weren't going off, I agreed.

On the way back to the campground, my senses seemed to heighten. I glanced around nervously. It felt like we were being watched. We probably were, given there were all sorts of wildlife and magical creatures in the forests, but this felt different. I realized that I was glad to have George by my side.

We returned to the campsite just in time to find Herne heading in our direction.

"Ember! I was beginning to get worried—" he paused. "Who's this?"

I crossed to him and gave him a quick kiss to reassure him that I was all right, then motioned for George to step closer. "This is George Shipman. He's a puma shifter. I met him near the showers and at first thought he was going to attack me—he was in cougar form—but then he changed and everything was all right." Realizing I was rambling, I stopped.

Herne held out his hand. "Hello, George. I'm Herne, the Hunter. I'm in charge of the Wild Hunt Agency."

At that, George's demeanor changed. He relaxed and nodded, as though he suddenly understood. "I've heard of you. How-do?" He took Herne's hand and shook it.

"Not bad," Herne said, glancing at me. "Thank you for walking Ember back. I was beginning to worry about her."

I tapped Herne on the shoulder. "Here's the thing. George said he comes out to the campground a lot. I thought that maybe he's seen something on one of his hikes that might help us. So I was bringing him back to the camp so we could ask him if he knew about Lazerous and where he might be."

Herne slid his hands into his pockets. "That's a good idea. George, would you have time to come talk to us for a few minutes? We've got cookies and coffee, though nothing to spike it with, I'm afraid."

George let out an easy laugh. "I'm not much of a drinking man, so that's not a problem. But some hot coffee would be good. Even in puma form, it gets chilly out here in the forest."

The three of us headed to the firepit, where Viktor was making coffee while Yutani was studying something on his tablet. He had brought a couple external power supplies and had plugged the device into one of them. When they saw us walking up with

George in tow, both of them put aside what they were doing.

I made introductions all around.

George shook their hands, each in turn, and settled himself on a log. "I belong to the White Peak Puma Shifters Pride."

"Is Mount Rainier your territory?" I asked. I knew that wolf packs and puma prides had definite territorial boundaries, though the two could overlap, but only in terms of interspecies. One puma pride wouldn't intrude on another pride's territory, but outside of their specific species, the Shifter Alliance provided for areas to house more than one shifter group.

He shook his head. "No, the White Peak area is our territory. Mount Rainier is far too large for one Pride to stake claim to. There are at least five different puma prides throughout the area, and I think about six wolf packs." He accepted a mug of coffee from Viktor and cupped his hands around it. "Thank you."

Viktor handed me a mug and I accepted it, stopping to add sugar and cream from the picnic table. We brought individual packs of creamer and sugar when we went on trips so it wouldn't get messy. I turned back to George.

"Cream and sugar?"

He glanced up from staring at the fire. "No, thank you. I like it strong and black."

"Trust me, Ember likes it strong," Yutani said with a laugh. "She can down more caffeine than anybody I've ever met."

I stuck my tongue out at him. "I may like it strong, but I also like it flavored." I settled down on the log next to Herne. "George, we're on a specific mission, and we're hoping that maybe you can help us. The fact that you've been out here a lot means you might have seen something that may give us a lead to…" I paused, glancing at Herne, wondering how much I should say.

Herne pursed his lips, then gave me a nod. "Let's tell him. He might as well know, given his people could be in danger." He set down his cup and propped his elbows on his knees, bending toward the fire. "George, do you know what a liche is?"

George frowned. After a moment, he gave a quick shake of his head. "I can't say that I do. I've heard the term, I think, but I can't remember where, or even what the context of the conversation was. What is it?"

Herne explained what a liche was, and how we knew he was in the area. "A friend of ours was attacked by this particular liche centuries ago. She was a harpy—well, still is, but he drained her of her powers. He's killed most of his victims, but a few managed to escape—" Herne paused as George interrupted.

"The kids from the college. I've read about several attacks where kids from the Winter Hall Academy were found dead. Is that why you're here?"

I nodded. "We're trying to find Lazerous so we can destroy him. Or rather, that's the long-term goal. Right now, we're out here to hunt down two students. Twin brothers went missing a day or so ago. They came out to this area. All the attacks have been near where the old White Peak Copper Mine was based. We start searching for them at dawn." I paused, a thought hitting me. "I know this is a beautiful area, but I wonder why so many of the students want to hike around this particular place. There are so many areas they could explore, instead."

George lifted his coffee, taking a long drink. "I think I might know the answer to that."

"Oh?" Viktor said.

"Yeah. What do you know about the White Peak Copper Mine?" George set his cup down. By the firelight, he made me think of Yutani, and I wondered if he was part Native American.

"Not much," Yutani said, glancing at me. "I haven't had the time to research it. Ember, what about you?"

"Nothing, really. Talia may know something because she's been researching this area, but I didn't even think to ask."

George finished off his coffee and accepted a cookie. "Thank you. Okay, so the White Peak Copper Mine was, as the name implies, mostly focused on copper. And it was fairly lucrative, but the mine shut down abruptly after an accident that left thirty-one miners dead."

I winced. "That's horrible. What happened?"

"Cave-in, due to a mistimed explosion. The mine insisted it was the fault of the miners, the miners blamed the supervisor who was part owner of the company. Fifty miners were seriously injured. Nineteen managed to escape. But thirty-one were buried under a ton of rubble. The courts ruled that it was the mine's liability, given what evidence the men who escaped were able to present, and the owners went bankrupt paying off lawsuits. The bank foreclosed. About three years ago, a group of dwarves bought it."

"So the mine's still in operation?" I asked, surprised.

"Yes, though that's not well-known. The dwarves have never made any official statement. I think that the group who owns it is waiting for a long-enough time to pass so that people don't associate them with the deaths of those men. But I know there are dwarves out here on occasion, digging around." George paused, then touched his finger to his nose. "Rumors are, through the grapevine, that they've dug deep enough to discover a pocket of ilithiniam."

Herne straightened up, staring at George. "Ilithiniam? Are you joking?"

George shook his head, a grave look on his face. "I don't jest about things like that. The dwarves can dig deeper and faster than any human or contraption on this planet. They have delved deep into the earth. They've also disturbed the spirits of the men who died in that explosion, or at least so the shaman of my pride believes."

"What's ilithiniam?" I asked. "I've heard of it, but I thought it was supposed to be like…some urban legend."

I'd heard of the magical metal, of course, and how it was worked into most magical weapons. Only small amounts of the ore was needed to give the weapon or item a magical signature, but I had thought it was more myth than truth.

"No, it's very real, and it's prized more highly than diamonds. The gods have it—not in abundance, but more than we do here. Over here, in this realm, ilithiniam is rare. It's found in small pockets near copper and other ores, but usually deep in the earth, which is why humans seldom if ever find it. That's how Excalibur was forged, you know. But for the most part, human miners simply can't dig deep enough, safely enough, in order to uncover it. Dwarves possess most of it, of course, and some sub-Fae like kobolds or knickerknackers. But they don't announce it when they find it, because it would put them in danger from claim jumpers, or worse." George gave me a long look. "Your kind, for example."

"What do you mean, *my* kind?" At first I thought he was making a reference to the fact that I was a tralaeth.

"The Fae, I'm talking about. Dark, Light, doesn't matter which side. In the past, they've raided some dwarven mines and stolen their ilithiniam. There's a reason the dwarves aren't keen on your kind," George said.

"Excuse me, but the Fae..." I drifted off. I was about to say they weren't *my people*, given the precarious relationship I had with both sides of my heritage, but that wasn't the truth.

"The Fae are who they are," George said, then paused. "I'm not casting aspersions on your nature, Ember. I know full well you probably live between the two worlds. I'm not dense in terms of what I know about your kind. But still, they are your blood, so I didn't misspeak, did I?"

I shook my head. "No. I just don't claim allegiance to either court. Given the way they feel about me, I tend to ignore the connection most of the time. So you think the students were looking for ilithiniam?"

"Think what a coup it would be. Though most of them probably know it's dangerous, you know how the young think of themselves as immortal. They never think that *they'll* be the ones in danger." He rubbed his chin, then shrugged. "My guess is that's what the allure to this area is. Somebody probably spread the rumor that they saw— or found—a small piece of the metal and it blossomed into a full-blown story. You know...*My friend's friend had a friend* or *I heard about this guy who...*"

"My guess about the urban legend was right, then. Just

not quite in the right way. It's not the metal that's a legend, but the finding of it." My mind began to wander to what we could do if we actually found a patch of the elusive metal, and before I realized it, I was halfway to fantasizing about creating my own bow out of it. "Crap, it's easy enough to get carried away," I said, looking up. "It's almost as if the metal has a glamour of its own, even when you aren't around it."

"It's like gold. The miners during the gold rush suffered gold fever. If word got out to the general public that these old mines contained ilithiniam—even a *hint* of rumor—we'd have a mad rush out here. And injuries would follow." Viktor glanced toward the road. "No wonder the dwarves keep quiet. Ten to one, they are mining in the deep areas, but in stealth."

Yutani had been listening the whole time. Now he spoke up. "What if the liche finds some? Could that help Lazerous in any way?"

Herne let out a sharp breath. "I don't even want to think about it. It would be disastrous if he were able to forge weapons as well as drain powers. I don't know enough about liches to know if they can create weaponry infused with their ability to drain energy. But if any metal could do it, it would be ilithiniam."

"As for where to find your liche, I think I may have some leads for you. For one thing, if the students are coming out here in search of ilithiniam, then they're congregating around the mines, so if—what's his name? Lazerous? If Lazerous is keeping an eye out, he may have figured that out and staked out his territory there."

"He's killed several students already, so there's a chance he's forced them to tell him what they're after,"

Yutani said. "Someone who drains powers isn't likely to be squeamish about torture. Or maybe he has the power to charm—surely someone he's drained over the years has had that ability, and so he would have it as well."

"I think his lair has to be near the mines," George said. "One of the reasons I've been out here scouting around so much lately is because Eliza, our shaman, asked me to come. I'm one of the best scouts in the White Peak Puma Shifter Pride. There's been a rift in the spiritual energy out here—a dark rift—and it's unsettled the creatures who live in this area. We talked to the local mountain lions and they have begun avoiding this place. They say there's a monster near the mines, and that it's a danger to anyone or anything that comes near."

"Lazerous," I said.

"Yes, I now believe that's who they're talking about. They don't have the words for what he is, so *monster* has to suffice. And twice now, Eliza has dreamed of the dead walking through the forest here, swallowing the light. Whenever our shaman dreams of such things, we know there's a problem." George leaned back, bracing his hands on the log as he stared into the sky. "If what you say is true, I doubt she'll be able to counter him. That was the plan—for me to find out what's going on and then for her to take care of it."

"I'm afraid Lazerous would suck your shaman dry. Leave him to us. But I'd like to meet Eliza, if she's willing, as well as the leader of your Pride." Herne stood, pacing around the fire. "It would be good to start forging alliances with some of the local leaders. There are things in the offing that I think you should know about, beyond the issue of Lazerous."

"Typhon?" I asked, glancing up at him.

He nodded. "We need to form a network, because when Typhon rises, we're going to need all the help we can get." He turned to George. "The world is about to get a lot more dangerous, and it would behoove us to create alliances for when it happens."

George hesitated, then held out his hand to Herne. "I can't answer for my Pride, but I sense you are offering us an alliance that could prove a lifesaver. For my own part, I'm thankful I ran into you tonight. Or ran into Ember, rather. Everything happens for a reason, even if we don't know what it is at the time."

The men shook, and then Herne glanced at his watch. "We should get some rest. George, what do you think about going out with us tomorrow morning to look for those kids?"

The puma shifter nodded. "I can do that." He yawned. "I think you're right, though. It's time for sleep."

"Would you like to stay in our camp with us?" Viktor asked.

"Sure, but I'll have to run back to my truck and drive over. It will take me about ten minutes." George headed out of the camp.

Viktor stoked the fire, then stood, stretching his arms wide and yawning. "Do you think we should keep watch?" He rubbed his eyes.

Herne shrugged. "I don't think it's necessary. I doubt if Lazerous is going to venture out here to the campground. He'd be risking exposure. No, why don't you and Yutani wait for George and help him set up, then get some sleep. We'll want to start at daybreak."

As I crawled into the tent with Herne, I realized I was

wiped. The adrenaline rush had vanished, and now I was left with the dregs of a day that had been too long, and too worrisome.

"I'm so tired," I said, yawning as I stripped off my jeans, panties, sweater, and bra. The chill hit me like a slap in the face and I shivered as I pulled a pair of sweatpants and a long T-shirt out of my pack. I slipped them on and burrowed into the sleeping bag. Herne and I could have zipped them together, but it was warmer to just burrow into a single bag with one of the thermal blankets Viktor had brought.

"Get some rest, love," Herne said, leaning over to give me a long kiss.

I drifted in the feel of his lips against mine, briefly entertaining the thought of a little nookie before sleep, but before I could do anything about it, my eyes closed and I was out for the night.

CHAPTER TWELVE

"*E*mber, wake up. Ember?" Herne shook me out of my dreamless sleep, and I blinked, my eyes stuck together with goop. I rubbed them before I remembered that I had forgotten to remove my eye makeup the night before.

"You look like a demented raccoon," Herne said, snorting. "Come on, the coffee's ready."

"You say that now, but I bet I'd be a big hit with the boy raccoons," I mumbled. "Eh, let me get dressed. I'll join you in a moment. Just make sure there's coffee."

He laughed, kissing me on the top of my head. "Get dressed. There will be coffee. I promise." As he exited the tent, I sat up.

The morning was chilly and rain was spattering on the tent.

I pulled my pack onto my lap and sorted through until I found my wet-wipes. They worked on makeup, not as well as makeup remover, but they did the job. I held a small hand mirror in one hand while I wiped the residue of makeup off with the other. Finally, my face was reasonably clean and I could smell coffee wafting through the tent flaps from the campfire. That was enough incentive to get me into a clean pair of panties, my bra, jeans, and a lightweight sweater. Over that, I slid on my rain jacket. If the rain stopped, I'd switch to a denim jacket.

After strapping my daggers to my thighs again, I slid on a pair of clean socks, laced up my hiking boots, and pulled my hair back into a ponytail, then followed the trail of coffee that beckoned so enticingly.

"Morning, sunshine," Yutani said, holding up a mug of coffee.

I accepted it gratefully. Viktor and George were crouched by the fire, holding long sticks over the fire.

"What's for breakfast?" I asked, heading their way.

"Brats, skewered and cooked over the open fire. We've got buns, condiments, and chips." Viktor motioned to the picnic table, where a line of sausages was spread out on a tinfoil platter. A bag of buns along with condiments sat next to them, and next to that was an open bag of chips.

I slid three of the brats on a long skewer and headed over to join Viktor and George. Herne was eating a handful of chips, while Yutani was already chowing down on a couple of the meaty sandwiches.

"It smells wonderful," I said, balancing my mug of coffee on the log next to me as I held the sausages over the fire and watched them start to sizzle and pop. "How long till they're done?"

Viktor grinned. "They take about ten minutes. Not long at all. I thought this would go down better than something cold. Plus, lots of protein and carbs to sustain us on the search."

I glanced at the sky. The rain was trickling down now, a fine mist, but it wouldn't be long before we were in the midst of a downpour. "Better make sure everything's tucked into the tents or the car before we take off on the hunt today. It's going to rain and it's going to rain hard." I could feel the water in my bones. Which brought up another thought.

"Listen, is there a creek near the mining site?"

George nodded. "Yes, Copper Creek. Why?"

"I can see if I can find a water elemental and ask if it's seen anything out of the ordinary. If there's one near the mining site, it might know what happened to Chaz and Branson." My Leannan Sidhe abilities came in handy around the area, given we got so much rain, and there were so many bodies of water weaving through the woods.

"That's a good idea." Herne crouched beside by me. He draped his arm around my shoulders and hugged me to him. "Give me a kiss, love," he said.

As I kissed him, I got a sudden flash. Yes, Herne wanted to kiss me, but he was doing this for George's benefit.

Of course. He's at it again, I thought. But at least this time he was trying to be subtle.

Herne had a way of claiming ownership over me that annoyed me yet made me feel safe. However, he was usually less subtle about it, to the point where I wanted to punch him. Like when he got into it with Kipa. At least now, with Kipa occupied with Raven, Herne wasn't nearly as aggressively possessive as he had been. Especially after he and Kipa had inadvertently thrown Raven and me into the clutches of one very big etho-spider.

I kissed him back, lingering for a moment in the warmth of his embrace. "I love you, you nit," I whispered, coming up for air. "Even if you *are* staking your claim again. At least you aren't peeing on me."

Herne snickered. "Deal with it, woman. You're my mate, my woman, and my love. I just want to establish that fact. And while I promised to stop picking fights, I didn't promise to stop making the point clear." His voice was low, but I glanced up and caught George staring at us, a wide grin on his face.

"My brats are done, so let me eat, you big lug, you." I lovingly flicked the end of his nose with my free hand, then stood, carrying my skewer of sizzling brats over to the table where I eased them onto a paper plate. I prepared three buns with ketchup and stuffed them with the sausages, then added a pile of chips to my plate and returned to the fire, where I settled in to my breakfast.

After we ate, we doused the fire, tamping it down to make sure all the embers were extinguished, and then prepared our daypacks. I added clean socks and under-wear, a thermal blanket, and enough food for a couple of meals to mine, along with a first-aid kit, two more bottles of water, some rope, and a flashlight. As I strapped a water bottle to my belt, I made sure that my daggers were secure, then slid a whistle over my neck. We all wore them. They came in handy if we got separated and some-body found something.

"Ready?" Herne asked, turning to me.

"Yeah, I'm ready," I said, looking around. We had locked most of our expensive items in the SUV.

"Then let's get moving. We'll visit the bathrooms first, then head over to the boys' campsite where they were last seen. The rangers found their things and returned them to the school, but I know where they set up camp." He led the way out of the tent, and we found Yutani, Viktor, and George waiting for us. Herne gave George the boys' campsite number and led us out onto the road, and we started our hike toward where the boys had last been seen.

THE SKY GREW DIMMER AND MORE OMINOUS WITH EVERY step, and I shook out a rain poncho I'd brought. It would not only keep me drier than just my jacket, but it would keep my pack dry, too. I paused in the middle of the road to slide it over my head. I felt like an olive-green balloon, but the poncho had a good hood on it, and I'd be grateful for the protection before long.

"That's a good idea," Yutani said. "Hold on a moment." He, too, pulled out a poncho and slid it over his head.

But Viktor, George, and Herne opted to brave the rain. As we set in for the hike, the rustle of leaves warned us that the wind was rising. A gust blew past, whipping the hem of my poncho, and as it did so, a bevy of birds broke out of one of the nearby trees and went winging off, their calls echoing through the sky.

"The storm's going to be a doozy," George said, gazing up at the clouds. "Be cautious when we near Copper Creek—the white water can churn up out of nowhere when there's a sudden downpour. It's a narrow creek, but deep, and it can sweep you under and slam you against the rocks before you even realizing what's going on."

He was right. I could feel the storm coming, and it was

a big one. The scent of ozone hung heavy in the air. Thunder and lightning couldn't be far behind.

We found the campsite where the boys had been staying, but there wasn't much to see. The rangers had gathered up all their goods after Nanette had talked to them. I wondered what she had told them. Had she mentioned they were missing? Or had she just said the boys had forgotten their things? I hated being suspicious of her motives, but given the circumstances, I couldn't help but question her agenda. Was it for the safety of the students? Or did she have the welfare of the school at heart? Were the shareholders more important than *collateral damage,* like Branson and Chaz?

"Here," George said, as he was poking among the undergrowth. "Here's a trail that somebody made through the forest, not long ago. And it's in the direction of the mines. I'm guessing that your missing students headed this way."

He set out on the path, leading us into the woodland. The ferns were waist-deep here, slapping against our thighs as we pushed through them. The huckleberry bushes were just budding out, but the skunk cabbage was thick and starting to reek. I avoided a large patch of stinging nettle. While it didn't bother me as much as it would most humans, it still produced an irritating rash. And the last thing I needed right now was another irritant.

I held tight to my walking stick as we slogged through the foliage, moving cautiously along the spongy forest floor. Thick with moss and debris from the annual autumn leaf-drop, the forests in Western Washington could be dangerous if you didn't focus on where you were stepping. It was easy to sink into the detritus, or to step on a hidden stone and turn your ankle.

The conversation quieted down as we moved along, following George. He seemed to be a natural-born guide, and I began to understand why his Pride considered him their best scout. It was as though he and the forest merged to become one. He moved effortlessly, picking out the path through the dense vegetation with barely a pause. Once in a while, he'd motion for us to stop, and he'd lift his head, listening to the creaking boughs as the wind set them to moaning. Then he'd nod, as if to some invisible guide, and start moving again.

We were deep into the woods when the storm broke. Lightning lit up the sky, breaking through the clouds with jagged forks. Shortly behind it, thunder rumbled, rolling like a wave. I shivered, grateful for my rain poncho. I wasn't cold so much as apprehensive. The poncho kept most of me dry, the water beading to bounce off. But the storm was angry. I could sense it in my core as it echoed from hill to hill.

If this were summer, I'd fear wildfires. I'd seen one once, some years back, when Angel and I went camping in the lower foothills near Mount Baker. The fire had caught in midsummer, and we woke to the smell of smoke rising from the ridge. We hastily packed our gear, heading out as the fire threatened to come our way. I'd been watching out the window as she drove, doing her best to navigate the forest road during the night. At one point, the fire exploded, cresting the ridge as it crowned from tree to tree, sending me into a panic. It raced along the ridge next to us, threatening to come down the ravines onto the road. The fire had felt like a predator, hungry and furious, aching to devour anything it could touch and when we managed to get past it, I had breathed a deep sigh of relief, realizing just how big of a danger we had been in.

Now, of course, I realized that elementals had been dancing in the flames, driving them on. But then, all I could see were sparks and embers flying through the air, and I had whispered prayers to whatever gods might be listening to help us escape.

Shaking the thoughts from my head, I caught my breath, trying to center myself in the present again. I wondered how long we'd been hiking. We were lost in a sea of green, and I had no clue of which way we had come, or how to get out should we get separated.

A few moments later, George let out a "Yes!" and turned around to face us.

"We're near the turnoff that leads to the mine. And look—over there, do you think that belonged to one of the students?"

I craned my neck to see what he was talking about. There, on the side of the trail, was a candy wrapper. It was from a Big Mountain bar.

I was closest to it, and stepped to kneel beside it. "Should I pick it up? Is there any reason we'd want to preserve any fingerprints?"

"Pick it up with these and put it in a paper bag, just in case." Herne opened a small case from his pocket and handed me a pair of tweezers from it. Viktor produced a paper bag from his day pack, and I cautiously lifted the wrapper and slid it into the bag. After folding the bag shut, I returned the tweezers to Herne and Viktor stashed it in his pack.

"It might be someone else, but I have a feeling our boys

came this way. Let me see here..." I knelt again, brushing aside the foliage till I came to a sizable puddle of water. I reached out, placing my fingertips in the liquid, and closed my eyes.

Is anyone there. Can you hear me? I reached out with my thoughts, touching the water lightly, searching for any spirits that might be living in it. While most elementals inhabited large bodies of water, there were smaller water spirits that could be found in puddles, and—in rare cases —even in one drop of water.

Hello? Anyone? I pushed out the questions, impressed into emotions, with my thoughts, then waited quietly.

Water could move mountains, and it could tear a town to pieces with a swiftly moving tsunami. Or it could lie placid for days, its currents shifting with a subtlety so sublime that no human could see the gradual difference. Water wouldn't be rushed, and at other times, it refused to be slowed. The nature of water worked at its own pace, without thought for what anyone or anything wanted. Mother Ocean and her kin could be merciful and life-giving, or she could be relentless, destroying everything she touched.

Another slow minute crept by, and then, very softly, I received the impression of a hello.

Welcome to my world, came the thought. Of course, I didn't hear the actual words, but more the sensation and feeling of the greeting. When I dealt with water, I worked on an entirely different level.

Hello, and thank you. I do not seek to disturb you, but I have a pressing question. Will you answer if I ask? Again, I formed the words into a feeling and laid it out to the water sprite. Water sprites were like baby elementals.

Maybe sometime, in the distant future, the sprite would make her way to a lake or a pond or an ocean and grow, but for now, she was a young spirit, newly born from the rains.

Another pause, and then, *I will answer. What do you seek?*

I am wondering if you noticed two boys—barely of age—come through here in the past turn or two of the sun? I tried to project their images.

The water sprite hesitated, then with almost a whispered kiss, once again touched my thoughts. *Yes, I watched them pass by three turns of the sun past. One left a marker for the world to remember him by.* An image of the candy wrapper sprang to mind.

I let out a long breath. So Chaz and Branson *had* created this trail, and one of them had dropped the candy wrapper. That was a big help.

Do you know if they returned this way since then?

This time, the water sprite was quick to answer. *No. No one has been by since then, not of your kind or their kind. Not since I last saw them.*

I sat back on my heels, trying to think if I should ask it about Lazerous. Finally, I decided that it couldn't hurt.

There is a fiercesome monster who lives near here. Have you seen him? I did my best to conjure up a picture of what I thought Lazerous must look like and added the sense of fear and destruction that surrounded the liche.

The water sprite shivered, jiggling the puddle so the water rippled. *No, I have not seen such a creature, neither do I wish to do so. I will return to my thoughts now.*

And just like that, the touch of the water sprite faded from my mind and I opened my eyes. Herne reached down to offer his hand and I took it as he pulled me to my feet.

"Did you learn anything?" he asked as I rubbed my eyes. I felt like I had just returned from another world, where time ran slowly. Yawning to replenish my oxygen, I nodded.

"Yes, I did. The water sprite saw the boys come by here and verified that one of them dropped the candy wrapper. Three turns of the sun ago, so three days ago. But it did *not* see them return. Nor did it know anything about Lazerous, though I'm not sure if it was telling the truth or just trying to avoid talking about him. I got a definite blast of fear when I asked about him."

"I'd be afraid too, water sprite or not." Yutani shook his head. "So we know that Chaz and Branson came this way, and most likely didn't return. Do you think the sprite could have missed them on the way back?"

"It's possible, but I think the sprite's right." I frowned. "I don't think they came back to their camp. At least not along this trail."

There was always the possibility, but water sprites and elementals didn't forget what they saw, and they didn't sleep, though at times they hibernated, especially when the waterways were covered with ice. In the far north, the ice elementals were more active than the water elementals.

George nodded. "All right, then we continue to the mine. From here on out, keep your eyes peeled. The liche could be hiding anywhere, though I'm fairly certain it wouldn't be too close to the mine because the dwarves would figure it out and there would be hell to pay. While they wouldn't want to expose what they're doing, they aren't the types to sit back and let some creature prey on themselves or others. So keep alert, and if anybody sees anything, speak up. I don't care if it's a wild goose chase, we want to know."

He led the way through the next bend in the woodland trail, then out into a clearing.

We entered a wide quarry—or at least it looked like it had once been used as a quarry. There was a mound in the center of the clearing, built up and into the hill, which rose behind it. There was an entryway into the mound, with a STAY OUT sign posted on a rough fence that circled the area. Over the entryway hung a faded sign that read WHITE PEAK MINING COMPANY.

The wide bowl-shaped area hadn't been reclaimed by the forest yet, or if it had, the dwarves had driven it back. The ground was exposed in several places, though grass had grown over what was obviously a deforested patch.

I slowly pushed past George, into the clearing, senses on high alert.

On the opposite side of the large opening, I could see an old logging road leading into the woods, and running parallel to the logging road, a two-lane drive, no doubt to keep cars from having to navigate the massive timber trucks that had once ruled over the forest.

I cautiously began to circle the mine, slowly becoming aware of whispering from all around. I closed my eyes, the rain streaming down my face, and listened, but while I could hear the voices, I couldn't catch any of the words. And then I knew what it was.

"There are spirits here. I can hear them." I opened my eyes and turned to Herne. "I think they're the miners who died here. I can't make out what they're saying, though.

Their words are just outside my perception. I wish we had Raven with us. She would understand them."

Herne gave me a short nod. "You're right. I can feel them pass by. Shades of the men long dead. I think they're trapped here."

"They were sleeping until something woke them up. We thought it was the dwarves, but now I'm thinking maybe it was the liche's presence." George shook his head. "This is a dangerous area. The spirits are angry and afraid, and they crave companionship—something to wipe away their fear. But the only thing that can help is if someone could move them along—" he paused, tilting his head. "Did you hear that?"

"What?" I hadn't heard anything, but George was heading toward a patch of rocks off to one side. He cautiously swung himself over the edge of the rockpile, dropping down behind it. A moment later, we heard him cry out.

"Hurry, we need help!"

As we raced across the clearing, a moan rose from behind the rocks. I dashed around to the side, skidding to a halt at the top of the slight ravine. The ground sloped downward, gently at first, then steeper, but the ravine ended far short of what I had expected, shallow by comparison to some that riddled the forests.

And there, behind the pile of rocks, inches away from the slope, George crouched next to a young man who was babbling incoherently. One look told me that, even though he looked drawn and gaunt, we had found Chaz. And he was alive.

CHAPTER THIRTEEN

"hat's Chaz!" I said, scrambling down the slope to George's side. "He's alive?"

"He is, but he's hurt badly. That I can tell just looking at him." He paused, stroking Chaz's face. "It's all right. We're here. We've found you." He gazed down at the boy. "Not only is his body thrashed, but there's something else. His soul is off wandering. He can't hear us. He won't know we're here—or that we've rescued him."

"How's his body? You said he's hurt?" I looked around for blood but saw nothing to indicate any open wounds. "Do you think he's got any broken bones?"

George nodded gravely. "Yes, he does. I'm not sure, but I think his spine may be injured. We need an ambulance, but..." He paused, glancing around. "Will it be safe to call them out here? I can tell you right now that Chaz's magical signature doesn't feel right for one of the magic-born. If I didn't know any better, I'd say he was human."

"Crap. Lazerous must have drained his powers," I muttered.

Just then, Herne, Viktor, and Yutani came rushing up. George quickly laid out what he had told me. "What do you think we should do?" he asked. "If we wait here, it could take a couple hours for help to get here."

"I have friends nearby. Let me see if I can find cell coverage here." Herne held up his phone and started wandering around the quarry.

Meanwhile, George was examining Chaz as best as he could. "I think he's got a broken leg, maybe a broken spine. It's hard to tell." He shook his head. "Whatever the case, it's bad. He needs a doctor."

Herne fist-pumped the air. "Yes! I've got reception."

He quickly punched in a number on his cell phone, and then walked off to the side, chatting with somebody. I wanted to tell him to hurry, to quit taking his own sweet time, that the boy was in danger, but before I could, he had returned, his phone back in his pocket.

"I called Justin and Irene Summers. They're a shifter couple I've known for years, and they live out in this area. He's a nurse, she's an EMT. They were home and they'll be here in fifteen minutes with medical supplies and transport. Meanwhile, Viktor, Yutani, and Ember? Keep watch for anything that comes our way. George and I will stay with Chaz."

Viktor, Yutani, and I fanned out.

I shivered, more from the situation than the cold. It was barely noon, which was one blessing. With any luck, we'd be out of here by dark. As I walked to the edge of the mining site, I felt something brush past me. It was a ghost, that much I could tell, and I tried to focus on the sound of the wind in the trees, of raindrops dripping from the boughs, anything to drown out the faint hush of whispers that permeated the area.

The heavy melancholy that seemed to cling to the very air made me weary, as if I was a thousand years old. I glanced over my shoulder at Herne and George. Herne was kneeling by Chaz, and I couldn't tell what he was doing, but George was watching him carefully. A moment later, George knelt beside Herne and placed his hands on Chaz's shoulders.

Why have you come to this place...

The voice echoed through the clearing as I stood there, a column of mist swirling around me. I froze, waiting to see what it would do. A moment later, it spun into a vortex, almost knocking me off my feet before rising and, like a serpent, striking the ground and disappearing into it.

"Crap, the ghosts here can get physical!" I whirled around, glancing at Viktor, who was by my side in a moment.

"Are you all right?" he asked.

I nodded. "Yeah, but that felt like a close call. I don't know what it was—"

"Oh, it was a ghost," Yutani said, joining us. "I could feel it from where I was standing. And if *I* can feel them, you know they're strong. This mining site is filled with spirits. I don't think it's just the men who died here, either. As soon as we can, I suggest we leave here."

As he finished speaking, a large, heavy SUV came rolling up the access road. Herne stood up, running toward it, waving. A man and woman jumped out, the man carrying a large case. They greeted Herne, briefly stopping to talk, then followed him back to where Chaz was sprawled on the ground.

Irene went down on her knees next to Chaz, while Justin opened up the case. While she was examining him, Justin began pulling out supplies. From where I was standing I could see a stethoscope, a blood pressure cuff, and several other medical devices.

I wanted to join them, ask how Chaz was doing, but I stayed at my post. I turned back to face the forest, wondering how he had managed to escape. From there, I segued into wondering if there had been some similarity between Claudia and Chaz that had allowed them to survive. Of course, we didn't know if he was going to survive yet, so speculation might be premature.

Viktor wandered up, folding his arms as he stared toward the tree line along with me. "Do you suppose Lazerous can control the spirits here?"

I frowned, then shook my head. "I don't think he's focused on the dead. He only derives his energy from the living, so he probably ignores them, if he hears them at all. But with how strong their presence is, surely he has to know they're here. It's a good thing Angel isn't here or she'd be in trouble."

"How are things going with her psychic protection class? Isn't your mentor Marilee helping her with that?"

I nodded. Angel was so open that it was easy for spirits and other astral entities to jump her. She needed to learn how to protect herself, so my magical mentor—Marilee—had taken her on and was teaching her basic psychic protection and warding techniques. Eventually, Angel wanted to be able to protect and ward the house. Marilee said she had the potential, and she was willing to teach her, as long as Angel was willing to work long and hard.

"She's actually coming along with it. Marilee plans on testing her come this autumn, near Samhain. And Raven has offered to help her too, after she gets her feet beneath her. Who knows, Angel may just become an even more integral part of the Wild Hunt once she's fully trained."

"Do you think she'd like that?" Viktor asked. "Angel is an incredible woman, but she's never seemed comfortable with the thought of combat, or anything like that."

"I think that's because she didn't feel like she had any way of protecting herself. She's been training in the gym, and now she's training magically. I think it's helping her self-confidence a lot. And I think that's only going to grow."

I wanted to see Angel feel like she could handle situations on her own, that she could take on an opponent and come out victorious. It never felt comfortable having to be reliant on other people for protection. While we all had our strengths and weaknesses, Angel was beginning to feel that she could manage on her own when it came to combative situations.

"That would be a good thing," Viktor said. "Especially given what we're facing with Typhon. Hey, do you think the ghosts here are agitated because of *him*?"

I shrugged. "I don't think we can know for now. But I'll bet you every single person who knows about Typhon's approach is asking themselves the same questions we are. We're all going to be walking on eggshells until he actually makes himself known. And then, ten to one we'll be wishing we were back at this point, where we weren't sure. I have the feeling reality is going to be far worse than imagination in this case." I pressed my lips together. Waiting for an enemy you knew was on the way was never an easy task.

Herne called us over at that point. Irene and Justin had fitted Chaz into a stretcher, and Herne motioned to Viktor.

"If you'd help Justin carry the boy to their SUV. I want to talk to Irene for a moment."

Viktor could have easily carried the entire stretcher by himself, but with two of them, it was better balanced and less likely to tip over.

As he and Justin carried Chaz away, I turned back to Herne. "There are spirits all over this mining camp. I've been feeling them since we got here."

"I know," Herne said. He turned to Irene. "Where are you going to take him? We need to be careful who works on him. He's magic-born, not human. We can't just take him to a general hospital, given what George said."

My ears perked up. "What did George say?"

"Chaz's soul is out of his body. He's going to need a soul retrieval."

I blinked. "Who can do that?"

"Eliza, the shaman of my pride. I'm going to call her and ask her to meet us at the hospital." George pulled out his phone, looking expectantly at Irene.

"There is a private clinic that's not very well known
—"

"Breaknight?" Herne asked.

Irene nodded. "I think that's the best place to take him, considering how much damage there is. It's still touch-and-go. Even if we heal his body, it will do no good if we can't retrieve his soul."

"I'll call Eliza now and have her meet us there. Can you text me the directions?" George asked.

Irene pulled out her phone. "What's your number?"

As they exchanged numbers, I quickly typed them both into my phone as well.

"Can you send me the directions, too?" I asked.

"Of course," she said.

Herne tapped me on the shoulder. "We need to get back to camp and get on the road. You head directly toward the clinic and we'll meet you there," he said, glancing back at Irene. "Thank you. And don't stay out here by yourselves. Don't even *come* out here unless you're in a large group. Lazerous would love to gobble up your abilities."

I wanted to ask just what abilities she had. Most shifters didn't have much magic to them, other than their natural abilities to transform, but there was something different about Irene and Justin. I just couldn't put my finger on it.

She nodded, sticking her phone back in her pocket. "We'll make sure we don't come out here alone. We'll meet you at the clinic. Is the boy a minor? Do we need his parents' permission to work on him?"

Herne glanced at me. I pulled out my notes and rifled through them. "No, he's not. He was twenty a month ago."

"Good. The longer we wait to start treating him, the less chance he has of making it. See you in a bit," she said, walking back to the SUV where Justin was waiting.

As Viktor rejoined us, they drove away. I watched them go, and then shivered as another gust of spiritual activity fluttered past, swirling around me like a shroud.

"Can we leave?" I asked. "I really don't feel like staying here."

Herne swung his back pack over his shoulder. "Let's get moving. We want to get back to camp as quickly as possible."

As we took off hiking away from the mine, I glanced back over my shoulder. For a moment, I thought I could see figures—misty and insubstantial—wandering around the camp. But I brushed it out of my mind. The last thing I wanted to do was to go back and investigate all those trapped ghosts.

BY THE TIME WE REACHED THE CLINIC, I HAD CLEARED MY head from the fog and cobwebs the spirits had left behind.

Breaknight was on the Eastside, not too far from the Medina district in Bellevue—an upper-crust area that used to be the rich part of the city, but was now mostly upper middle-class shifters and their families.

I pulled out a candy bar and began to eat as we veered off of I-405 onto the exit.

"Should we have searched for Branson?" I asked, thinking that if he had managed to escape as well, we might have signed his death warrant by leaving so quickly.

"Unfortunately, finding Chaz cut that option short. Besides, I doubt if both had the luck to escape." Herne glanced at me, his expression stoic. "Either we rescued Chaz or we risked his life to try to find Branson. And there's no way in hell I was leaving you and the others out there to search while I came back with Chaz. It's just too dangerous."

I nodded. It wasn't the best answer, but it made sense. "What do you think of George?"

"I think George is a valuable ally. I'll tell you this, if his shaman can retrieve Chaz's soul, we'll owe her a huge favor." Herne paused, then added. "I think it was more than coincidence that we met George. There's usually a reason to things, even if we don't understand why at the time, and I have a suspicion that we'll be seeing more of George in the future."

He swerved into the left lane, then turned onto Martin Street, a private lane. Up ahead at the end of the road was the Breaknight Clinic. Herne swerved into the parking lot and we tumbled out of the SUV, heading for the emergency entrance.

The clinic was two stories, smaller than the average hospital, about the size of a moderate grocery store. The sliding doors opened automatically with a soft *swoosh*, and as we passed through, I felt like we had entered a library. The atmosphere immediately felt muted, and the sounds were muffled. People were moving quickly, there was a bustle of activity, but the sound felt magically suppressed.

I tapped Herne on the shoulder. "Why is it so quiet?"

He wrapped his arm around my waist. "Because shifters built this place and they took into account the specialized needs of their own kind. Shifters in pain don't react well to noise, so they built in magical wards to filter sound. And it's not just the shifters. The magic-born can have an issue with loud sounds. Come on, let's check in at the reception desk."

He led us over to a wide counter, behind which a

woman with skin as dark as her brown eyes gazed up. There was a golden glow to her eyes, and I realized her pupils looked different. She was some kind of shifter, but I wasn't sure just what type.

"May I help you?" She paused, then abruptly stood. "Lord Herne, I'm sorry, at first I didn't recognize you."

I blinked. Herne had been here before?

"Not a problem, November. We're here to see Chaz— oh, what is his last name? Irene and Justin should have brought him in within the past hour or so."

She consulted her charts, then nodded. "Yes, they're with the doctor now. He's in room 115. You'll go through that door there," she said, pointing to a door that cordoned off the reception area from the rest of the care clinic. "Take a right, and follow the red stripe to the second turnoff. Turn left, and you'll find the room. It's the third door on the right."

"Thank you." Herne motioned for us to follow him. Nurse November didn't seem to mind that we were all trailing him. She just buzzed us on through.

The clinic was a maze, like most hospitals. The walls were painted a pale blue, and the lighting was cool—not fluorescent, but definitely not the warmth of incandescent lighting. Everywhere, nurses seemed to be on their way to some destination, hurrying but careful in their movements. The scent of disinfectant hung heavy in the air, but so did the smells of herbs, and the crackle of magic flickered through the hallway.

The nurse's directions were clear and we arrived at room 115 within a couple minutes. Herne tapped on the door, then peeked in. I heard a muffled "Come in" and he led us through.

The room held only one bed, and Chaz was in it. He was being held very still, strapped into place so he couldn't move. Irene and Justin were there, along with someone I didn't recognize.

The man was tall, with a buzz cut, and his ears were ever so slightly pointed. He was razor-thin, and he was one of the first people I could truly say had beady eyes. His pupils seemed abnormally small in the large pools of white, and his nose was hawkish. A stethoscope hung around his neck, and he was wearing a pale blue doctor's coat. The man looked up as we entered, then went back to reading the chart that he held in his hand.

I glanced at Chaz as we slid past the bed to join Irene and Justin. They were seated on a long banquette that spanned one side of the room. As we sat down, I scanned the room. It was filled with machines of various sorts—many that I recognized from typical hospitals, but I still wasn't sure what they were. Chaz was hooked up to a heart monitor, what I assumed was a blood pressure machine, and there were several IVs already in place. He was still unconscious.

"What has the doctor said?" Herne asked as we joined Irene and Justin.

"Not much yet. Just that George was right. Chaz's soul's detached from his body. We're waiting for Eliza. George called ten minutes ago to say he'd be here in about twenty minutes and that she was on the way." Irene shook her head. "The boy has taken a lot of damage, but the doctor is trying to stabilize him now. They've already taken x-rays and we're waiting for the results to come back."

The doctor suddenly closed the chart and turned to us.

"I'm Dr. Neilson. I specialize in treating the magic-born. Are you family?"

"No," Herne said. "We have yet to notify them. But he's of age, so you can treat him without repercussions."

"I see. Well, what I can tell you right now is that he's suffering from hypothermia, soul-loss, energy drain, and multiple broken bones. As to what bones, we're waiting on the x-rays. We also did an ultrascan to look for internal injuries and he's a lucky young man. I found some bruising on his lungs, but if we treat him with the right herbs, he should recover from that."

Ultrascans were new. Similar to ultrasounds, but far more accurate, they allowed doctors to see organs and look for tumors, bruising, or perforations. I wasn't sure how they worked, but they were an expensive leap in treating the injured.

At that moment, a tech swung through the door, handed the doctor a large folder, and then left, all without a word. The doctor flipped on a lightbox on the wall and opened the folder. Inside were the x-rays. He flipped through them, then clipped them on the screen. The box was big enough to hold three at a time.

"All right, let's see what we're dealing with here." Dr. Neilson said. "I can tell you right off he has four broken ribs. He's a lucky man—none of them have perforated his lungs. All right, let's take a look over here." He pointed to the second x-ray, which was of Chaz's right foot.

"His right ankle has four fractures in different places. But we can treat them with pins. He should heal up from that." As he came to the third, he let out a sigh. "Here's the biggest issue. His right wrist has been shattered beyond repair. There's no saving the bones and there's been a horrendous amount of nerve damage. We're going to have to amputate his hand."

"He's going to lose his hand?" I asked. For the magic-born, that could spell the end to their career. No pun intended. But then again, if he already had lost his powers, the wrist might be a moot issue.

"Yes, I'm afraid so." He changed over to the next set of x-rays. "He's lucky, however. His shoulder is dislocated, but that's an easy fix. And he's suffered no permanent spinal damage. He'll be able to walk again once his ankle heals up."

He flipped off the lightbox and turned around to face us. "The biggest obstacle we face is that if we go in and amputate the hand right now, with his soul still out of his body, it could affect his recovery. Attitude and will make a world of difference, even through the actual surgery. Where's the shaman?"

Dr. Neilson had no sooner asked the question than George walked through the door with a woman behind him. She had dark hair that hung down to her knees, caught back in a ponytail, and she was wearing a kimono-like gown. Her eyes flickered with a green that made my own eyes seem pale, and she was wearing a necklace that sizzled with power. By the looks of it, it was a massive smoky quartz surrounded by smaller stones, all in a large silver setting. The central stone was at least three inches in diameter.

"Are you the doctor treating Chaz?" George asked.

Dr. Neilson nodded.

"May I present Eliza, the shaman of the White Peak Puma Shifter Pride," George said, standing back so Eliza could enter the room.

She took one look at Chaz, then turned to the doctor. "I need to work on him immediately. He's a long ways from his body and if I don't retrieve his soul now, I might never be able to bring him back." Then she glanced at the four of us sitting there. She fixed her gaze on me. "I need *you* to help me. The rest of you, out. Go."

And with that, everyone including the doctor filed out of the room, leaving me alone, wondering how the hell I could be of help to a puma shaman.

CHAPTER FOURTEEN

"*W*hat can I do?" I had no clue what Eliza wanted me for, but whatever it was, I would do my best.

"You understand the nature of the hunt. So does Lord Herne, of course, but I can't work with a god the way I need to in order to retrieve his soul. I mean to send you after Chaz's soul." She stared at me. "Can you take orders?"

"Take orders? Wait, where are you sending me? Why aren't you going yourself?" It dawned on me that if she planned on sending me after Chaz, it was unlikely that I'd do so in my body.

"I'm sending you into the astral, to follow Chaz's signature and bring him home. I have to hold the door open. While I could do it myself, it would take a lot longer and we don't have the luxury of that extra time. Given his physical injuries, we need to find him as quickly as possible, and that means working with a partner. My assistant is pregnant and didn't come with me. I wouldn't take a chance on her at this point in time anyway. Too much chance of some walk-in trying to come through her child." Eliza shrugged. "Will you do it?"

I was about to ask if I had a choice, but then realized that yes, I did. If I declined, though, it would most likely mean Chaz's death. "Tell me what you need."

"Good. I have my equipment with me," she said, motioning to a couple of large bags that George was carrying in. "George, she's going to help. I'll need you to drum. I'll be the conduit and Ember will be the arrow."

George said nothing, simply pulled a large drum out of a bag and set it on the floor. Then he folded a blanket and put it behind the drum. "Where's Ember going to be?"

"She needs to lie next to Chaz. Since this is a private room, we'll need a cot for her. Please have the nurse bring one in. Also, extra blankets, for both Chaz and Ember." Eliza looked around, then pulled an armchair over next to the drum. "Ember, take this and then lie down as soon as they bring in a cot. It's safe for Fae, so no worries there." She handed me what looked like a thin wafer.

"What is it?"

"A mixture of herbs. Do you have any known allergies?"

"Just iron, and that should be obvious." I stared at the wafer in my hand. It was thin, about a quarter-inch thick and the size of a fifty-cent piece. I brought it to my nose and my skin tingled. *Strong magic*, I thought. *Whatever this is, it contains stronger magic than I've felt in a long time, except for when I'm at Marilee's.*

I glanced up, catching Eliza's gaze. The woman reverberated with strength. The magic flowed around her in a cloud that seemed to constantly shift and churn. It was as though it emerged from her pores, from her aura, from her core to surround her with a nimbus of power. And her eyes—they were so green that I found myself in the deep forest at nightfall. I could practically hear the call of the birds echoing in the deepening sky. Eliza was rooted in the woodlands and forest the same way that Herne was. She was part of it, drawing her strength from it, and it graced her every touch and word.

"You begin to understand," she said softly.

"I think so," I answered. I held out my hand, the wafer on my palm. "When should I take this?"

"Go ahead and eat it now. It will take a few minutes to fully enter your system." She tilted her head. "I'll tell you what to do once we've started. Don't worry. Your nature will take over. You'll understand what's required."

As I chewed the wafer, which tasted like a combination of licorice and honey, I could feel the magic running down my throat. It was a wave, the energy cool and resonant.

I'm drinking silver, I thought. *It tastes just like I'd think silver would taste.*

George reappeared with a nurse, who had two orderlies behind her. They were carrying a portable cot, and they set it up beside Chaz's bed. It had a thin mattress on it. Another orderly entered the room, carrying a stack of blankets and an extra pillow. They made up the cot in silence and, just as silently, vanished.

George shut the door behind them, then took his place by the drum.

"Lie down and make sure you're covered up and comfortable," Eliza said.

I took off my shoes and coat, then slid beneath the

covers. As I pushed my feet down under the covers, a shiver raced through me and I felt everything shift.

"What?" I blinked.

"Is it starting to take effect?" Eliza asked.

I nodded. "I think so. Everything moved out of phase for a moment."

"It's called an *earth shift* and it means the magic is working. There will be more of those. Take them as they come, calmly. Eventually, they'll help you move over to the astral so you can travel easily. Listen to *me*. Talk to no one while you're out there, unless it's Chaz. Don't engage, don't do anything to attract notice." Eliza stared at me sternly. "Do you understand?"

I nodded. "No engagement. Just…hunt and retrieve. I'm on a search-and-rescue mission, aren't I?"

"Of a sort," she said. "I suppose that's exactly what this is."

I started to say something, but before I could, again everything around me shifted. It was like the floor moved beneath my feet and when it stopped, everything was the same, and yet different. This one had been stronger than the first.

"Another earth shift," I said, a quiver of fear creeping through me.

"Relax. Close your eyes and they'll be easier to navigate. They should come more quickly now." Eliza motioned to George. "You may begin. Make sure you've gone to the bathroom so you don't have to take a break."

He thought for a moment, then nodded. "I'm good."

And then he began to drum out a beat. Whatever the drum he was using, it was more than a simple percussive instrument. I didn't know how it was made, but as he tapped out a four-four beat, it quickly took on a steady but intricate rhythm.

I leaned back and closed my eyes. The drumbeat echoed loudly through the room, and I could feel it down to my core. I could see it, a line of colors echoing through my thoughts, ebbing and flowing with each note. Fuchsia and purple, magenta and teal, and then into deep indigo and silver. The colors expanded and contracted with the beating of the drum, and as I watched them shimmer around me, once again, the world shifted.

This time, while I wasn't prepared, I wasn't caught totally off guard.

A spiral of sound spun around me, like the echoing of a flute, only the thread of melody was smooth, washing through me with a vortex of song. Every time a note played, I felt my body expand and contract. Part of me wanted to ask where the music was coming from, but before I could open my mouth, the question vanished in another wash of sound, and I found myself dancing on the music clef, spinning as I leapt from note to note, my feet bouncing as they landed. The moment I touched them, I jumped to another, and the sound melted away into the next phrase of the song.

I don't know how long I danced with the music, but then it began to fade and the rhythm slowed, taking on a somber tone. I straightened up, looking around me.

All around me were mist and fog, rolling along the ground in every direction. Shivering, I folded my arms across my chest, trying to remember what it was I was looking for. I was on a hunt, that much I knew, and I was searching for something.

*No...*someone. The words echoed through my mind.

Trying to focus, I narrowed my vision to straight in front of me, to the mist rolling along a darkened patch of grass on which I was standing. I glanced up and saw the moon cycling through the sky across the darkened panorama. It spun like a wheel, soaring through the heavens, and then it was gone again and a blaze of light blinded me. I had no more than shaded my eyes from the brilliant sun than it was dark again, and the stars came wheeling overhead. And once again, the moon rose and shone down on me, edging through the sky.

Where are you going so swiftly? I asked it.

But the moon told no tales, and she whispered no secrets.

I cast around for the reason I was out here, and then...*Chaz.*

Chaz's face came to mind and I remembered. I was searching for Chaz.

No, you're hunting, my mind whispered, and I recognized that my father's blood was rising strong.

Can you help me? I whispered.

Give me the helm, came the answer.

And so I did. I gave over to my Autumn Stalker nature. Instantly, my senses heightened, and through the eternal night and mist, I could hear a young man crying. He was calling out for his mother, and he was terribly frightened. I took a moment to catch the thread of his voice and began to follow it, moving soundlessly through the mist.

A small part of me wondered why I didn't stub my toe, or trip over anything, but then I remembered I was out of my body, and while I could be attacked or hurt, it wouldn't be on a physical level unless my soul took too much damage.

Chaz's cries continued, and I focused on the direction, as though I had an internal compass. I began to move faster, until I was racing as fast as thought. The cries were still distant, but they were beginning to grow louder.

I ran, the mist swirling around me as I slid silently through the fog. I'd been on the astral before, especially when working with Marilee, and also in my dreams, and I recognized the sensations. It was as though I were hovering lightly above the ground.

All around me were dim silhouettes of trees and rocks amid the unending field of mist. Out on the astral, I couldn't see the horizon—the distance faded off into a murky gray blur, and at some points, it was hard to know whether I was even moving. My legs pushed me along, but everything including my body felt insubstantial.

Then, as the cries grew louder, I knew I was zeroing in on Chaz. His sobs sounded so much like a frightened child that I stopped for a moment. He was lost, and didn't know what was going on. In some ways, we were all like that. We all had our moments where we felt lost, where we felt as if there was no one in the world to help us, and all we wanted was a friendly hand to reach into the mire in which we were immersed and draw us out.

I had no way of knowing how far I had come, but the mist opened ahead to reveal Chaz, sitting on a stone, his arms crossed across his chest. He was rocking back and forth, his face a mask of fear and uncertainty. He was sitting within a sparkling membrane that reminded me of water, and yet it wasn't fully liquid.

I had no clue what the substance was, but he was immersed in it.

Cautiously, I tested the glasslike surface with one foot.

It held my weight—if I had weight on the astral—and I inched forward, sliding along the top of the membrane until I was almost directly over him. Kneeling, I placed my hands on the surface of the bubble holding him captive. It felt smooth, like glass, but there was a spark running through it.

Magical.

I slowly pressed my hand against the surface, pushing hard. My fingers penetrated the bubble and I plunged my hand through, calling out to Chaz. Like reaching through water to rescue a drowning man, I held out my hand.

"Take my hand, Chaz. I've come to help you back into your body. I know you're scared and lost, but trust me, please."

He sobbed again, then froze. Slowly, he looked up and his eyes widened as he saw me.

"Chaz. I need you to trust me. Can you do that? Can you take my hand?" I focused on putting as much warmth in my words as I could. He was traumatized and probably afraid of everything that was going on, including me.

He hesitated for a moment, saying nothing, but his tears slowed and he slowly unclenched his arms, looking around.

"Chaz, I know you're unsure of what's happening, but take my hand. I can help you get back to your body. I promise that I won't hurt you. You have my word…" I paused, wondering what would be sacred to him. I could promise on my honor, but he had no idea who I was. And then, an idea came to me. "Triston is waiting for you. He's worried about you. You want to see Triston again, don't you?"

That seemed to jog him along. He blinked and shook

his head, as though he were trying to clear his thoughts, then hesitantly, he began to reach for my hand.

As our fingers met, I focused on lifting him up. I reminded myself I wasn't dealing with a body here—I could lift his spirit as easily as lifting a feather, unless I allowed my mind to get mired down in appearances. This wasn't Chaz's body, but his soul.

And with that thought, I gave one final heave and he broke free from the bubble, breaking through like it was an amniotic sac, and he was standing beside me.

He shook his head again, looking around. "Where am I?"

"You got lost out on the astral. I've come to rescue you and bring you back to your body." I kept hold of his hand, not wanting him to wander off again. It was easy to get lost out here, especially when you weren't used to being out of your body. And even though he was used to magic, that didn't mean he was proficient in working sans physical form.

"You're deep on the astral plane. You got separated from your body and I'm here to take you back. You're in the hospital right now, and…" I didn't want to tell him they were going to have to amputate his hand or that he had lost his powers. I wanted him to be in the best of fighting form when he went into surgery. "Come with me, please."

He nodded, his face a blank slate. "I don't know what's going on, but all right. It feels…safe…to go with you."

"It is, I promise you that." I turned back the way I'd come and I projected my thoughts, reaching out to Eliza. *I found him. Lead us back.*

Follow the beat of the drum.

A drumbeat reverberated in my ear, though Chaz didn't seem to hear it. But I could pinpoint the direction from which it was coming and I began to run, Chaz in tow. I followed the rhythm, not allowing myself to get lost in it, even though it beckoned me to dance with it again. Chaz gave me no resistance. He allowed me to pull him along, and we skimmed over the surface, through the fields of mist, through the unending fog.

As we silently ran, I began to see a silver glow from up ahead and I recognized it as Eliza's signature. I zeroed in on it, heading directly toward her.

"What's that?" Chaz asked.

I glanced back at him. His eyes narrowed, and he looked more puzzled than frightened at this point.

"That's our destination. It's the signature of a shaman whose name is Eliza. She's skilled in soul retrieval and she's the one who sent me out to look for you. She's leading us back now. You might not be able to hear it, but I'm keying in on her drummer."

Chaz stared at me for a moment, then said, "Do what you need to. Take me home."

I tightened my grip on his hand and followed the silver glow. As it began to brighten, I felt Chaz stiffen. He shielded his eyes, but I kept mine open, wanting to find the precise point where we could jump off the astral.

You are near Chaz's body. Tell him to focus on diving back into it. Tell him to focus on breathing, and then to jump directly into the mist in front of him. You need to stand back.

I relayed the message, moving out of the way.

"I didn't realize I wasn't breathing," he said, looking startled.

"We don't, out here on the astral, but we're so used to

it that it might feel like we are." I turned to him, holding both his hands. "I'm going to let go and as you jump, focus on your body, on opening your eyes, on breathing through your lungs. Are you ready?"

"How am I?" he asked, licking his lips.

I didn't like lying, but I wasn't going to scare him. "Fine. Don't worry…just do it before you psych yourself out." I dropped his hands and stood back, pointing to the spot in the mist where he needed to jump.

Chaz placed a hand on his chest, then closed his eyes. All around us, the drumming increased, and I once again felt the pull to dive into the rhythm, to dance with it. Then Chaz bent his knees and leapt. He slid through the mist, down below the clouds, and vanished from my sight.

I waited for Eliza to give me the go-ahead.

We've got him. He's back. You do the same, now.

I glanced around. Part of me wanted to stay out here, to dance through the mists with the rumbling song that seemed to beckon me, but I knew that wasn't a good idea. I placed my hand on my breast, feeling the rise and fall of my chest from a distance. With one last look at the fog surging around me, I made the leap of faith, back into my body.

"Ember, Ember, can you hear me? Wake up, Ember." The words cut through the fog in my head, and I blinked, opening my eyes to see the overhead light of the hospital room glowing. I squinted, trying to fend off the glare as I sat up.

In the bed next to me, Chaz was listening to the doctor

and mumbling something in response. Eliza and George helped me sit up, and I warily swung my feet over the side of the bed. Dizzy, I took a moment to try to get my wits about me.

"You did great," Eliza said, smiling. She was really a lovely woman, and having seen the intensity of her energy signature—or aura, some would call it—I would never make the mistake of underestimating her.

"Thanks," I said, shifting my shoulders. I was tense from lying in one spot without moving. In fact, it felt like my entire body had tensed up. "Is he...he's back, right?"

Eliza nodded. "Good job, by the way."

"I didn't tell him about his injuries," I said. "I was afraid he might not want to come back if he knew, and he didn't seem to remember anything."

"...brother. He was still..."

I caught some of what Chaz was telling the doctor and Herne, who had returned to the room, and I motioned for Eliza and George to quiet down so we could hear.

"My brother, he's still alive. He's out there. Or...he was..." Chaz caught sight of me. "I know you—you're... You brought me back."

"Yes, I brought you back," I said, standing up and moving to the bedside. "What were you saying about your brother?"

"Branson...the skeletal mummy-like thing got him. He seemed to freeze Branson in place and carried him away like a spider carries away a fly to eat later." Chaz groaned, trying to move his arm but the moment he did, he let out a shout of pain. "Oh my gods, my arm..."

"Stop trying to move," Dr. Nielson said. "I need to get

you into surgery right away. I'm so sorry that things are this bad, but we have no choice."

"No choice?" Chaz's gaze darted nervously around the room. "What do you mean?"

The doctor looked at me. "You didn't tell him?"

I shook my head. "I thought it best to wait so you could explain it better." I wanted nothing so much as to be outside that room. I didn't want to see Chaz's expression, to hear his agony as he learned he was going to lose his hand. In fact, I wanted nothing more than to curl up on my sofa with a warm cup of broth and a fuzzy blanket. Being out on the astral had been strain enough—I felt insubstantial, like a flag blowing in the wind. I didn't feel strong enough to handle anybody else's pain at the moment.

"I need to get out of this room," I said. "I'm feeling claustrophobic."

Herne seemed to catch the fear in my throat and he quickly bundled me up in his arms and carried me out the door. In the hallway he carried me to the seating area where he settled me on a chair and knelt beside me.

"Are you all right, love?"

"No, I'm not. I'm…" Overcome by emotion, I leaned forward, elbows on my knees, resting my chin on my hands. "I'm feeling weak and vulnerable and on the verge of collapsing."

"Take a few moments. Going out of body like that for any length of time can throw you a real curve." He began to rub my neck and I silently let him continue.

Viktor and Yutani joined us then, along with George and Eliza.

"We really should discuss everything that happened,"

Herne said, looking up at them. "Can you meet us back at our office? I know it's nearly five-thirty, but we can order in some takeout and if the drive home is too long for you, you're both welcome to stay at my place," he said.

"Not a problem," Eliza said. "Text us the address and we'll meet you there. Ember, you be sure to eat plenty of protein tonight and drink lots of water. And rest. You need a lot of rest."

And with that, we headed out, splitting into two groups—Eliza and George taking his car, and the rest of us heading back to Herne's SUV. Within another moment, we were on the road, headed for the Wild Hunt, and I closed my eyes for a brief rest.

CHAPTER FIFTEEN

I opened my eyes as Herne pulled into an open space in front of the building. As we entered the office, Angel directed us to the break room.

"Herne called while you were dozing and told us what happened. I ordered food, so you can have something to eat. Ember, make sure to get enough protein and carbs to ground you, considering what he told me about your day." She motioned to Herne. "Do you want me to join you?"

"As soon as George and Eliza get here, yes." Herne vanished into his office as the rest of us headed for the break room. I was in sloth-mode, more tired than I wanted to admit. It had been a nonstop past few days, and then to go out on the astral after Chaz had been the final straw in my *I've-reached-my-limit-go-away* mood. At least we had found him alive, though.

The break room smelled like soup and bread. Angel had spread out a feast from Anton's Fish Shack. There was chowder, fried fish, French fries, bread, and coleslaw in abundance. As I wearily dropped into a chair, too tired to even fill a plate, Talia took one look at me and jumped up.

"I'll get you some food." She looked worried. "Did you find the boys?"

"One of them. And then I had to go out and hunt down his soul on the astral. But he's back in his body, and the hospital is treating him." I paused, shaking my head. "You're really lucky, you know that? Lazerous is so incredibly dangerous. Not only did he drain the boy, but he knocked him out of his body. I'm dreading going up against him." I shook my head, realizing just how much I meant that. "Talia, how you ever survived, I don't know. You must be incredibly strong to have made it through what he did to you."

She stared at me thoughtfully for a moment, then turned to get my food. When she brought me back a large bowl of chowder, a couple fish fillets and some fries, and a roll, she seemed deep in thought.

I wearily began eating the soup.

By the time we were all gathered around the table with George and Eliza there, I was trying not to nod off. My body felt bone-weary and I wanted nothing more than to sleep for a solid twenty-four hours.

"George, I want to thank you and Eliza for your help. We'd like to keep in touch. There are troubled times ahead of us and it will help everyone to have allies." Herne paused, and Eliza took the opportunity to speak.

"I know something large and frightening is coming. I've been dreaming of the dead, and when I dream, there's always some meaning behind it." She leaned back in her chair. "I believe it was more than chance that brought George and Ember to the same meeting place."

"I do too," Herne said. "And your dreaming of the dead could easily relate to the fact that Typhon, the father of dragons, is waking. As he wakes, he will bring the dead with him."

Eliza nodded, a frown creasing her face. "I feared it might be something like this. Typhon is large enough and powerful enough to rock the entire world when he reappears. The Titans were world shakers…and world destroyers."

"What about Gaia?" Angel asked. "I thought she is the soul of the planet. Isn't she a creatrix rather than a force of destruction?"

Herne gave her a short shrug. "Gaia creates, yes, and is a life force. But she also destroys as well—the storms that ravage the planet, the volcanoes that destroy life around them so that new life will spring from their ashes. Gaia sends disease to cull the herds when they grow too large, unchecked by predators. That includes humans. She eats her young if they get out of hand."

I was doing my best to focus on the conversation but found myself drifting off, my thoughts a pleasant blur. A moment later, Angel was shaking my shoulder.

"Ember, wake up," she was saying.

I blinked, yawning as I realized that I had fallen asleep in my chair. I rubbed my head. The weariness had turned into exhaustion and was rapidly descending into the beginnings of a migraine.

"Crap, I'm sorry. I didn't mean to be rude, but I'm so damned tired. I need to sleep, and I need to get away from the damned light."

"It's the astral reconnaissance you did. It takes an extremely strong focus to hunt on the astral plane, and not only were you on a hunting mission, but you also had to return with Chaz. People never realize just how much energy it takes to work with magic like that." Eliza pushed back her chair. "I think George and I should go now. It's a long drive back to our Pride, so I think we'll find a hotel for the night. I'm also tired, and it's been a long, long day."

"Are you sure you won't stay at my place? We can talk further, and I've got guest rooms that are far more comfortable than any hotel." Herne turned to Angel. "Can you make sure Ember gets home safe?"

"Of course," Angel said. "I'll need help putting her gear in the car, though."

I pushed my dishes back. "I need to sleep," I said. "Now."

"We'll break for this evening then. Meeting tomorrow morning at ten. Sleep in, Ember. Everyone can come in late, given how long today has been." Herne stood, turning to George. "Let me give you directions. I need to drop off Viktor and Yutani before I go home."

"I can drive them," Talia said. "You go with your guests."

"Then tomorrow, at ten A.M." As he turned to George and Eliza, I tried to pick up my pack and promptly failed.

"I need help," I grumbled.

"I'll carry it out to your car for you," Viktor said, shouldering my gear. "Talia, give me five?"

"Not a problem."

As we headed out, Angel carried my purse as well as her own. Viktor stashed my gear in the car, then headed back up to the office to get his own. On the way home, I told Angel what had happened.

"I'm worried that we can't handle Lazerous. Sure, we've taken on some nasties, but…"

"Well, if you can find a sorcerer or sorceress, it will be much easier."

I blinked. "What are you talking about?"

"Don't you remember what Eliza said? That we need a powerful necromancer or sorcerer to take on a liche?" She frowned, then let out a laugh. "Oh, that must have been when you nodded off at the table. You were out for at least five minutes before anybody noticed."

"What else did I miss?" I didn't like losing time, but at least I had a good excuse.

"Herne's going to ask Kipa to join us tomorrow morning, because Kipa knows some extraordinarily powerful sorcerers. After that, I think you woke up." Angel shook her head. "When we get home, let me get your pack. You just go on up to bed. You aren't fit to do anything else right now."

"I want a shower," I said. I felt cold and grungy from the walk through the woods.

"I'll draw you a bath, then, and sit with you to make certain you don't accidentally drown yourself." She eased the car into the driveway. "Now, come on, let's get you inside. Mr. Rumblebutt will be glad to see you."

She took my pack away from me and lugged it into the house, dropping it to one side in the foyer. Then, as soon as I took off my coat, she led me upstairs to my room, while she drew a bath full of vanilla-scented bubbles. As I stripped and lowered myself into the steaming water, I quickly lathered up and scrubbed my legs and arms and feet, then leaned back and closed my eyes. When Angel woke me up, the water was getting tepid.

"I'll just rinse off in the shower quickly and then get into bed." I braided my hair back. It needed washing but that could wait until tomorrow. The headache had backed off a little, but I still felt it lurking on the horizon.

"I'm waiting until you do. I don't need you passing out in the shower." Angel sat on the vanity bench until I finished, then held out my towel. I wrapped it around me, and padded into my bedroom. Angel pulled the covers and I toweled off, then crawled into bed.

As she tucked me in, I let out a long sigh. "Thanks for being here, Angel. You really make life a lot more bearable. Thanks for being you." I yawned on the last word, and she finished tucking the blankets around my shoulders.

"That's what we do, Ember. We take care of each other, like best friends should." And with that, she turned off the lights and quietly left my room, leaving the door open so Mr. Rumblebutt could come and go.

I closed my eyes, grateful for the soft mattress, grateful for the warmth of the house, and most of all, grateful that Angel was my best friend. As I fell into a dreamless slumber, I basked in the feeling of how lucky I really was.

NEXT DAY, I WAS SORE BUT AWAKE, AND AFTER A HUGE breakfast of waffles, bacon, and coffee, Angel and I drove down together to work. I felt much clearer and realized that any fog that had remained attached to me from the astral plane had cleared out of my aura during the night, along with the threat of the migraine.

Herne was waiting by the reception desk, a worried

look on his face. "Angel, check the messages, please. Talia's not here yet. But Kipa is, so we can start the meeting if she's going to be late."

"That's odd." Talia was never late. But traffic being what it was, there was always a first time. I spotted Kipa in the break room. "So he made it?"

Herne nodded, absently staring at the contents of a folder in his hand. "Yes, Kipa made it. He's been a lot better about following through with his commitments since he started dating Raven, that much I'll say for him."

I laughed. "I happen to know she makes him toe the line on several issues. That's probably one of them."

"More power to her, then," Herne said, then looked up. "Good morning, love. How are you feeling today?" He closed the file folder and pulled me in for a long kiss. His lips tasted like apple juice and sausage.

I grinned. "Let's play twenty questions. Ten bucks says I can guess what you had for breakfast!"

"I'm glad to see you're back to your obnoxious but lovable self." He rocked me back and forth in his arms. "I was worried about you last night. By the way, speaking of worries, my mother and father persuaded the Triamvinate to hear my case against Myrna."

"Good. When?"

"A week or so from now." He kissed me again, then let go. "We'd better get the meeting started. Angel, call Talia before you come in and ask her what's keeping her."

We headed for the break room.

Kipa waved as I entered. "Raven sends her love," he said.

As we gathered around the table, Viktor finished

making a pot of coffee. He had also fixed a mug of tea for Angel. By the time she entered the room, we were all set.

"What did she say?" Herne asked.

Angel shook her head. "I couldn't get hold of her. I tried three times and nobody answered. I left a message but I have an odd feeling about this, Herne. I'm worried. And I don't usually have premonitions unless there's some reason."

A veiled look crossed Herne's face. "She was really quiet last night. Did she say anything to anybody?"

"She was worried about me, that much I know." I was concerned, too. It just wasn't like Talia to not show up for work and not leave a message. "I wonder if an emergency called her away. Maybe her family is sick?"

"Surely she would call us before leaving, though?" Viktor cupped his coffee mug, staring at it, his brow furrowed.

"Well, there's one way of finding if she went out of town." I pulled out my phone and punched in Ronnie Archwood's number. "She would never leave her dogs unattended." After three rings, Ronnie came on the line. "Ronnie, did Talia call you about her dogs? Are you taking care of them for her?"

"Yes, she did. She called last night around ten-thirty. She asked me to check in on them starting today, and she said she'd be back later. That she had something important to attend to. I walked her dogs this morning, and I noticed an envelope on her kitchen table. It has Herne's name on it. I was going to call and tell you after I finished up with my next two clients. I'm almost done. I have to go back there in the afternoon to walk the dogs again. Do you want me to pick up the envelope at that point?"

"Hold on. I'll call you back in a minute." I set my phone on the table, shaking my head. "Something's wrong. Talia called Ronnie last night and asked her to come over and start walking and feeding the dogs this morning. She told Ronnie she had something important to do. Ronnie just told me that she saw an envelope with your name on it, Herne, on the kitchen table. She's offered to pick it up and bring it over later this afternoon, but we need to look at it *now*."

Herne shifted, concern turning to worry in his eyes. "I don't want to wait until this afternoon."

"I have a key to her place," Viktor said. "We look after each other's houses when needed. I can drive over there right now and grab it."

"Go ahead." Herne looked at me. "Call Ronnie back and tell her we're going to get the envelope now. Tell her if she finds out anything else, to let us know."

"Will do." I called Ronnie again and relayed the message. She promised to keep her eyes open for anything unusual. By the time I was done, Viktor had already headed out. "Should we start the meeting now?"

"We might as well. We can fill Viktor and Talia in later." Herne turned to Kipa. "All right, we have a powerful liche on our hands. Eliza, the shaman from the White Peak Puma Pride, told us we need at least an equally powerful sorceress or necromancer to even think of fighting Lazerous."

"Right," Kipa said, the smile sliding off his face. "I know several of them who could do the job. The question is, will they help us, and how much are they going to ask. None of them are what you would call philanthropic. The one I think most suited for the job is named Louhia. She's sort of a combination sorceress and necromancer, and she lives in Finland. Or rather, Pohjola. Louhia has a high standing among the royalty there. She's deadly, but she will work with others when it suits her needs." He looked a little queasy. I took that as a bad sign.

"What do you think she'd ask in payment?" I asked.

"Whatever it is, it's going to be expensive. She tends to like gems—sapphires, diamonds, white topaz…"

Herne looked relieved. "For a moment I thought you meant she was going to ask for a baby or something. You know, a pound of flesh?"

"Louhia is more than capable of picking out her own sacrifices. No, she's going to want gems and/or silver and gold." Kipa shrugged. "The only way to find out how much is to ask her."

"Can you bring her here? To talk to us?" Yutani asked.

Kipa shook his head. "No, we're going to have to go through the portal to Mielikki's Arrow to meet her. I'll have to call ahead and get permission, given the fact that I'm persona non grata over there." He arched his eyebrows, flashing me a naughty schoolboy grin.

Herne guffawed. "I *have* to see this. Ember and I will go with you. That is, if Mielikki even grants you an audience. Kipa, go ahead and call her. And for our sake, let's hope that she relents."

Mumbling something under his breath, Kipa headed out into the hallway. He was Lord of the Wolves, much like Herne was Lord of the Forest, and he was gorgeous in an entirely different way than Herne. Kipa wasn't quite as tall as Herne, his skin was rich and golden, and his eyes were pools of chocolate. He had dark brown hair that brushed his shoulders, and a dolphin bite piercing through his lower lip. Kipa wore four earrings in each ear, and at times I wondered if he had any tattoos under those clothes of his. I could ask Raven, but I didn't want her telling Kipa that I had entertained thoughts about his naked body. That could lead to a lot of trouble for everyone.

"Where do you think Talia went?" Yutani asked, tossing a pencil on the table as he leaned forward to rest his elbows in front of his laptop.

"I'm hoping it's a family emergency," I said. I was nursing a suspicion, but I didn't want to bring it out into the open until we knew for sure. With Angel's uneasy premonition, I had the feeling I was right. And I didn't want to be.

"I think we should wait until Viktor gets back before we start speculating." Herne spoke in an even tone, but as I gazed into his eyes, I saw the worry there. He gave me a subtle shake of the head, and I knew he was thinking the same thing I was.

There was a loud burst of noise from the hallway, and we could hear Kipa stuttering. After a moment, he quieted down. When he returned, about five minutes later, he looked wrung out.

"Okay. This afternoon at two. And she said to be there promptly or don't come at all."

"*She* being Mielikki?" Herne asked, trying to suppress a grin. But it peeked out from the corners of his lips, and I wondered how long he could sustain a straight face before he burst out laughing.

"Yes, smartass. She's granted me a special dispensation. I'm allowed to return if there's an emergency. I explained the situation to her, and Mielikki agreed. I'm to be on my best behavior or Tapio will thrash me within an inch of my life. I agreed that I understood this, and that I would act like a gentleman." He snorted and shook his head. "Honestly, I don't know why Tapio got his nose so out of joint. All I did wa —"

"All you did was try to cop a feel," Herne said. "Don't blame Mielikki for giving you a black eye, or Tapio for banning you from the agency."

"Did Mielikki really give you a black eye?" I asked. "She must be a firecracker."

"Not only is she goddess of the Hunt, but she's a goddess of the Dark Fae. She doesn't put up with anything from anybody, and she makes no bones about how far she's willing to go to pay back an injury." Herne was shaking his head as he laughed. "Her husband is easier going than she is, but if she gets angry, he gets angry on her behalf. If she had accepted the advance, Tapio probably would have gone along with it. But she didn't, and that made all the difference in the world."

"Can we stop discussing my egregious behavior? I suppose in hindsight, I should have just asked her instead of playing touchy-feely. But she doesn't have anything to worry about this time. I'm with Raven right now, and I promised on my honor that I wouldn't do anything behind her back." The smile on Kipa's face vanished. "I really don't want to fuck things up. I like Raven in a way I never knew I could like a woman."

"You mean, she's your friend as well as your lover?" Herne asked.

"Precisely. To be honest, I've never had many female friends. And I never knew I could also be friends with someone I wanted to bed. Raven keeps me on my toes.

She's always got some surprise up her sleeve, and she's not afraid of me. I like that. I like a woman who challenges me."

Whether or not he knew it, Kipa was in love. I wasn't about to mention it—some things you have to find out on your own—but I wondered just how long it would be before those three little words came popping out.

Just then, Viktor entered the room again. He held out the envelope to Herne.

"I didn't open it," he said. "I thought it best to wait until I got back."

Herne gingerly took the envelope, staring at the front of it for a moment. Talia had written his name in an elegant scrollwork. He opened it, shaking the single page out in his hand. As he scanned the words, I knew immediately what she had written.

"She's gone after Lazerous," Herne said. "She left last night."

And with those words, my heart dropped a million miles.

CHAPTER SIXTEEN

*H*erne stared at the paper as though it might burst into flames.

"Damn it. Why the hell did she do this? She says here that she doesn't want any of us hurt because of her, and that she feels like he's her responsibility. I don't know what she hopes to gain. She's smart enough to know that she can't take him on by herself." He tossed the paper on the table, folding his arms across his chest. He looked like he wanted to punch something. Or somebody.

"That's what I was afraid of," I said. "Do you think we can catch her?"

"She left last night. She's already up there. And thanks to us, she knows where to find him. I'm going to call George and ask if he can look for her in the campground. He can get there before we can." Herne pulled out his phone and moved off to the side.

I turned to Angel. "Do you have any premonitions? Any hunches you can share?"

"I get a bad headache when I think about this. She's in

danger, and I know that seems like a given, but I have a feeling that she's still alive. But she's in a precarious place right now, and I can't see, because something is blocking the way."

Yutani tapped away at his laptop. A moment later, he looked up. "Eliza was right. The only way to take on a liche is to have the help of a good sorcerer. We *have* to get Louhia on our side."

I glanced at the clock. It was nearly quarter of twelve. "When do we have to leave to get through the portal? If we need to be there on the dot at two P.M., shouldn't we head out now?"

Herne's face was pasty white. "Yeah. There's not much we can do without a sorceress with us. Ember and I are going over with Kipa. Viktor, get ready for a trip back to the campground. Everything needs to be ready when we get back. Angel, you'll hold down the fort here."

"Should I call Raven and ask her to come with us? She's a bone witch, and she *is* one of the Ante-Fae."

"No," Kipa barked. "Raven's a capable bone witch, but she is *not* powerful enough to take on Lazerous. All that will happen is that he'll steal her powers."

Herne glanced at him, and for a moment I thought he was going to yell at the Lord of the Wolves. Instead, he just muttered, "Kipa's right. Raven's too new to her magic to be a help rather than a hindrance. I don't want to put her life in danger as well."

He stood, shoving his hands in his pockets. "Ember, grab your jacket and come with Kipa and me. Yutani and Viktor, start packing for the trip. Get your asses in gear, because we don't have time to waste."

We scrambled, me to my office to grab my coat, and

Yutani and Viktor toward the storeroom. Angel stopped me as I headed toward the reception area. "Herne's right. You have to go now. She's alive for now, but if you don't get to her soon, she'll die. That much I know."

I started to retort that her observation was obvious, but bit my tongue. I knew Angel better than to make light of her premonitions. Instead, I just gave her a quick hug. Herne and Kipa were waiting for the elevator and I joined them. Angel came out to see us off, and as the elevator door closed, I couldn't help but wonder if we were already too late. Was Talia really still alive?

WE TOOK ONE OF THE NEAREST PORTALS, WHICH WAS located between two trees near Herne's home. Technically, it was in a park, but one of the park workers who was always there also worked for the Wild Hunt as an adjacent member.

There was a network of portals all around the country, and each one—of the ones that weren't natural—had a gatekeeper to watch over the portal and tend to the needs of visitors going either way. I stared at the oak trees between which the portal vibrated. The vortex was an icy blue color in terms of the energy, and Kipa had called ahead so that Orla, the gatekeeper, could set the coordinates for Mielikki's Arrow.

"What's the proper way to address her?" I asked. It seemed every god or goddess had their own specified title they chose to be addressed by. Some, like Morgana or Cernunnos, tended to use their first names when they were on a friendly basis with others. But I knew that there was a subset of gods who insisted on a long, elegant title.

"Lady Mielikki, or Lady of the Hunt, or Queen of Fae. Those three all work for her." Kipa was straightening his jacket, and I realize he was trying to make himself as presentable as possible.

"Getting yourself all spiffed up?" I asked, taking the chance to needle him.

Kipa gave me the side eye. "Don't be a smartass. And yes, I am. She demands cleanliness and order. And once you've been scolded by her, you learn very quickly to avoid doing whatever it was she found objectionable. Let me put it this way. Mielikki is far scarier than just about anybody you've ever met when she's pissed. When she's happy, she's a gem. But don't ever cross her, because in my culture? An angry woman is a woman to be afraid of."

I laughed, grateful to Kipa for breaking the tension. "That's why you like Raven, isn't it? I take it women in your culture are outspoken."

"Let's face it, my culture tends to be a little bit crazy. All of us. If it weren't for their mothers, some of the heroes like Väinämöinen would have been killed off long ago. Some were, and their mothers rescued them and brought them back to life. And if you think *Mielikki* is nerve-racking to deal with, you should meet Rauni. She's the mother of our pantheon, and nobody but nobody goes up against her. Not even her husband, Ukko. He might control the thunder, but she controls lightning." Kipa glanced at Herne. "You've met them, haven't you?"

Herne nodded. "Kipa's not exaggerating."

As we exited the building, the rain began to fall again. The buds on the trees were blossoming out into leaves, but it felt as if all the skies were crying, and I raised my face, letting the rain stream down my cheeks.

As we crossed through the portal to Helsinki, I wasn't sure whether we would come out in the middle of the city, or inside the agency itself. But we arrived in what looked like a small park off of a street named Merikatu. It was pitch dark, except for the streetlamps, and far colder than it was in Seattle. There was still snow on the ground. Patches of it looked like they had been melting, but the weather was cold enough that the remaining snow had frozen over again, into ice.

"Do we have much of a walk? I'm wearing boots, but they aren't fit for snow like this." I glanced at the ice nervously, wondering how many times I'd fall on my ass.

"There will be someone along to pick us up in a moment. We don't have far to go, but we didn't have time to go home and change clothes. And it's too cold right now to walk far, anyway. At least, if you're not used to the weather." Kipa rubbed his hands together, then jammed them under his armpits. I thrust my hands in my pockets, shivering. Herne wrapped his arm around me as we stood there.

"I should have thought about both the time and weather difference, but I didn't. I was too worried about Talia."

A gust of wind came flying by, catching us in its wake. It had to be below freezing. In fact, it was probably in the low twenties, if not colder.

"What time is it?" I asked glancing around. The sky

was clear, sparkling with stars, but that only made every-thing seem colder.

"It's a little after midnight," Kipa said.

Just then, a black sedan drove up, slowing down at the edge of the park. Kipa waved for Herne and me to follow him as the driver got out and opened the back door.

Kipa nodded to him, saying nothing, and slid onto the seat. I scooted in next, and Herne sat on the other side of me. Once we were buckled in, the driver started off again.

Kipa said something to him in Finnish and the driver answered. "He said it will take us about twenty-five minutes to get there," Kipa told us. "He'll wait, and when we're done he'll take us back to the portal."

"So she's seeing us in the middle of the night?" I asked. "That's nice of her."

"Mielikki tends to be more nocturnal, depending on her mood."

I noticed the driver had straightened his shoulders and seemed to be eavesdropping on our conversation. I poked Kipa in the arm, jerking my head toward the front seat. He glanced at the driver, then surreptitiously held his finger to his lips. We spent the rest of the ride in silence.

I wasn't sure if we were outside the city proper when the car began to slow, but I decided to keep quiet. I didn't need to know and, if the driver was keeping tabs on Kipa, I didn't want to inadvertently cause any infrac-tions by asking questions out of turn. Herne would know if we were headed in the wrong direction and put a stop to it.

I glanced at Herne, who was staring out the window. "What are you thinking about?"

"Talia. How could she just run off like that on her

own? She knew better than that. What the hell was she thinking?"

"I think I know why she did that, and it's partially my fault," I finally said.

"What are you talking about? How is it your fault?"

"Last night when I came in so tired and wiped out from locating Chaz's soul, I said that I was afraid we might not be able to take on Lazerous. I guess I was rambling, but I remember that she gave me an odd look, like…like she was sorry I had gotten mixed up in this. I think she's worried we'll get hurt and is feeling guilty. I think that clouded her common sense."

Herne groaned. "Okay, that answers that. Well, I wish she would have talked to me because now, not only do we have to take out Lazerous, but we've got to rescue her as well. I swear, once we get her back safe and sound, I'm going to have a talk with her."

Kipa leaned forward, turning to look at Herne. "For fuck's sake, Herne. Don't blame Talia. That liche stole her powers, left her for dead, and look at all the trauma she went through until she met you. Is it any wonder that she's got PTSD from it? I don't care how long it's been, this has to dredge up horrendous memories for her. Talia would never knowingly put her friends in danger. This has to be a stress reaction."

"You're probably right," Herne said after a while. "Talia's very sensitive, even if she doesn't openly show it. She must blame herself for him being here in the first place, even though that's not at all the truth."

"Speaking of trauma," I said, "Did you call the school and tell them about Chaz?"

"Yes, I did. And I warned Nanette, in no uncertain

terms, that she needs to lock down the school until we take care of this. You were right about her agenda. She argued with me until I told her that if she didn't institute a curfew and warn the students that the area around the mine is dangerous, I'd get my father out there. I told her that if Cernunnos has to enforce it, he's not going to be a happy camper. That seemed to do the trick. After that threat, Nanette agreed with no hesitation. It's a wonder what a little name-dropping can do."

The driver swung into a parking lot beside a tall stone building. Three stories high, the building reminded me of the Wild Hunt, and I wondered whether it shared space with other businesses like we did.

"Is this entire building Mielikki's Arrow?"

"No, the first floor is a free clinic, a lot like the urgent care clinic below the Wild Hunt. And I think the top floor houses a series of lawyers' offices. I'm not sure, though, because it's been quite a while since I've been here." Kipa gazed up at the building as we walked toward it.

"How long ago did she kick you out?" I asked.

Kipa sighed, staring down at his hands. "Oh, it's been a good...five...six decades? Maybe longer. I tend to run dates together in my head, so I'm not sure exactly when it happened."

"And in all this time you haven't apologized, so you could go back?" I was surprised that it'd taken this for Kipa to make amends.

Herne snorted. "Of course it took this long. Kipa never thinks he's the one in the wrong. Do you, bro?"

Kipa waved him off, then laughed. "Raven's teaching me how to say I'm sorry. The list of people I should probably apologize to is just so long that it's going to take quite some time."

And with that, he led us down the snowy sidewalk into the spacious first floor.

THE BUILDING FELT NEWER THAN THE ONE THE WILD HUNT was in, but the emergency care clinic looked remarkably like the urgent care clinic at home. Some things never change. A medical office was still a medical office.

We rode up the elevator until we reached the second floor. Very much like our own agency, the doors opened into the waiting room. A gorgeous blonde sat behind the desk, and she flashed us a dazzling smile as we entered the room.

"Welcome to Mielikki's Arrow. My name is Katia. Please have a seat and I will let Lady Mielikki know you are here." As she rose, I noticed that she looked uncommonly strong. She had quite a figure, and her muscles rippled, and I wondered if she was something other than human. She certainly wasn't Light or Dark Fae, and I doubted if she was one of the magic-born.

Kipa led us over to the leather chairs and sofa that lined the waiting room walls. Two large windows overlooked the street, and I peeked out, staring into the darkness. It felt odd to think that we were half a world away from home, and that we had gotten here within the blink of an eye. Somehow, we seemed closer to Seattle when we were in Annwn.

As I sat down, I shivered again. A chill seemed to permeate the building, and I couldn't throw it off. Herne sat down beside me and took my hand. Giving me a soft smile, he leaned over and pressed a quick kiss to my lips.

"Feeling overwhelmed?"

I nodded. "Overwhelmed, and worried. I can't stop thinking about Talia. It feels like we're so far away from her. Anything could be happening and we aren't there to help."

"I understand. I feel the same way. But love, we can't *do* anything unless we have the help of a sorcerer. Or a necromancer. We need help, and that's why we're here."

I knew what he said was true, but I also knew how deadly Lazerous was. I entwined my fingers in his, and tried to change the subject.

"Did your parents say anything else about the Triamvinate?"

"No, but they were royally pissed at Myrna and what she's trying to pull. In fact, I had to stop my father from paying a visit to her. If you haven't noticed by now, Cernunnos can be kind of a hothead." He smiled, shaking his head. "When I was a kid, I was scared to death of him when he got angry. He never threatened me, nothing more than to tan my hide, but he was so dour when he got angry. And I've seen what he can do to his enemies. I know better than to ever do anything that would truly piss him off."

"Speaking of Cernunnos, what do you think he did to Ray?" I had avoided this question for weeks, not wanting to know. But now that Herne brought up the Lord of the Forest and his moods, I couldn't help but ask.

"Ray isn't dead. Cernunnos respected your wishes on that. But there's no chance that he'll ever walk free. He's not being tortured. He'll just live out his life somewhere else, doing hard but fair work, thinking about what he lost because of his stupidity."

Ray Fontaine had been my boyfriend at one time, and when I had broke up with him everything seemed fine... for a while. Ray developed an obsession with me. It had started small but ended up with him trying to torch my house. I had begged Herne not to kill him, and he had acceded to my wishes. But rather than turn him over to the cops, Herne had taken Ray home to Cernunnos, who had effectively made Ray a *non*-problem.

At that moment, Katia returned, motioning for us to follow her. "Lady Mielikki is ready to speak to you."

We followed her down the hall into a spacious room. A small refrigerator sat against one wall, and a microwave sat on the counter. There was a sink and cupboards, and two rectangular tables with chairs lining the sides. At the head of one of the tables sat a woman. She stood as we approached, and I gasped.

Mielikki was tall, well over six feet, and hair the color of midnight flowed down to her ass. Her skin had the faintest green tone to it, and her eyes shimmered, the color of lilacs in spring. She was wearing a pair of leather pants, and a leather halter top. Her wrists and her neck dripped with gold and silver chains, each chain sporting an array of charms. Around her head, she wore a circlet, a woven leaf pattern in silver, with delicate gems inset within the leaves. A central stone, a moonstone, rose above the intricate metalwork.

A polished longbow sat on the table. It was one of the most beautiful bows I had ever seen, and when I glanced at Mielikki, her eyes twinkled as she met my gaze.

"Well met, Herne. It's been a long time. This must be Ember."

Herne bowed, as did Kipa, and I curtsied.

Mielikki bade us to sit, and I sat down next to the bow. I knew better than to touch it, but I couldn't help but lean in to gaze at the intricate patterns carved into the wood.

"So, you are to meet Louhia?"

Herne nodded. "We have a problem at home, one we need to take care of as soon as possible. When Kipa put forth Louhia's name...well, we have no other options whom we can engage quickly enough. We have a liche on the loose, and he's on a killing streak. And right now, one of our own went after him. He stole her power centuries ago, and I think she's out for revenge. We have to reach her before he does."

Her voice dripping with golden honey, Mielikki said, "Then yes, Louhia is your best bet. I just wish you all the luck of the gods in dealing with her." She snapped her fingers, and Katia opened the door.

Without another word, Mielikki nodded, and Louhia, the Witch of Pohjola, entered the room.

CHAPTER SEVENTEEN

*W*hen Louhia walked into the room, the temperature dropped nearly twenty degrees. I scooted my chair closer to Herne's. The power emanating from the sorceress was palpable, rolling out before her like a carpet, announcing her presence. She was wearing a pristine white cape that fluttered around her as though it were caught in a magical wind. Beneath the robe, her dress sparkled, ice blue beaded with sequins. Louhia's shoulder-length hair was black at the crown of her head, fading into silver, fading into platinum. But her eyes captivated me most of all. Instead of a colored iris in a sea of white, her eyes were like snowflakes shining in a sea of glossy black.

I leaned close to Herne. "Does she belong to the Force Majeure?"

Louhia must have overheard my whisper, because she answered in perfect English. "No. They offered me membership, but I turned them down. I choose to live outside of this realm, and I forge my own path, in my own country. I have the ear of Pohjola's Chieftain, and her will is my will."

I frowned. "Pohjola? I thought Finland had a prime minister."

Mielikki touched her nose. "Ah, but Pohjola resides in the realm of Kalevala, as does my own land of Tapiola. Just as Herne's land of Annwn resides in the realm of Otherworld."

Understanding hit me like a ton of bricks. Louhia wasn't from Earth. She had come in from a different realm. Which meant we were dealing with someone who was a wild card.

"Would you be willing to help us?" Herne asked, leaning forward to stare at the sorceress. "Kipa tells us you are powerful enough to take on a liche."

Louhia glanced at Kipa, then back at Herne. "Kipa is correct. I have gone up against several liches in my life, and in all cases, I have emerged victorious. But they are not easily subdued. As to whether I'm willing to help you, that depends on what you can do for me in return. I neither offer my assistance for free, nor am I swayed by sob stories."

Her lips turned up very slightly at the corners, reminding me of a predator. I realized right then that Louhia scared the crap out of me. She radiated power, backed by a ruthlessness and neutrality that made me all too aware of my mortality.

"I'm prepared to offer you a small fortune in gems and jewels, if that is to your liking." Herne reached in his jacket and pulled out a small pouch. He opened it and poured a heaping mound of sparkling gems on his palm. Diamonds and sapphires, aquamarine and blue topaz—all were represented in quantity. There were enough stones there to fund a small jeweler's shop. I wondered where he had gotten them, but decided that some questions were better broached in private.

Louhia glanced at the gems impassively. "Gems are well and good, but they cost you little to offer." A sly smile stole across her face, and she turned to me. "How much do *you* want this liche caught?"

Taken aback that she had actually spoken to me, I wasn't sure how to answer. I didn't want to mess things up, and I had no clue what to say. If I answered honestly, it might put us more in her debt. If I lied, she might dismiss our request.

Herne reached under the table to take my hand and squeeze it. I glanced up at him, and he nodded for me to answer.

"Very much. He's killed a number of students at a magical school, and he's also hurt a friend of ours." I tried to keep my voice from wavering.

Louhia looked pleased. "Very well, then. I shall help you in exchange for the jewels…"

"Wonderful—" Herne started to say, but Louhia interrupted him again.

"And in exchange for one night with you, Lord of the Hunt." And the crafty smile blazed across the table.

"What?" My stomach lurched and before I could stop myself, I let out a cry of dismay.

"You can't be serious," Herne said, leaning forward to stare at her intently. "I'm no pimp, nor am I a gigolo."

"You asked for my terms. You have them." Louhia shrugged. "Take the offer or leave it on the table. It's no matter to me."

"You're just doing this to hurt Ember," Herne bellowed. "You delight in inflicting pain, don't you?"

Louhia laughed. "Oh, son of the Forest Lord, by now you should realize that I do so enjoy playing chess. Only my pieces are very real, and remember—the queen always wields the most power. So, do we have a deal or not?"

I stared at the table. We needed her help, and we needed it now. We didn't have time to find another sorceress and I knew it. Talia was out there, looking for Lazerous and if he found her, she wouldn't stand a chance.

"I'll do it," Kipa said, breaking my thoughts.

We all turned to stare at him. He didn't look enthusiastic, but his jaw was set and he looked determined.

"You're asking Herne to service you right in front of his girlfriend. I can guarantee, your victory would be a hollow one. I know my cousin well enough to know that whatever pleasure you'd derive from your victory would be lackluster at best. If you must extract your pound of flesh, I'm the better choice."

"Kipa, what about Raven—" I started to say, but he waved me off.

"Raven will understand, and it won't hurt our relationship as much as this would impact yours. You two are practically engaged." Kipa shook his head. "Let me do this, Herne, as a way to make amends for the past."

Herne slammed his fist on the table and stood. "No, I won't have you compromising yourself for me. Or for anyone, regardless of what happened in our past. Louhia, you may think you're the one with the upper hand, but I refuse to put anyone in my company—and Kipa now belongs to the Wild Hunt, even if he doesn't want to admit it—on the line as a bargaining chip. There are other ways around this. I can ask my grandfather, the Merlin. It may take a little longer, but he won't refuse me."

I knew that we didn't have that amount of time. "It's all right, Herne. Do what you need to. I understand. Talia's life is on the line."

"You seriously want me to sleep with this bitch?" Herne stared at me. "I refuse. Talia knew better than go out there alone. I will not be blackmailed into unreasonable demands. I'm offering this woman a small fortune in gems. That should be enough." He turned back to Louhia, hands on his hips.

Mielikki shot out of her seat and cleared her throat. She looked pissed.

"Louhia, you may not be one of my subjects—Pohjola and Tapiola aren't allies even on the best of days—but I warn you. *Do not meddle with the Dark Huntress.* I command an army of Dark Fae, as well as the animals of the forest. Even the animals in *your* forest. How would you like a famine to sweep through Pohjola? Your people would blame Loviatar, your queen, and she in turn would blame you. Loviatar may be a goddess, but *so am I.* Is it not better to return home rich with gems and remain my reluctant ally, rather than to return home to find the bear has turned his back on your people, the deer no longer runs through the woods for the hunters to catch, and hunger is widespread throughout Pohjola?"

"We have the fish of the sea—" Louhia started to say, but Mielikki cut her off.

"Tapio, my consort, rules over the fish of the sea, and the wolves of the mountains. One word from him and the fish will no longer bite at the bait, and the wolves will come down from the crags on high to seek their prey. Your people will die, and I will make it known that you angered me. That by *your* actions, their larders are empty and their children in danger."

As Mielikki drew herself up to full height, she lowered her masks and all around her, a swarm of dark sparkles radiated power and strength. I realized I was down on my knees, in awe of her power, and saw that Kipa, too, was down on one knee. Herne bowed his head.

Louhia flinched, her eyes so dark that the snowflakes almost vanished. "You tread dangerous waters, Lady Mielikki, but I acknowledge that you are often at home there. You are known as treacherously beautiful for a reason."

Mielikki's smile was feral and wild, and I feared her more than I had feared any goddess I had yet met.

"My waters are indeed treacherous, and so are my forests. They can also be pleasant and rewarding, if I so choose. Bear this in mind, Louhia: Should you run tattling to Loviatar, she would not look favorably upon her favorite witch putting the people of Pohjola in danger. I am no gamboling maid of the forest. I am the Queen of the Darkest Woodlands, and I ride both under full and moonless nights. I am the Ancient Mother of Reindeers, Mother Bear, Queen of Bees. I am the beckoning lure of the Dark Fae, and I nurture the bog in which the unwary traveler meets his end. *Do you dare deny my power? Would you dare cross me?*" Mielikki's voice was no longer wind chime lovely, but low and throaty, a sultry warning backed by all the power of the deep woodland.

Louhia crumbled then, lowering herself to her knees

and pressing her forehead to the ground. "Lady, I abide by your will."

"And you will no longer complain?"

"No." Louhia raised her face, her expression a mask of anger and awe.

"Then do the work well, without spite, and I will double what Herne offers."

A spark of greed filled those onyx eyes, and Louhia's smile returned. "That will make me wealthy, indeed."

"And, I hope, will serve as a reminder that good deeds are rewarded more than blackmail. Very well. Go with them, and I'd better not hear any complaints or I will have words with your Mistress. We may not be friends, but in the past, we have worked together, and we shall in the future, when need calls again. Remember, Louhia, *no one* is indispensable. Not even a powerful sorceress." Mielikki stood, turning to us. "I wish to know how things turn out. You will return when the task is done, Kipa, to let me know how the mission fared." She paused, then added, "You are slowly earning my respect again. It's not returned yet, but in time…perhaps."

I realized this was her move to dismiss us. She waved her hand and Kipa rose, bowing as he motioned to us. We followed him out of the room. Louhia stayed for a moment, but quickly joined us in the waiting room. She looked miserable, but all that mattered was she do her job and do it right.

"So you're coming with us?" Herne asked her.

Louhia glared at him, but nodded. "Yes, apparently so. I'll do my job, like I'm supposed to. But know this, Lord of the Hunt. Favorites don't always stay on their pedestals, and when they fall, they're fair game."

And that was all she would say as we headed toward the sedan waiting to take us back to the portal, through the long Helsinki night.

"WELL, NOW I CAN SAY I'VE BEEN TO FINLAND," I SAID AS Viktor, Yutani, Angel, and I gathered in the break room. It was seven-thirty, and Herne had been locked up in his office for over two hours, talking to Kipa and Louhia. I had the feeling that he was laying down the law on what was and wasn't acceptable behavior.

"That woman scares the hell out of me," Angel said. "She's got more power in her little finger than I do in my body."

"I think she's got more power in her little finger than the rest of us combined. Herne being the exception," Yutani said. "She's a freakshow, and I say that as someone who makes chocolate look vanilla." His eyes darkened, and once again, I spotted a glimpse of Yutani's wild child that lurked beneath the surface.

Viktor shook his head. "It's not a good thing, working with her. But we can't wait. I wish to hell Talia hadn't gotten it into her head to go out there on her own."

I groaned. "As I told Herne, I made the mistake of talking about how dangerous Lazerous was and how scared I was of going after him. She saw how wiped out I was after going out on the astral to retrieve Chaz's soul. Now I feel responsible for whatever happens to her."

"Don't blame yourself. You couldn't have known she would take it into her head to run off like that." Yutani shook his head.

At that moment Herne entered the break room, followed by the others. He looked exasperated, as did Kipa, while Louhia was wearing a smirk that wouldn't quit. Kipa gave her a nasty look, then stomped out of the room.

Looking pained, Herne pulled out a chair for Louhia and she settled herself at the table.

"Well, you all look like you're having a chatty little time."

I stifled a smartassed retort. I *really* didn't like the woman, and I *really* didn't want to have anything to do with her.

She turned to Angel. "My, my. Aren't you a reservoir of untapped powers?"

Angel looked like she wanted to dive under the table rather than answer. She glanced at Herne, who shook his head.

"Leave my staff alone. There will be no goading or bating them. You've already chased Kipa away for the time being."

"You need *my* help, not his," Louhia said, brushing off his complaint.

I jerked my head around, staring at Herne, but he shook his head, warning me with his eyes not to ask. I bit my words back, but wondered what the hell had happened.

To the rest of us, he added, "We're heading out to search for Talia. She has a twenty-four hour head start on us, and we can't afford to let the gap get any wider. Louhia has everything with her that she needs in order to combat Lazerous, but we'll need to be her backup. She can't do it on her own. Louhia, if you would tell them what you told me."

"It's likely that your liche has animated several skeletons to be in his attendance. While you cannot bring *him* down, you *can* take care of them. And you will need to protect me, because I guarantee that Lazerous will sense my power once we arrive. He'll know that I'm capable of defeating him. Obviously, once he realizes that, he will be focused on destroying me. So you'll need to run interference. Bows will do no good, nor simple swords. You will need magical weapons."

I had to hand it to her. Once Louhia turned on her professional mode, she went full-bore.

"I have Brighid's Flame, a magical sword forged by Brighid herself. Will that do anything against him?" I asked.

Louhia's eyes lit up. "Yes, actually it will. You wouldn't be able to kill him with it, but you can damage him enough to put him at a disadvantage. And he can't take it away from you. Wielding a sword forged by a goddess who would be aligned against him would only put him at further disadvantage."

"Also, my bow was forged by Herne. Would it still be useless?"

Louhia nodded. "Think about it for a moment. The most likely scenario is that he will have animated skeletons at his beck and call. Arrows don't pierce magically enhanced bone, even if the arrow is magically charged. A sword can do damage, but the arrows would just bounce off. Any striking weapon—a hammer, a sword, even a magical pipe if you had such a thing—would be your best bet. You can use the sword with the flat of the blade as well. The magic inherent within it will cause some disruption to the system."

Viktor looked over at Herne. "So, what should Yutani and I bring? We don't have magical weapons—"

"Actually, I do."

We all turned Yutani's interruption. Last we knew, none of us had heard that he owned any magical weapons.

"And *what* exactly do you have?" Herne asked. "Have you been holding out on us?"

Yutani shrugged, looking a little sheepish. "I felt awkward talking about it. And I just got it a couple weeks ago. There was a package on my doorstep when I got home one night, from my father. Here, I've got it in my pack. Let me show you." He slipped out of the room, leaving us to wonder just what he was going to produce.

"Who is his father?" Louhia asked.

"The Great Coyote." Herne leaned back in his chair, his arms folded. "Yutani didn't find out until recently. He's still new to whatever his heritage will bring him."

Louhia let out a cackle. "And you worry about having *me* in your party, Lord of the Hunt? I should think it better to have an honest enemy than an unwitting if friendly chaos monger."

"Enough, Louhia," Herne said. "You will not harass any member of my team."

"Or you'll tell Mielikki?" She sighed. "You don't have to answer that. Of course you would. I will abide by your wishes, but once I am free of this task, I warn you, Lord Herne: Do your best to never again cross my path. The Witch of Pohjola will not be trifled with."

Once again, the temperature in the room felt like it dropped twenty degrees. I sidled a glance at Angel, who rolled her eyes. But neither of us said a word. Sometimes it was better to just keep out of things.

Yutani returned at that moment, his backpack in hand. He sat it on the table and opened it up. As he reached inside, I wondered what Coyote had given him. A dagger? Maybe a hammer? But the next moment, Yutani withdrew a whip. It was black as night, with blue strands interwoven throughout the black leather. And it emanated a faint blue aura.

"Oh good gods," Herne said, straightening up. His gaze was fastened on the web. "Does that have ilithiniam in it? And if so, how the hell did Coyote manage it?"

Yutani laid the whip out on the table and we all leaned in, even Louhia.

"You see the thin blue metallic threads woven in with the leather? Somehow, my father managed to spin ilithiniam into threads and when he fashioned the leather, he embedded them into the strips. So this whip not only contains the magic he infused into it, but the magic of ilithiniam. I don't know if it will harm Lazerous, but I might be able to grab hold of him with it. I'm extremely good with a whip," Yutani added.

"Oh, if you can wrap that around his arm, it will burn if nothing else." Louhia smiled a genuine smile for the first time since we'd met her. At least, a smile that was even remotely friendly. "You intrigue me," she added.

The look on Yutani's face almost made me laugh. He managed to keep his feelings to himself, but he looked like he had just been propositioned by a goblin.

Viktor cleared his throat. "Unfortunately, I don't have any magical weapons to speak of. But I do have brute force, and I can take on his minions and—hopefully—break their bones."

"I'll make sure you have something to carry," Herne said. "I've made a number of weapons in my life, including a hammer I intend to take with me. It's not exactly Mjolnir, but it will do the trick. Ember, why don't you head home with Angel to pack fresh clothing, and any other supplies you might need. Don't forget Brighid's Flame, and you might as well bring Serafina just in case. We'll pick you up in about ninety minutes. Viktor and Yutani, go home as well and pack. We'll need fresh supplies. I'll tend to things here. We're getting a late start, but we don't dare wait until morning. The minute we set up camp out there, we're going to start looking for Talia, even through the dark. Louhia, what do you need beyond what you've got packed in your bag?"

She snorted. "Nothing. I can go for days without sleep, and I come from the north. The chill in the air here is as good as summer for me."

"All right. Let's get going. Meet back here in an hour at the latest. Angel, tomorrow, come in and open up as usual. If anything earthshaking happens, let me know, but otherwise put all appointments on hold." And with that, Herne motioned for us to get moving. I tried to linger long enough to find out what had gone on with Kipa, but no such luck.

But by the time Angel and I reached the car, Herne had texted me.

KIPA AND LOUHIA GOT INTO AN ARGUMENT AND I FELT THE BEST THING TO DO WAS SEPARATE THEM. WE NEED LOUHIA'S HELP MORE AT THIS POINT, SO I TOLD KIPA TO TAKE SOME TIME OFF.

"What I wouldn't give to know what went on in that office. It's hard to needle Kipa into blowing up, but it looks like she managed it," I said, telling Angel about the text.

"Cripes. That's bad." She eased the car out of the garage and we headed for home.

On the drive, it occurred to me that Chaz must have been through his surgery by now. I put in a call to Breaknight.

"I'm checking on the condition of a patient who came in yesterday? He was undergoing surgery last we left him." I gave the receptionist both Chaz's and my names.

The nurse came back in a moment. "Chaz made it through surgery, and he's resting. The amputation went well, and the doctor asked me to thank you for your help."

I paused, then asked, "Are Chaz's parents coming?"

The nurse hesitated, then said, "I'm afraid that his parents have declined to visit. But his boyfriend is here."

"Triston? Is there a chance I could talk to him?" My heart sank. I wondered if it was the fact that Chaz had lost his powers that caused his parents to turn their backs on him.

The nurse brought Triston to the phone.

"Triston, I'm so glad to talk to you again. This is Ember Kearney, from the Wild Hunt."

"Thank you so much for saving my boyfriend. He's got a long road ahead of him to recover, but he's alive. Did you find Branson?" Triston's voice was shaky, but I could hear the relief in it.

"No, I'm sorry. We didn't see any sign of him. Though since Chaz escaped and survived, maybe there's a chance Branson did too. We're headed back out there tonight.

We'll do our best to find out what happened to Chaz's brother." I paused for a moment, then added, "I understand Chaz's parents didn't come when they found out he was in the hospital?"

Triston's voice darkened. "No, they didn't. The nurse mentioned to them that I was here, and she made the mistake of mentioning that I was his boyfriend. That clinched it. Second, Branson is still missing. When they found out there was no word of what happened to him, I think they blamed Chaz. Third, while they agreed to pay for Chaz's medical treatment, his family puts a great deal of emphasis on looks and the nature of their powers. Chaz is missing a hand now, and he has no powers."

My stomach sank. "I'm so sorry. It's hard to imagine, but...I guess there are people like that."

"Oh, they gave some flimsy excuse—they can't make it out right now because they have obligations they can't get out of, but we know it's an excuse. Eventually, they'll fly in. They'll blame him for Branson's disappearance, and they'll conveniently be too busy when he needs to talk to them. His father will have the 'I'm so disappointed in you, son' talk with him. They'll give him a small settlement and write him off."

I frowned at my phone. Chaz's family sounded like a genteel bunch of assholes. "Well, we'll come see Chaz as soon as we can. I'm glad you're there for him. And Triston —don't let them poison your love. Trust me, I know all about families turning on each other. If they can't support Chaz and his love for you, fuck 'em. They aren't worth it."

After saying good-bye, I pocketed my phone again. We were almost home. It was time for *Nightmare in the Woods*, part deux.

CHAPTER EIGHTEEN

*T*his time, we chose a campsite that was close to the copper mine. We had to set up in the dark, but Herne turned his headlights onto the campsite to make it easier. Viktor and Yutani quickly set up the tents, including one for Louhia, even though she insisted she didn't need it.

"You might change your mind," Herne said, fore-stalling her protests. "I'm going to call George and see if he'll come out and help us."

"So are we going to look for Talia?" I asked. "Maybe we should look for her car first. We can drive through the various campsites."

"That's not a bad idea," Herne said. "As soon as we get everything set up and the fire ready to light, we'll do that. Let's get to work."

We had eaten on the way, stopping for fast food so we didn't need to cook. It was edging toward midnight, and even though I had rested well the night before, I found myself yawning. I pulled out a bag of chocolate-covered espresso beans and began munching on them.

"Can I have a few of those?" Viktor asked.

"I brought plenty," I said, tossing him one of the other bags.

Viktor and Yutani made quick work of setting up the tents, while Herne prepared the fire for when we got back. When they were done, we piled back in the Expedition.

As we drove slowly through the campsite, looking for Talia's car, I found myself clinging to a shred of hope that she had changed her mind and gone somewhere else. But twenty minutes later, as we threaded our way through the campsites, Yutani shouted. He pointed out the window to the right, at one of the smaller campsites.

"That's her car. I recognize it." He pressed his face out the window, staring intently at the gray sedan parked at the dark campsite.

"How do you know that's hers?" I asked. "Don't all gray sedans look alike?"

"Look at the left bumper. See that dent? She just got that the other day. Some idiot backed into her in a parking lot. She told me about it when she came into work. Also, the glow-in-the-dark bumper sticker gives it away. That's not a common one."

I looked again, squinting. Yutani must have very good eyesight, I thought, but then as we neared the car, the bumper sticker became clear. It read HARPIES PUT THE HARP IN HARPSICHORD.

I blinked. "Yeah, that sounds like her." I had been over to Viktor's a couple times, but Talia and I mostly inter-acted at work. I considered her a friend, but she was a private person, and I didn't like intruding on her personal space.

"She thought it was cute, and seeing as how she used to play the harpsichord, it seemed perfect for her. I bought it for her birthday a couple years ago," Viktor said, his voice quivering.

I knew that Viktor and Talia were good friends, and it hurt me to hear the fear in his voice.

"All right, we have a place to start. Does everyone have their flashlights and walking sticks?" Herne asked.

"Ten-four," Yutani said.

Herne parked the car, and we slipped out into the chilly night. At least it wasn't raining, I thought. That was one bonus. Viktor immediately headed over to Talia's car to check it out, and I began searching around the campsite. There was no sign she had set up a tent or anything of that nature. And if she had been out here since last night, that meant something had happened.

"There's no sign that she spent the night here, other than her car." Yutani turned to Herne, a contemplative expression on his face.

"Her car is locked," Viktor said. "But I'm good at getting locks open, and I checked inside. Her purse is under the seat, and it doesn't look like anybody's been through it. I also found her phone, sitting in the cup holder," he added bleakly.

"You don't think that she...didn't expect to return, do you?" I asked, hating to even voice my thought.

"I think exactly that," Viktor said. "I think Talia expected that she would be coming out here to finish off Lazerous as her final act, however stupid that was. And I don't think she expected to survive the battle."

"There is no way a harpy, even one *with* her powers, could survive taking on a liche," Louhia said.

"Start looking through the undergrowth for any sign she went cross-country. I'm hoping against hope, but there's still a chance that she hurt herself trying to find him, and could be laying there injured." Herne stood over to one of the huckleberry bushes and began prowling around, looking for any sign that Talia had pushed through them. As we joined him, I only hope that he was right.

TWENTY MINUTES LATER YUTANI LET OUT A CRY. "HERE! I think she went through here."

Herne got to him first but I was close behind. There were several large ferns crowded together, but some of the fronds had been broken, and when we knelt, looking with a flashlight, we could see footprints in the thick mulch of the forest floor. They looked about the right size for Talia's boots.

"Did you find her?" The voice echoed from the other side of the campsite.

I whirled around, surprised to see George there. Herne strode past me to shake hands with the puma shifter.

"Thank you for coming," Herne said. "No, but we think we found the point where she went into the forest. She drove up here last night, so she's been missing since then. Her car's over there, with her purse and phone in it. Nothing looks like it was broken into."

"And you know for sure that she came up here to find Lazerous?" George asked, his eyes lighting on

Louhia. He stiffened, though it was subtle, but I still noticed it.

"Yes, she left us a note," I said. "I don't think she planned on returning. If we don't find her before Lazerous finds her, she's a dead woman. We brought a sorceress who can handle the liche, as long as we cover her ass." Even though I didn't like acknowledging her, I gestured to Louhia. "George, meet Louhia, a sorceress from Pohjola. Finland. Sort of. Louhia, this is George, he's part of a puma pride near here."

George inclined his head, but his arms remained at his side. "How do you do, ma'am?"

Louhia stared at him for a moment, then murmured something none of us could hear and turned away, staring at the forest.

George arched his eyebrows, but said nothing more to Louhia. Instead, he turned to Herne. "What do you need me to do? Whatever you need, I'm here."

"Will you search for her with us? If we happened to stumble over Lazerous, stay out of the way. I don't want you hurt." Herne motioned for him to follow as we returned to the undergrowth.

George knelt by the broken fronds. "Yes, she's definitely come this way, and within the past twenty-four hours. I can still smell a faint whiff of...lavender perfume?" He looked up at me. "Did she wear lavender?"

"Yes, she just bought a new bottle," I said. "I asked her what she was wearing last week and she said that she found a new fragrance. It's French, and yes, it is lavender."

"It would be easier to track her if I changed into my puma form." George moved back away from the prints.

"Do you mind? That would probably be a good idea,"

Herne said. "I don't have that good of a nose, even in my stag form. And while Yutani probably could pick up her scent as well, you know these mountains better than any of us."

George stepped behind a bush, and a moment later, his shirt and pants came whipping over one of the branches to drape on it. "Can someone put my clothes and boots in their pack?"

Viktor swiftly folded them away into his pack. "Got them."

Within another moment, George stepped out from behind the tree in his puma form. He was gorgeous, as big as he had been when I first met him, and he padded over to my side, letting out a chuffing sound. I couldn't help myself. I reached down and scratched him behind the ears. He let out a low rumble, but nudged against my thigh in a playful manner. I glanced up to see Herne staring at me. *Oops. Too friendly.* I backed up a step, giving George a final pat on the head.

"Whenever you're ready," Herne said, still holding my gaze.

George let out another chuff, then plunged into the undergrowth, moving quickly but not so fast that we couldn't follow him. Herne and I swept in behind him, then Yutani, with Louhia and Viktor bringing up the rear.

It was a good thing we had George to lead us, otherwise we would have gotten lost. The undergrowth was thick, and even though it was barely spring, the winter die-off still left enough junipers, ivy, ferns, and other bramble bushes to create a labyrinth in green.

My sweater caught on one of the brambles, and I had to stop to free myself. I shuddered, remembering Blackthorn, the Bramble King. One of the ancient Ante-Fae, he was safer at a distance. Herne must have sensed what I was thinking because he took my hand, leading me around the brambles so I didn't get caught again.

Overhead, the moon shone down through a break in the cloud cover, and a hazy mist rose from the forest floor, rolling along as it crept around our ankles.

I shivered. I wasn't really cold, but if I had to admit it, I was frightened. We were in Lazerous's territory now, I knew it as sure as I knew my own name. And I couldn't help but wonder whether he had found Talia yet. And if so, was she still alive? I flashed back to Chaz and his injuries, especially his shattered hand. From what Chaz had remembered, Lazerous had picked him up by the wrist and launched him headfirst into the pile of rocks. The thought of the liche doing that to Talia made my stomach churn.

Up ahead, George began to slow, then suddenly turned and walked back to us. He nudged Viktor, and Viktor held out his hand.

"Do you need your clothes?" Viktor asked.

George bobbed his head, then headed toward a stand of ferns. Viktor shrugged off his pack, pulled out George's clothing and boots, and set them behind the biggest fern there. We turned to give George a little privacy, and a couple moments later, he was standing beside us, fully dressed.

"Did you lose her scent?" Herne asked.

"No, in fact it's grown stronger. However, I know what's up ahead beyond that patch of huckleberry. I can hear the water from here. That leads out to Copper Creek, which runs near the mine. We'll have to go upstream a bit to find the bridge that crosses the water, off of a hiking trail." He frowned, staring at Viktor for a moment. "The bridge is made of rope. It's old and unsteady. It will probably hold your weight, but I recommend that you wait until the rest of us cross first. We should go one at a time. As I said, the bridge is old, and since it's privately owned, nobody feels the need to keep it up. The dwarves who mine this area don't like strangers around here, and they don't make it easy for them."

Viktor snorted, but said nothing. George turned back to the makeshift trail that Talia had left, and we began moving along it again.

He was right. Before long we broke into the open and found ourselves on the bank of a stream that was raging through its channel. It was highwater season for sure, and the whitecaps foamed along, deep and dangerously swift.

"There's the bridge," George said, pointing toward a rickety-looking rope structure. The wooden slats looked old, and even in the dim moonlight, I could tell that some of them had rotted through. There were two thin ropes—one on either side—for hand railings, and the stakes anchoring the bridge into the ground on our side looked makeshift at best.

"Okay, I'm not exactly thrilled about this. Do you want me to try to find a water elemental down there? Maybe it could calm the stream long enough for us to cross without danger," I asked.

"No," Herne said. "We need to make haste. We'll take

our chances." He motioned toward Louhia and me. "The women go first. That way, you'll be on the other side if anything happens."

"You mean, if the bridge doesn't cave in first, taking Ember and me with it." Louhia shook her head, giving him a pathetic look. But she set foot on the bridge and, as it swayed from side to side, she quietly crossed the footpath, as easily as if she were walking on solid ground.

I couldn't let her show me up. I took a deep breath and put my foot on the swaying bridge, holding tight to the ropes. I wasn't worried about drowning, but the fall onto the rocks was another matter. I could easily call up a water elemental to help me, but unless I contacted them first, they couldn't cushion the blow onto granite.

Halfway across, I saw three broken boards in a row. I took a giant step over them, grimacing as the bridge swayed even more. But I made it to the other side safely, and as I stepped onto the ground again, I let out a sigh, only then realizing how tense I had been. I walked over to stand next to Louhia, and watched as Herne crossed over next. Yutani came afterward, and then George. Viktor was last.

As the half-ogre set foot on the bridge, there was a cracking sound, and he moved just quickly enough to avoid slamming one of his feet through the planks. The broken wood fell into the creek, swept away by the raging water. Viktor paused, glancing back at the footpath, before he shook his head and thundered across, leaving a trail of broken planks in his wake. But he made it, and the bridge remained more or less intact.

I walked over to him, slapping his arm. "Don't scare me like that again, you big lug."

"Scare you? Hell, *I* thought I was going to end up in the drink. And even at my size, those currents could sweep me along just like that." He snapped his fingers.

"Well, we're all here. What next?" Herne asked.

"I'll see if I can pick up her scent again, so at least we'll have a direction to go in." George said. He leaned over, smelling the ground. A moment later, he motioned for us to follow him, and set off on a narrow footpath that had been blazoned through the woods.

ANOTHER TWENTY MINUTES AND WE STUMBLED OUT INTO yet another clearing, but this wasn't the bank of the creek. By the light of the moon, I could see a sign next to the hillside. I tried to remember where we were, tried to remember the map, but I couldn't seem to pull up the image in my mind.

George held his fingers to his lips, then motioned for us to creep back behind the cover of the trees. He leaned close, whispering, "That's one of the old White Peak Copper Mine shafts. It's still being used by the dwarves, though they've made some changes. I can smell Talia's perfume. My guess is she may have entered the shaft."

"Do you think Lazerous is in there as well?" Yutani asked.

"It's impossible to tell at this range. Unless your sorceress knows of a way?" He glanced at Louhia.

She paused, then said, "I may be able to tell. I need a little room. And I need silence."

We scooted away from her as best as we could,

keeping quiet. I crept back to the edge of the clearing, peeking out to see if I could catch anything.

Once again, I saw the figures of spirits wandering through the area. They were all over the mines, and I couldn't help but think that more than just the thirty-one men had died. I thought about bringing Raven up here. But that wouldn't happen unless we caught Lazerous first.

A few moments later, Louhia spoke. "All right, I sent out feelers. There is a large source of powerful energy somewhere in the area, but I can't tell if it's within this mine shaft, or someplace else."

"Powerful enough to be a liche?" Herne asked.

Louhia gave him a nod. "Yes. I'm assuming this Lazerous is a king among his kind. If the energy is all from him, it's a good thing you sought me out. If we make it through alive and come out victorious, I'm charging you extra." She wasn't joking.

Herne nodded. "If we make it out alive and take him down? I'll pay you extra. And even more if we can get Talia out of here alive. Did you sense if she's around? Was there a way to—"

"No. I have no clue," Louhia said. "The liche's energy drowns out everything else. It's like looking at a blazing light. You can't pinpoint where it is, it's difficult to see anything surrounding it, and you don't know how to get a better read on it. If your friend's alive and in that mine shaft, the only way we're going to know is to head on in. The question is, are you willing to do this? You'd better decide now because once we enter the mines, the liche will probably know we're there. He will be able to sense me even as I can sense him. And I can't guarantee that he hasn't already sussed me out."

"Then we have no choice. We go in. George, I'm not asking you to go with us. This isn't your battle."

"I'm going," George said. "After seeing what happened to that boy, how can I *not* go? By the way, how is he doing?"

"I called the hospital. Chaz made it through surgery. He should recover, but he's been drained of all his powers. And on top of that, his parents have turned their backs on him. They found out he was gay. What a time to let your son down," I said, shaking my head. "Anyway, we need to keep a lookout for his brother. Maybe Branson managed to escape and hide in the mines, and he can't find his way out. One way or the other, I'd like to settle the question for Chaz as to whether Branson is alive."

"All right, I guess this is it. We're heading in, let's hope to hell that we can handle the fallout." Herne stepped back, allowing Louhia to go to the forefront. "Do you want us to cover you in front, or should we flank your back? Choice is yours."

"I'm going to need to prepare spells. Give me about fifteen minutes, and then I would ask that you, Herne, be at the front. Chances are good the liche won't be able to drain you. Liches aren't as powerful as gods, even though some may seem so."

She moved off to the side, settling herself on a fallen log where she closed her eyes and began to meditate. The rest of us milled around, but I kept an eye out on the entrance to the mine shaft. I wondered if the dwarves had been around lately, or if they knew about Lazerous at all. Perhaps winter wasn't mining season, and they didn't know he was here. Surely they wouldn't cover for him?

Finally, Louhia was ready. We formed a line, with

Herne and Yutani in front. Louhia stood ready behind them. Then Viktor and me. Finally, George would bring up the rear. Without another word, we headed out into the clearing, quickly crossing to the entrance of the mine.

Here goes nothing, I thought. Or perhaps, here goes everything.

CHAPTER NINETEEN

*a*s we prepared to enter the mine shaft, I glanced over my shoulder and whispered to George, "Are these mines still as dangerous as they were when the men were buried?" The image of tons of dirt and stone tumbling down on our heads was fucking with my mind.

"The dwarves have shored them up, so they should be safer—dwarves are natural miners—but there's always the chance of an earthquake or other natural disaster. You can never entirely negate the dangers," George said. "But I'm far more afraid of the liche than I am of a cave-in."

"I find it odd that no dwarves are out here working right now." The absence of the dwarves made me wonder if they knew about Lazerous. Or maybe they were just taking time off.

George reassured me. "We're smack in the middle of the dwarven spring holidays. They take three weeks near the equinox to celebrate their traditions. They have a similar holiday in the autumn. No occupational work is permitted. All families must take care of themselves—

servants are given time off, as well. The only dwarves still working are government workers, healers, and members of the clergy." George shrugged. "As to what they're celebrating, I don't know."

"So Ginty's probably not at the bar," I murmured.

"Unless he has a special dispensation or has turned his back on his people, no, he wouldn't be." George gently pushed me forward.

I stepped into the mine shaft, prepared to feel the weight of the world pressing down on me. All I could think about was the stone and rock overhead, and how this hill was riddled with tunnels. But once we were in past the entrance, I suddenly realized this was like no mine I had ever seen. The dwarves had, indeed, been here and their influence was everywhere.

The timbers shoring up the ceiling were huge, as though the trunks of old trees had grown through the ground into the earth, planting their roots in the soil and rock. Lights lined the side of the tunnel—swirling colors in translucent sconces. The glowing lights whirled and dipped, contained within their glass enclosures, lighting the way with a gentle glow. The floor of the mine shaft had been paved, at least where we were, and deep tracks embedded within the asphalt provided mining cars an easy path along which to move. The gentle whir of a motor came humming through the air, and I realized a current was flowing by as we moved forward.

"Do they have fans?" I asked, wondering at the detail the dwarves had gone to. The entire operation had a sophisticated feel to it.

"Yes, I think they do. Great, monstrous machines spaced throughout the shafts keep the air circulating. I'm not sure what energy they run on, but I'd guess some sort of magic." Herne paused, gazing up at the ceiling. "They certainly upgraded this operation, but then, as George said, dwarves are natural-born miners. It's in their blood."

We followed the mining car tracks back into the hill. As we continued, the path slowly descended, the gradient gradually increasing. On either side of the passage, the dwarves had built sidewalks of a sort, textured so that when the pavement got wet, it wouldn't be terribly slick. Railings had been driven into the sides of the walls, allowing for handholds as we descended. However, they were created for the dwarven physique, and therefore were lower, making them awkward for us to use. But it made sense, given dwarves owned the mines and operated them.

"How deep are these mines?" I asked.

"They're fairly deep and extensive. Copper mines are usually deeper than coal mines. I believe most of the mining in this area was done for copper or gold. I have no idea how deep into the earth the dwarves have excavated, but knowing them, it's likely that these mines go very deep indeed." George kept his voice low, but still it echoed in the mine shaft.

"Do you really think we're headed in the right direction?" I asked after a few moments. "Surely Lazerous isn't hiding out in these mine shafts? The dwarves would find him."

Herne turned around to look at me. "What did you say?"

I shook my head. "Do you really think Lazerous is in the mine shaft? I would think he'd hole up near it, in an abandoned section. Because if he's down here, the dwarves are going to run into him. Dwarves don't have much magical power, but they've got a lot of brawn. I would think that if there were enough of them, they might be able to take him down, or at least kick his ass out of here." Suddenly, the whole decision to poke into the mine seemed futile. And the more I thought about it, the more sense it made.

Herne looked like he had just swallowed a frog. He cleared his throat, and glanced at the others. "Do you think she's right? I just assumed he'd be down here, I guess."

Viktor let out a groan. "I can't believe we didn't discuss this beforehand. Ember, why didn't you bring this up before we came this far?"

"I thought that you understood liches better than I did. But it just struck me a moment ago that Lazerous wouldn't choose a place where he could be easily found. Then it occurred to me that there have to be other abandoned mine shafts around here. From the little I read about it, the White Peak Copper Mine had an extensive array of shafts. But it looks like the dwarves have focused on this area in particular. Aren't there a few other entrances around here?" I strained to remember what I had read about the mining company, and I was positive that there had been at least four different entrances into their mining operations.

"Oh, for fuck's sake." Yutani pulled out his tablet, and as he turned it on, the screen illuminated the area around us even more so than the light sconces that the dwarves had installed.

"I don't think you're going to get any reception—" Viktor began, but Yutani interrupted.

"I don't need to. I saved a copy of the information we gathered on the mining company to my files. I'm pulling it up now." He paused, scanning the screen for a moment. Then he let out a long sigh. "Ember's right. There were three other entrances to the mines, and while the dwarves own the land they're on, from what I can see two of the entrances are so precarious that they're still walled off. The dwarves haven't had a chance to open them up yet."

"Why the hell didn't we sit down and plan this out better?" Herne sounded grumpy.

"Because we were worried about Talia. We didn't have time to plan it out in detail."

Louhia gave us a disdainful snort. "If you run your agency as smoothly as you're running this operation, I feel for Cernunnos and Morgana." She leaned back against the wall of the mine.

Herne ignored her. "All right, let's get out of this shaft and go look at the other entrances. My gut tells me Ember is right. I just wish we would have thought of this beforehand."

We had been walking for about twenty minutes, so we had a bit of a hike ahead of us to reach the entrance. But we poured on the speed and moved as quickly as we could. As we stepped out into the night, once again the swirling vapors from the spirits surrounded us.

"I wonder why they aren't down in the mines where they died?"

Louhia answered that one. "I can tell you why. Dwarves may not like magic, but they've used it to keep the spirits out of the mines. And it's a good thing too, because some of the spirits have no desire to see people leave here alive. Watch your step around them."

Yutani pulled up a map of the area showing the other entrances to the mines. One of them was near where we had found Chaz. He tapped that one. "This one is still abandoned, and it's near where we found Chaz, and where the school found three of the students who died. Want to bet that Lazerous is holed up there?"

"You're probably right," I said. "And Talia's smart enough to have figured that out. How far is it from here?"

"Less than half a mile. Ten minutes' walk at most if we keep moving. There's a narrow trail that leads to it, over there." Yutani pointed to the other side of the clearing. "It's probably overgrown, but it was used for a long time so there should still be a rudimentary path that we can follow. If not, George can blaze the way for us."

"George isn't going in front of us this time," Herne said. "Considering we're likely on the right track this time, I don't want him in front when we're heading into Lazerous's territory. All right, let's head out. Same order as we went down the mine shaft. Yutani, you're up front with me. Louhia, you're next. Then Viktor and Ember, and finally, George. Yutani, can you use the map to make sure we don't get off track?"

"Yeah, I think so." Yutani airdropped the map to his phone, which was easier to carry than his tablet. After tucking his tablet away in his pack, he pulled up the map on his phone, and we headed out once again.

THE GOING WAS A BIT TOUGHER, GIVEN THE PATHWAY WAS so old and so overgrown, but it was still visible, even amidst the thick layer of foliage and mulch that lined the forest floor. Every now and then, I thought I heard a rustle in the woods and my Autumn Stalker blood whispered, *Animal.* Now and then it whispered, *Spirit.* As far as the animals went, they would probably be frightened off by a party of our size, so I wasn't worried about running into an actual puma or a bear. And if either one of them were near, George would probably sense it. Come to think of it, since he was a coyote shifter, Yutani would probably sense a big predator around as well.

The moon remained out, the clouds scattered around her. She shone down, offering us a cold beacon through the trees. We walked in silence, making as little noise as possible, and true to Yutani's prediction, ten minutes later Herne held up his hand.

He glanced over his shoulder and whispered, "There's a small clearing up ahead. I think that we've found the mine shaft. We'll have to be very—" he stopped as Louhia interrupted.

"Your liche is ahead. I can feel him from here. I thought his magical signature was strong before, but this is rather overwhelming, and my guess is that he can feel my presence, if he's paying attention. I don't think you realize how strong he is." For the first time since we had met her, she looked a little shaken.

"Do you still think you can go against him?" Herne asked.

Louhia nodded. "Yes, I can, but I'll need your help. I need you to distract him, and that's a dangerous task. From the moment we step into that opening, you have to be on your guard. I cannot tell you if he's on the surface, or if he's inside the mine shaft. But his energy is strong enough to make my teeth ache."

"Holy crap, I wonder if he's got Talia." Viktor sounded frightened.

"If he does, I think you can kiss her ass good-bye," Louhia said. "We make our plans now, before we go out there, but we have to hurry because if he is paying attention and he does sense me, he won't wait for us. He'll make the first move."

"Weapons at ready," Herne said. "We have enough magical power in our weapons to at least hurt him, even if we can't kill him." He paused, then added, "I'll go in with Louhia. The rest of you focus on protecting her. I don't need the protection. Even if he can wound me, he won't be able to kill me. But Lazerous *can* destroy her. Whatever happens, focus on first protecting Louhia, and then yourselves. If things get really bad, run like hell."

"What about Talia?" Viktor asked.

Herne stared at him for a moment, then said, "Do your best to save her if she's there, but when push comes to shove, we'll have to let her go rather than let Lazerous destroy us all. I'm not sacrificing my entire crew just for her. And I'd say that no matter *which* one of you was out there."

"Are your spells still prepared, even though we made a detour?" George asked Louhia.

She nodded. "They're prepped until I actually cast them. Or I fall asleep. Then the energy dissipates. But I'm ready. I warn you, though, don't get caught between me and Lazerous. Because my spells can kill you as well. And I'll try to be careful, but if you're caught in the cross fire, there are no guarantees."

"George, I want you to stay here," Herne said. "What we're headed into, you're not prepared for. But you can take word to my father if we end up on the wrong end of the blade. Your shaman will know how to reach him. Promise me, you won't follow us in?" He held out his hand. "I want your word."

George looked ready to argue, but finally, he gave Herne a nod. "All right. I promise."

"Then we're ready. And pray for us while we're in there. To whatever gods you follow."

We were about as prepared as we could be, so we turned back to the edge of the forest. Herne and Louhia stepped into the clearing, and we followed.

CHAPTER TWENTY

*a*s we eased into the clearing, I immediately scanned the area, looking to see if Lazerous was in sight, but there was no one around. However, the entrance was there, not twenty yards away, and it was boarded up. Several of the boards had been ripped off and a faint light emanated from within the shaft.

I stared at the broken boards, and a voice entered my mind.

Be careful. Run while you can. The voice echoed as though it came from a great distance. It wasn't Talia, nor anyone else that I recognized.

I looked around, and realized I was standing in a puddle. The voice had come from the water and I bent down, dangling my fingers into it. Immediately, I could sense a very small spirit. She felt so fragile that my first instinct was to sweep her up and nurture her, but I caught myself before I did so.

Who are you? I forced the words into emotions, projecting the question to it.

Either the spirit didn't understand, or she just ignored my question. But again, the soft voice filled my ears, echoing through my body like rain beating against the window.

Go. There is danger here. You are creature of the water as am I. Escape while you have the opportunity. The voice drifted off, melancholy and haunting.

I wasn't sure whether to say anything, so I reached forward past Louhia to tap Herne on the shoulder. He turned around, and I crooked a finger at him. He slipped back to my side and I whispered in his ear, telling him what had happened. He gave me a nod and returned to the front of the line. Silently, I thanked the spirit for her warning.

Herne and Louhia headed directly to the entrance to the abandoned mine, and I found my lungs getting tight. I scrambled, trying to figure out what was wrong, but the longer I stood there, the greater my fear grew. The thought of walking into the abandoned mine shaft nauseated me. The dwarves hadn't renovated it yet, and I suddenly felt absolutely certain that the moment we entered the shaft, a thousand tons of debris would come crashing down on us, trapping us in there without air, without the chance to ever be free again.

"No, no…no…" I began to back away, unable to think my way through the fear. As I turned to run, Yutani caught me by the arm and yanked me around, just to stare in my face.

Louhia turned, glancing first at Yutani, then at me. She reached out and placed her hand on my forehead, and the jolt of her touch chilled me into my core, but it seemed to strip away the fear. I shook my head, startled to realize that I had been about to run out on my friends.

"I almost ran away... What the hell..."

"It's Lazerous's magic," Louhia said softly. "He can cause fear, and he can also cause dissension, so watch yourselves."

As she turned back toward the mine, I tried to calm myself. I felt embarrassed, and used. The thought that I had almost fallen for one of his spells—when he wasn't even in front of us—was unnerving enough. But to know that I had almost abandoned my friends made me queasy. Yutani tapped me on the shoulder and held out his hand. As I took it, he squeezed my fingers, and a warmth raced through me, easing the knots in my back. Startled, I glanced at him again but he just shook his head and mouthed the word *Later*.

Feeling shored up and steady again, I let go of his hand. For a moment, I worried that I might slip back into my fear, but it seemed to have drained away at his touch.

We reached the opening to the mine shaft, and Herne broke apart the remaining boards. "It doesn't matter if we talk. He obviously knows we're here." He glanced back at us and with a nod, led the way into the tunnel.

As we followed, the eerie light intensified, but we soon found the reason for it. The light was coming from glowing sticks placed against the wall, like LED torches.

There were signs of cave-ins everywhere along the path, rocks that had tumbled down, broken timbers, rubble all over the place. It occurred to me that any loud noise could bring the whole thing down on our heads and that was enough to make me want to run out again, but I managed to control my fear this time—it came from within this time, rather than from Lazerous.

As we edged our way forward, another thought occurred to me. Lazerous probably wouldn't want to bring the house down on our heads. If he did, he'd be trapped here too, unless he had some sort of teleportation spell, and only the greatest magicians and witches could manage that. Granted, he was powerful, but to take down a witch who could do that would mean that he would have been able to kill us from a distance. And that he hadn't done.

We were nearing an entrance to what looked like a larger cavern when there was a sudden flurry of movement, and four skeletal warriors sprang out from the opening. They were larger than human skeletons, and I hazarded a guess that they may have been half-ogres or half-giants. Either way, they were huge, and they carried massive weapons.

One was carrying a sword, while another carried a flail with a spiky ball and chain on the end. A third had what looked to be an iron bat, and finally, the fourth was holding a gleaming bronze hammer.

There wasn't room to spread out, and Herne quickly pushed Louhia back through the ranks as we moved in to engage the skeletons.

I darted beyond the one with the hammer and the one with the flail, intent on engaging the one with the sword. At least the mine shaft was tall and wide enough to wield a weapon. I was intent on forcing the creature back through the opening in order to get a better aim. Immediately, I found we were in a large chamber.

As I pulled out Brighid's Flame, the skeleton recoiled,

seeming to stare at the blade instead of me. I took that moment to swing wide, hitting it with the flat of the sword so that the bag of bones stumbled back through the opening. Charging, I rammed into it, knocking it down and then danced away before it could grab hold of me.

The blood was pumping through my veins like fire, and I felt both sides of my heritage rise, intent on besting my opponent. I gave in to my predator, gave in to the desire to destroy and conquer.

I dodged the skeleton's sword as he rose to his feet again. The last thing I needed was to become a shish kebab on the end of his blade.

Swinging wide again, I came around hard and low, trying to knock him off his feet. I had been practicing with Brighid's Flame for the past couple of months and had become very agile with her. It felt as the sword had been made specifically for me, and her hilt fit snugly in my hand. I felt a sudden awareness as she woke, and she cheered as I swung her at the skeleton.

Brighid's Flame wasn't exactly sentient, not in the way humans were, but I was used to her joy in the battle. She rose to the challenge with a thrill that I seemed to match, and when she was excited, I tended to swing with a truer aim, and my fear decreased with every swing. She acted like a potion of courage, making me feel stronger than I could on my own.

The blade connected with the skeleton's knees, and I held my breath as the edge broke through the left knee joint, biting deep enough to sever bone from bone.

The skeleton wavered, then fell to the ground, sprawling on its side. But I hadn't destroyed it—it wasn't out of commission yet. As I watched, the skeleton warrior reached down, detaching its other leg at the knee, tossing the bones to the side. Then it grabbed its sword again and started toward me, balancing on the balls of its knee joints.

The skeleton was now about my height, and I darted back as it swung again. I dodged out of the way, the skeleton's blade barely missing me. Dancing back a couple of steps, I glanced up and happened to catch sight of the other side of the chamber out of the corner of my eye. I saw an exit leading into yet another tunnel, or perhaps another cavern.

But as quickly as I noticed the tunnel, my opponent swung at me again and I brought my attention back to the fight. I dodged his blow—again—and came back with another swing, this time raising the blade so that it was aimed toward the skeleton's neck. But my opponent skittered back, just out of reach. I drove forward, swinging again, aiming for a hit. I didn't care where my blade landed, as long as I managed to do some damage.

This time, Brighid's Flame slammed into its ribs. My blade cleaved through the rib cage and I jerked her upward, the edge slicing up through the bones.

Before the skeleton could pull away I managed to break its arm off at the shoulder and send it careening across the room. The arm still held the sword as it fell, and I jumped over it, chasing my adversary across the cavern.

I swung again, managing to hit the skeleton on the neck, and severed the head from the rest of the bones, sending it rolling like a bowling ball. The rest of my opponent's body began to lurch, its one remaining arm flailing as it tried to grab at me. But it didn't seem to know where

I was, and the body of bones jerked around like a chicken with its head cut off.

As I delicately stepped out of the way, I noticed that the arm that had been holding the sword was still trying to make its way over to me. It set down the sword, pulling itself along a few feet, then reached back for the sword again before eventually it stopped moving.

I ignored it, turning back to the skeleton's torso. I began smashing at it, breaking apart the bones. Brighid's Flame let out a laugh of glee in my head, so joyous she was.

When my opponent was nothing more than a twitching pile of bones, I looked around to see how the others were faring.

Herne had bested one of the skeletons—the one with the flail—and Viktor had smashed his to pieces. Yutani, however, had blood running from a gash on his cheek. Before I could move to help him, Viktor stepped in. Between the two of them they managed to take care of the last remaining skeleton.

At that moment, before we could even catch our breath, there was a noise at the entrance I had spied. As we turned to see what was happening, Lazerous entered the room.

SOMETIMES IN LIFE, THERE ARE MOMENTS WHERE everything goes into freeze-frame, where everything seems to stop and hang on a thread. At that moment, it feels like your entire life passes before you. You see all the mistakes you've made and all the good you've done. You tally up the list of all the things you've left undone, and all the things you're grateful you've finished. It's as though the world holds its breath for a moment, stopping time long enough to give you a long-distance perspective of this existence we call life.

In that moment that Lazerous entered the room, my life rolled out before my eyes. But in the midst of taking stock, I also noticed every single nuance and every detail of our enemy.

He wasn't particularly tall, about five-seven, and he looked like a mummy that had lost its wrappings. Like one of those screaming corpses caught in the ashes of Pompeii, or perhaps by a fiery wind that had desiccated his body and hardened it into living stone.

Lazerous was dressed in a black robe, cinched at the waist with a golden sash. But the robe was threadbare in places, and through those holes, glimpses of his skin, dried to the point of leather, showed through.

His face bore no expression. The skin was stretched over the bones so tightly that I wondered if he could even move his mouth to talk. Instead of eyes, his eye sockets bore gleaming red globes, glowing from within. A thin wisp of hair was still attached to his skull, straggling down to his shoulders.

Lazerous turned toward Louhia, and everything moved again—the world sped up, and I was back in the midst of battle. There was no time to think. Only time to act.

Herne raced forward, jumping between Lazerous and Louhia, a large silver hammer in hand. He swung it at Lazerous, but Lazerous swept his hand to the side and

Herne went careening across the room, sprawling in a heap on the floor.

While Herne engaged Lazerous, Louhia held out her hands toward the liche, her voice echoing as she incanted her spell.

> *From the grave thou hath come, to the*
> *grave thou shalt go,*
> *To the past thou belong, time now shall*
> *cease its flow.*
> *I strip you of your powers, I strip you of*
> *your life,*
> *Begone thou foul creature, born of anger*
> *and of strife.*

As she spoke, the words formed into a mist in the air in the shape of an arrow. The energy flew like a bolt, slamming into Lazerous and knocking him back, sending him to the floor. I held my breath, hopeful that we would luck out and that one spell would do it. But as he rose to his feet, the light in his eyes swirled and he opened his mouth, a greenish gas flowing out like a noxious vapor.

"Poison!" Louhia stumbled back.

Herne raced toward Lazerous again, screaming for the rest of us to get out of the way.

Viktor, Yutani, and I turned to run, scrambling out of the path of the noxious green vapor that seeped through the air. Even from where we were, I could tell by the smell that it was some sort of corrosive poison, some sort of acidic cloud.

I dumped my pack onto the ground and scrambled through it to pull out a handkerchief. Quickly pouring water over it, I tied it around my face. Then I grabbed Brighid's Flame again, trying to think of what I could do that would disrupt Lazerous long enough for Louhia to cast another spell. Whether the first had even weakened him, I didn't know, though it had obviously startled him.

As Louhia prepared for another round, Herne charged Lazerous again and this time he brought his hammer down, hitting the liche in the stomach with it. Lazerous went sprawling back from the blow, looking confused as the cloud of poison gas surrounded Herne but had no effect.

Doesn't he know Herne's a god? Then it occurred to me that maybe he *didn't* know. Maybe Lazerous had gotten so used to winning that he thought he could emerge victorious out of any situation.

Yutani pulled out a pair of daggers that gleamed with pale blue light. *Ilithiniam.* He had daggers with the stuff as well as the whip! He sent them, one after another, hurtling through the air. They hit right on target, both of them striking Lazerous in the shoulders. Their impact once again knocked Lazerous back a few steps.

Lazerous turned his gaze on Yutani and held out his hand.

Yutani clutched at his throat, gurgling as though he were being strangled. He fell to his knees, clawing at his neck, trying to unseat the invisible hand that was choking him.

Viktor roared, then sucked in a deep breath before he charged forward, barreling toward the liche. Herne joined him, hammer at the ready, as I raced over to Yutani's side, trying to figure out some way to break through the enchantment.

In the background, I could hear Louhia chanting again, as she let fly yet another spell.

> *Thunder take you,*
> *Lightning break you.*
> *Ice storm freeze you,*
> *Winter seize you.*
> *By the force of Ukko,*
> *Magic shall forsake you.*

A swirl of mist rose through the cavern as the temperature plunged by a good sixty degrees. It was well below freezing and frost began to form on the ground, on the ceiling, and I could see it forming a shell around Lazarus, like a suit of ice sealing him in.

Yutani fell forward, clutching his throat but he seemed to be breathing again. Deep bruises had formed on his neck, and his breath came in ragged pants, but he waved me off.

"I'll be all right," he said hoarsely. "Go help them."

Viktor reached Lazerous at the moment that Louhia's spell hit, and he slipped on the ice that had formed on the cavern floor. He immediately dropped his weapon and folded his arms over his chest, rolling into Lazerous's legs, knocking the liche down yet once again. As the liche came up on his knees, Viktor body-slammed him, landing hard on top of him.

The poisonous cloud had dissipated, and Lazerous was still encased within the shell of ice, but I could tell that it was beginning to melt. I raced forward, clutching Brighid's Flame. If I could decapitate him, that should take care of matters.

"Ember! Get out of there!" Herne shouted, darting forward from the other side.

But I didn't want to lose the chance. Sometimes in life we're only offered one opportunity, and we either seize it or lose it.

I was determined to get as much use out of this one as I could.

Viktor was still holding Lazerous down. But as the ice vanished from Lazerous's face, he opened his mouth and breathed onto Viktor. The half-ogre rolled to the side, weeping inconsolably like a child.

"No!" I screamed. I brought Brighid's Flame up and swung as hard as I could toward Lazerous's neck. As my blade touched the hardened flesh, Louhia shouted a word in the language I didn't understand, but whatever magic she used made me twice as strong and twice as sure. The momentum of my blade increased and all doubts evaporated. I focused every drop of my will into bringing Brighid's Flame down on his bony neck.

I let out a battle cry, so loud that I could hear rocks fall in the distance.

Lazerous reached up, trying to grab for my wrist, but it was too late. I drove Brighid's Flame down, putting all my muscle into it, and cleaved through his neck. The moment his head began to fall away from his body, I let out another shriek, embracing the destruction of my enemy, reveling in the kill.

His head tumbled away from his body and I jumped to my feet, giving it a hard kick, sending it skating across the ice that still covered the chamber floor. Bringing my sword up once again, I plunged it deep into the center of Lazerous's heart, so hard that the tip of Brighid's Flame bit deep into the cavern floor, pinning the liche down like a bug in an entomologist's display case. I staggered back, the sudden surge of energy draining out of me. The next moment, I was on my knees, throwing up.

Louhia raced over to kneel by Lazerous. She grabbed the head, holding it up, and in a language I didn't recognize, she incanted yet another spell. Spiderweb veins of ice began to cover the liche's head. Then the sorceress stood, waiting until the entire skull was encased in ice.

She handed it to Herne, who set it on the floor and raised his hammer. He brought the hammer down, striking the head square center, and it shattered into a thousand pieces. I glanced over at the liche's body, and it too, shattered, as though it too were made of ice. A gust of wind passed through the chamber, catching up the shards, and the next moment it blew them away.

Lazerous was gone. But where was Talia?

CHAPTER TWENTY-ONE

*H*erne knelt beside me, but I waved him off. "I'm fine. Check on Viktor and Yutani."

With a worried nod, he moved off. Using Brighid's Flame for support, I slowly dragged myself to my feet, more spent than I had felt in months. Louhia stood near me, watching with wary eyes. I glanced over at her, surprised to see what looked like a genuine smile on her face.

"You cast a spell on me, didn't you?" I knew it hadn't been all me at the end.

She inclined her head slightly. "I wanted to make sure that you wouldn't falter at the end. The fact that he was able to reach into your mind before and play on your fears, well—I thought he might be able to do it again."

Even though it had taken every ounce of energy we had, I still wondered at the fact that we had been able to defeat him. "Did he seem weaker than he should have been to you?"

She shook her head. "A liche he may have been, and

the possessor of great power, but with extreme power comes extreme ego. That's the downfall of almost every great villain. They don't believe they can be defeated, and they let down their guard. Never underestimate your enemies. That's the first great rule that all conquerors should learn and live by."

"Lazerous let down his guard?"

"He let down his guard when he allowed us into his lair. My guess is he was aiming for my energy. He wanted to add it to his collection. So he allowed us closer than was advisable. If he had killed you before you reached the cavern, I would have run and he knew it. No, he had to take a risk if he wanted to drain me. This time, he made a mistake."

I turned, glancing over at Herne and the men. Yutani's throat was coloring into a deep purple, but he seemed all right, though he probably hurt like hell. Viktor had stopped crying.

"What did he do to Viktor?"

"Played on his fears. Whatever the half-ogre was crying about, it was a wound that he probably hides on a daily basis. We should look for your friend. I'd like to get out of here as soon as possible."

"Is there any chance Lazerous could return? I mean, we destroyed his body. What about his spirit?" It chilled me to think that perhaps he might stick around, perhaps join forces with the other spirits in the area.

Louhia shrugged. "I don't know. He can't take form again, at least not in any way I know of. Whether he remains to haunt this area, however, is a problem for the dwarves who own the land. It's none of my concern."

Herne, Yutani, and Viktor joined us.

"Do you think Talia is in the other chamber?" I asked, dreading what we might find when we went through the door.

"I'll look," Herne said. "Better I should check first, considering what we may be facing." With a somber look on his face, he headed toward the door into the next chamber.

I reached out for Yutani's hand, and then took Viktor's with my other. We stood there, praying for good news.

A few moments later, Herne peeked around the corner. "She's not in here. But I found Branson, I believe, and several other bodies. Some of them don't look like students, so I have a feeling Lazerous has been preying on anybody he could find who met his needs. It's a charnel house in here. I'm going to call Akron to get his crew out here and clean up. They should hopefully be able to supply us with a list of names. Or at least descriptions."

Akron was a raven shifter—a priest of the Morrigan. He cleaned up after crime scenes for Herne and the Wild Hunt.

As Herne motioned for us to head outside, I wondered where Talia could be. If she wasn't in Lazerous's lair, then where the hell was she? And that brought another thought to mind.

"What does he have in there? Anything we could use? He's lived a long time, so he must have quite a stash of treasure and…well… Things he's gathered off of his victims."

"There was a good amount of loot in there. Akron will catalog it and bring me the list." Herne led us out of the mine shaft, into the clearing.

"Won't it be dangerous for Akron to go in there, given the shaky nature of the mine shaft?" Viktor asked.

"Akron's used to danger. Besides, he'll be able to take precautions. And I'm *not* leaving anything in there for the dwarves. They're too greedy for their own good at times. They can scream all they want to, but that's my final say on that."

George peeked out of the forest. "Did you…"

"Yes, we killed him. Come in." Herne waved for him to join us.

As George rejoined our party, I looked around. If I were Talia, where would I be? She had come searching for Lazerous, but as far as we could tell she hadn't found him.

I turned to Louhia. "Do you have some sort of location spell? And if you do, would you be willing to cast it for us?"

She let out an exasperated sigh. "Do you have anything of hers? Anything she's touched?"

"There are plenty of things back in her car." I looked at the others. "Did you bring anything out of her car, by any chance? Like her purse?"

Herne was staring at Louhia. He ignored my question, saying, "You didn't tell us you could do that. Why didn't you cast a location spell in the first place? I mean, yes, we had to defeat Lazerous, but wouldn't it have been easier to see if we could pinpoint Talia before we came out here?"

Louhia laughed. "You didn't ask, *oh mighty* Lord of the Hunt."

Though he looked ready to smack her, Herne restrained himself. He pulled a wallet out of his pack. "I brought her wallet, because her ID and all her credentials are in there and I didn't want anybody stealing it." He handed it over to Louhia.

She took the wallet and walked away from us to the side of the clearing, where she closed her eyes. A few moments later, she returned.

"The trail that we came through? She's along there somewhere, in the woods. I can't pinpoint her exactly, but there is life still, so she's not dead."

I glanced up at the sky. Dawn would be arriving within an hour or two, and a sudden weariness crept over me. I felt so tired I could barely move. In fact, I felt more tired than I had after retrieving Chaz's soul.

"I'm exhausted. Let's get a move on. I don't know how much longer I can stay on my feet. The adrenaline rush has worn off and I'm ready to drop." I stifled a yawn.

"All right, here's what we're going to do. Louhia, you and Ember wait here for Akron. If he shows up before we get back, Ember, tell him what he needs to do. Standard procedure, confiscate and log everything that's in there. Identify the bodies as best as he can, get me the information by tomorrow morning. And tell him to be careful, that mine shaft isn't all that stable. Meanwhile, George, you can help Viktor, Yutani, and me search for Talia. You're a scout, you should be of great help." Herne motioned to the three men and they all headed off into the woods again.

I walked over to a log as far away from the entrance to the mine shaft as I could find, and dropped down on it. I was exhausted, and I didn't care what Louhia thought.

She settled herself on the log next to me. After a moment, she said, "I know you don't like me, and I don't really care."

I gave her a weary look. "I don't know whether I don't like you, or whether I just don't trust you. I can still like someone I don't trust, I just never give them a chance to screw me over." I was too tired to be diplomatic.

"That's actually a very wise stance to take. This Talia. She means a great deal to all of you, doesn't she? You put your lives on the line to find her." She sounded almost confused.

I shrugged. "She's a friend. A good one. And she already had her life destroyed by Lazerous once. We weren't about to stand by and see it happen again."

"In my land, close friends are worth more than gold. I learned to rely on myself the hard way. I worked my way up in the court, and I've made myself as irreplaceable as possible. That's one way to ensure longevity. But I don't trust the queen. And I don't trust the gods."

I looked at her then, woman to woman. Beyond the sarcasm and arrogance, I saw a great weariness that tired me even further. And a life that seemed incredibly painful.

"Isn't it hard, living that way? Never letting your vulnerability show?"

"It's better than dying. Pohjola is a harsh land. Weakness will get you killed, and so will vulnerability. You learn to build walls. To build a fortress around you." She glanced up as a spatter of rain began to fall. "This land, your realm...it may have its problems, but you are blessed in many ways."

I pressed my lips together, thinking over her words. After a moment, I asked, "Why don't you move to—what is it? *Tapiola*? Mielikki's world? Or Finland?"

Louhia gave me a speculative look, then shook her head with a soft laugh. "Oh, Mielikki would never allow me in her land. I'm too intractable and I know it. As for moving into your realm, into Finland? I'm afraid I've lived too long in the lands of snow and ice. My light is the midnight sun. My first breath in the morning is a breath so cold it freezes your lungs. I file my nails on the shards of shattered dreams. No, whatever remains of my life—and I hope the end is far away—I will live serving my queen. I have given Loviatar my word. My heart is made of ice, but my oaths stand strong as the roots of the world itself."

I wasn't sure what to say. I didn't even think she wanted a response. But for some reason, her words made me like her a little bit better. She was honest. She didn't try to sugarcoat who she was, and I appreciated that.

"Do you have the Fae in your realm? In Pohjola?"

"Some. There are far more in Tapiola, under Mielikki's rule. You would fit in there, you know. Both sides of your nature would find a home there, if you ever should need it. Remember that, just in case the day comes when you need somewhere to hide. With what's coming into your realm, that day may be closer than you like."

"Are you talking about…" I wasn't sure just how much she knew about Typhon. But she answered for me.

"Typhon? The father of dragons? You are not the only ones who know about him. He is ancient beyond time. Even now the gods gather together, trying to smooth out their differences so they can align their forces against him. You see, he is one of the ancient pillars of the world. He and his kind go beyond the gods. Just as Gaia is the spirit of earth, Typhon is an elemental spirit conjured from the prime forces of fire, and his realm is that of death. He is bound to your world, where he is not bound to most others."

Her words were stark and harsh, but I knew in my heart she was right.

Before I could say anything, I yawned, so tired I could barely manage to stay awake. She must have seen this, because she held out her arm.

"Lean against my shoulder and rest. I will keep you safe."

I blinked, realizing that she had just probably made the most gracious gesture she had in years, and she was absolutely sincere about it. That much I *could* tell.

"I'm just so tired," I said, the weariness growing stronger. She enclosed me in her embrace, pulling me close to her, and I rested my head on her shoulder, for just a moment. She smelled like ozone and fresh snow, like the amazing clarity the air gets after a snowstorm. Before I could help myself, I closed my eyes and fell asleep.

SHOUTS FROM THE WOODS WOKE ME UP. I STARTED, wondering what the hell I was doing until I realized that I was still snuggled in the crook of Louhia's arm. She pulled away as I straightened up and yawned. I wondered how much time had gone by, and noticed that dawn was peeking through the clouds. At least a couple hours had passed. As we stood, I let out a little groan and arched my back, feeling stiff from the night.

They stumbled in from the undergrowth, Viktor carrying Talia. She was moaning, her head lolling against his shoulder. They had cut the legs off her jeans from the knee down, and her left ankle looked swollen to three times its normal size.

I started forward, terrified to ask what was running through my mind.

Herne glanced at me and shook his head. "Lazerous didn't find her. She never even made it here. She got lost in the woods, and stepped in a hole. Her ankle's broken, and she's suffering from minor hypothermia, although luckily she's not human. If she was, she might have died." He glanced around the clearing. "Any problems while we were gone?"

Louhia answered for me. "Everything's fine," she said. "We just sat and talked for a while."

Herne arched his eyebrows, but said nothing. "We need to get Talia back to town and to the hospital."

I knelt by her side as Yutani attended to her ankle. She was wearing Viktor's coat around her shoulders, and she glanced up at me, a sheepish look on her face.

"I'm so sorry that I worried you. I was just terrified that you would get hurt trying to help me. That's why I came out here on my own. I don't know what I was thinking. I guess…" She trailed off, staring at her hands, which were on her lap. "I guess I didn't think."

His hands on his hips, Herne loomed over her. "No, you didn't. What you did was stupid and you put everyone in danger. But most of all, it hurts me that you didn't trust *me*. That you didn't come to me and tell me your fears. We would have talked this through. You're one of my oldest friends, but I swear, if you pull a stunt like this again, I'm going to turn you over to my mother."

"Do you have to yell at her like that? She's hurt and scared," I said breaking in.

"Of course I do. I'd yell at you, too. Or Viktor, or Yutani." As he finished ranting, I caught the fear in his eyes and realized how afraid he had been. I backed off.

"All right, where's the fire?" a voice said from the opposite side of the clearing. As we turned, we saw Akron and his crew breaking through the undergrowth.

"In there," Herne said, pointing. "The mine shaft's not stable, so be careful. And make sure you catalog everything that's in there and bring me the list so I can figure out what to do with it. If any dwarves come around and give you lip, tell them to talk to me."

Akron, a tall, pale man with jet-black hair, nodded. "Got it. All right, get out of the way so we can get busy. I'll talk to you tomorrow." And just like that, he waved us away.

Herne glanced at me, grinning. "It seems we've been dismissed. Come on, Viktor, you carry Talia. Let's get out of here. I don't think I ever want to see this place again." Draping his arm around my shoulder, he paused. "You're tired, aren't you?"

I nodded. "I dread thinking of the walk back to the car."

"That's not a problem. I can carry the three women."

Herne moved to the side, and the air shimmered as he transformed into a great silver stag. Unlike most shifters, the gods didn't have to remove their clothes when they changed shape.

Herne knelt, and I climbed aboard his back. Viktor set Talia in front of me so that I could hold her around the waist. She moaned as her swollen ankle dangled down, but it would be quicker this way. Louhia skeptically allowed Viktor to help her straddle the massive stag behind me. She held onto my waist.

When we were set, Herne rose to his feet and then—without so much as a jostle—he began to race through the woodlands, heading back toward our campsite. He was faster than any stag of the forest, and the ride was smooth and comfortable, the wind streaming past us, blowing through our hair.

I breathed a sigh of relief. As soon as the men joined us, we'd be out of here, on the way home. And the best part? There was one fewer danger in the world.

CHAPTER TWENTY-TWO

*O*ne week later...

We were all gathered around the fire in Herne's living room, including Raven and Rafé. Talia's crutches were near the sofa and her foot was propped up on an ottoman, the cast already covered with doodles and artwork. Angel and I carried in large bowls of chips and popcorn, and the champagne was flowing. Danielle jumped up to help us as we brought in the food, looking far less sullen than the first time I had met her.

"I want to propose a toast," Herne said, raising his glass. "We not only defeated Lazerous, but I also have full custody of my daughter until she comes of age. Which won't be that long," he added, beaming at Danielle.

As I watched her return his smile, I couldn't help but notice the resemblance between them.

The Triamvinate had ruled unanimously in Herne's favor, decreeing that as long as she kept company with Thantos, Myrna was to have no visitation with her daughter. And Myrna had chosen Thantos over Danielle, telling Herne that she washed her hands of both of them. It made me incredibly sad to see a mother turn her back on her child, but Danielle snapped back quickly. She'd be returning to the island of the Amazons in another week to continue her training.

As everybody chatted—the chief topic being the fight against Lazerous—I walked over to the window and gazed out into the rain. It was warmer tonight, and the leaves were starting to open on the branches now. Nature was like that. One moment, the branches were bare, and the next moment, they burgeoned out with life and the world was young again.

"Mind if I join you?" Raven asked.

I shook my head. "I don't mind. How are you doing? How's Rafé?"

"He's agreed to see a counselor. Ferosyn has found someone who can help him. I think it'll work out. I just hope that Angel has the patience to wait for him. He truly wants to try to get over the shock."

"Torture can take a harsh toll on the victim." I stared into my champagne flute.

"You have to understand something about Rafé," Raven said, pressing her nose against the windowpane. "When he lost Ulstair, he lost more than he ever thought he had. Ulstair and I were together for what—almost fifty years? We were just starting to get comfortable with the idea of commitment. And honestly, as much as I loved him, it never felt truly right. It never felt *easy*, like it does with Kipa. But Ulstair was Rafé's *brother*. They were the only two in the family who understood each other. I think that losing Ulstair was actually more of the problem than the torture. Whatever the case, the counselor will help him work through it."

I glanced over at the sofa to see Angel sitting in Rafé's lap. They were smiling, with his arm around her waist. "I guess he's told her."

"So, what's on *your* mind?" Raven asked. "Something's bothering you. I can tell."

I bit my lip, then shrugged. "I'm just thinking about the future. I'm thinking about Typhon, and what he's going to do to the world. Louhia told me that I'd feel at home in Mielikki's world. She said that someday I may have to find a place to hide, if things get bad."

"That's good to know, I guess."

"Yeah, I suppose. But…I never thought that things might actually come to that. I mean, I've known for a couple months now that Typhon's going to bring massive chaos to the world. And all we can do is clean up the fallout. Take care of the collateral damage, I guess. It's the gods who are going to have to fight against him, and we have to put our trust in them. But…it's starting to hit home. Life's going to change. Even if it doesn't seem like it on the surface, we'll see the changes happening and have to face them."

"It's the lack of control that's bothering you," Raven said. "I know, because I feel the same way. My mother volunteered me to help with this, so I don't really have a choice. When your mother is one of the Bean Sidhe, you can't just walk away when she says jump."

"I guess not. Just like if we're assigned a case, we can't just say we don't want to do it."

Raven paused, then said, "It's already starting, you know. I can feel the spirits. They're more active lately. I'm afraid that we're standing at the tip of the iceberg." She folded her arms across her chest, shaking her head.

I thought about what she said. "You're right, I think. I've just gotten used to being on the front lines. And I'm getting used to being in a relationship with a god. Then I find out he has a daughter, so I'm kind of a surrogate stepmother, possible enemy all rolled into one. And then, I discover that I have a great-uncle who actually wants to be a part of my life. After years of avoiding my blood kin, I have to face what it means to...to have someone in my life that I didn't choose to be there. The last year has brought so much change that I'm feeling overwhelmed."

Raven clapped me on the shoulder. "There's something else. Something else that's bothering you, more than all of this. What is going on? Are you having second thoughts about Herne?"

I shook my head. "No, not at all. I love him more than I thought I could ever love anybody, even though that scares me." I paused. "Come with me in the kitchen for a moment."

Raven followed me into the kitchen, stopping by Kipa's chair beforehand to give him a quick kiss. He had just returned from Finland again and seemed pleased as punch at being able to visit Mielikki's Arrow again without worrying that Tapio was going to kill him.

Once we were in the kitchen, out of earshot, I turned to Raven.

"Promise me you won't say anything to Angel?"

She nodded, her eyes wide. "What's up?"

"All I can think about is...since the Cruharach, I've pretty much stopped aging. And now, I realize that in what...fifty? Sixty years if we're lucky? I'll lose her. I'm going to be just about the same as I am now. And she'll grow old and die."

I burst into tears. "I can't let that happen, Raven. I can't lose my best friend. She means more to me than anybody in the world. I can't handle the thought that someday she's going to die and leave my life, and that a thousand years in the future, I'll be sitting here…and maybe I'll remember her and maybe I won't. Her little brother will outlive her too because he's part shifter. There *has* to be a way to extend her life. There has to be a way to give her…"

Raven shook her head, a wary look in her eyes. "No one's immortal, Ember. Not you, not me. The gods, yes, but no one else. Promise me that you won't do anything until you think this through. There are spells out there that can help—and potions, but they're rare and some of them can be incredibly dangerous. Just promise me that you won't go off half cocked and do something you'll regret. Or that *Angel* will regret."

She reached out and took my hands, gazing into my eyes.

I found it hard to look away. The Ante-Fae were magnetic in a way that the Fae could never be. This woman was from the line that engendered my species, and her heritage was old as the earth. And yet, we were in this together.

I hesitated, then finally exhaled and nodded. "I promise. I won't do anything right now. We have some time. But I have to figure out a way… I can't sit around and just do nothing."

"I understand. But for today, try to enjoy the present. Stop being afraid of the future."

"There's a lot to fear," I said bleakly.

"Any one of us can find ourselves the target of a serial killer. My fiancé did. Or we might step into the street and get hit by a driver who turns the corner too fast. Against all odds, people get struck by lightning every year. A sinkhole could appear, an earthquake could take down the city. We can't control death. I should know, I work with it daily. It's part of my blood, it's part of my nature." Raven bit her lip, blinking away tears. "One of the hardest things I've had to learn as a bone witch is that I can't control the end result. All we can do is to prepare for the inevitable, but once that's done, we have to go out and *live* our lives." She kept hold of my hands, squeezing tightly. "Does any of this make any sense?"

I took a deep breath, hanging my head. "Honestly? It makes all the sense in the world. I guess almost losing Talia made my fear of losing Angel even worse. And watching Chaz lose the support of his family, well, it made me think about how Angel is the sister I never had. I can't imagine losing her. I'll be careful, though. I promise. I won't do anything before I talk to you and Herne, and Angel, of course."

"Then let's get back to the party. Because Typhon's out there, and he's waking up, and we need to celebrate every moment we can, because soon, the world's going to be a whole lot scarier."

As Raven walked me back to the living room, I thought about what she said.

She was right. There was so very little that we maintained control over in life, and what control we *did* have was a thin veneer, most of it lies we told ourselves at night for comfort. The universe was very big, and we were all just small souls, living on a ball of rock in the backend of a mediocre galaxy. All we had were the bonds we forged with those we considered family.

And we *did* need to celebrate every victory, every joy that came our way, because the odds were usually stacked against us. For everyone but the gods, life was a no-win scenario. No one escaped death, not even Lazerous. In the end, it would claim all of us.

But until that day—for however long we had on this planet—it was vital that we kept fighting for what was right, and that we celebrated the milestones of our lives with friends and family and loved ones. Because at the very end, only that love would carry us through. And at the very end, our memories were all we had to mark our time here.

IF YOU ENJOYED THIS BOOK AND HAVEN'T READ THE FIRST nine books of The Wild Hunt Series, check out THE SILVER STAG, OAK & THORNS, IRON BONES, A SHADOW OF CROWS, THE HALLOWED HUNT, THE SILVER MIST, WITCHING HOUR, WITCHING BONES, and A SACRED MAGIC. Book 11—SUN BROKEN—is available for preorder now. There will be more to come after that.

Return with me to Whisper Hollow, where spirits walk among the living, and the lake never gives up her dead. AUTUMN THORNS and SHADOW SILENCE return in January, along with a new book—THE PHANTOM QUEEN! Come join the darkly seductive world of Kerris Fellwater, spirit shaman for the small lakeside community of Whisper Hollow.

If you prefer a lighter-hearted paranormal romance, meet the wild and magical residents of Bedlam in my Bewitching Bedlam Series. Fun-loving witch Maddy Gallowglass, her smoking-hot vampire lover Aegis, and their crazed cjinn Bubba (part djinn, all cat) rock it out in Bedlam, a magical town on a mystical island. BEWITCHING BEDLAM, MAUDLIN'S MAYHEM, SIREN'S SONG, WITCHES WILD, CASTING CURSES, BEDLAM CALLING: A BEWITCHING BEDLAM ANTHOLOGY, BLOOD MUSIC, BLOOD VENGEANCE, TIGER TAILS, and Bubba's origin story— THE WISH FACTOR—are available. Book six— DEMON'S DELIGHT—is coming in February!

I invite you to visit Fury's world. Bound to Hecate, Fury is a minor goddess, taking care of the Abominations who come off the World Tree. Books 1-5 are available now in the Fury Unbound Series : FURY RISING, FURY'S MAGIC, FURY AWAKENED, FURY CALLING, and FURY'S MANTLE.

For a dark, gritty, steamy series, try my world of The Indigo Court , where the long winter has come, and the Vampiric Fae are on the rise. The series is complete with NIGHT MYST, NIGHT VEIL, NIGHT SEEKER, NIGHT VISION, NIGHT'S END, and NIGHT SHIVERS.

If you like cozies with teeth, try my Chintz 'n China paranormal mysteries. The series is complete with: GHOST OF A CHANCE, LEGEND OF THE JADE DRAGON, MURDER UNDER A MYSTIC MOON, A HARVEST OF BONES, ONE HEX OF A WEDDING, and a wrap-up novella: HOLIDAY SPIRITS.

The last Otherworld book—BLOOD BONDS—is available now.

For all of my work, both published and upcoming releases, see the Biography at the end of this book, or check out my website at Galenorn.com and be sure and sign up for my newsletter to receive news about all my new releases.

CAST OF CHARACTERS

The Wild Hunt & Family:

- **Angel Jackson:** Ember's best friend, a human empath, Angel is the newest member of the Wild Hunt. A whiz in both the office and the kitchen, and loyal to the core, Angel is an integral part of Ember's life, and a vital member of the team.
- **Charlie Darren:** A vampire who was turned at 19. Math major, baker, and all-around gofer.
- **Ember Kearney:** Caught between the world of Light and Dark Fae, and pledged to Morgana, goddess of the Fae and the Sea, Ember Kearney was born with the mark of the Silver Stag. Rejected by both her bloodlines, she now works for the Wild Hunt as an investigator.
- **Herne the Hunter:** Herne is the son of the Lord of the Hunt, Cernunnos, and Morgana, goddess of the Fae and the Sea. A demigod—given his

mother's mortal beginnings—he's a lusty, protective god and one hell of a good boss. Owner of the Wild Hunt Agency, he helps keep the squabbles between the world of Light and Dark Fae from spilling over into the mortal realms.

- **Talia:** A harpy who long ago lost her powers, Talia is a top-notch researcher for the agency, and a longtime friend of Herne's.
- **Viktor:** Viktor is half-ogre, half-human. Rejected by his father's people (the ogres), he came to work for Herne some decades back.
- **Yutani:** A coyote shifter who is dogged by the Great Coyote, Yutani was driven out of his village over two hundred years before. He walks in the shadow of the trickster, and is the IT specialist for the company.

Ember's Friends, Family, & Enemies:

- **Aoife:** A priestess of Morgana who guards the Seattle portal to the goddess's realm.
- **Celia:** Yutani's aunt.
- **Danielle:** Herne's daughter, born to an Amazon named Myrna.
- **DJ Jackson:** Angel's little half-brother, DJ is half Wulfine—wolf shifter. He now lives with a foster family for his own protection.
- **Erica:** A Dark Fae police officer, friend of Viktor's.
- **Elatha:** Fomorian King; enemy of the Fae race.

- **George Shipman:** Puma shifter. Member of the White Peak Puma Shifter Pride.
- **Ginty McClintlock:** A dwarf. Owner of Ginty's Waystation Bar & Grill.
- **Louhia:** Witch of Pohjola.
- **Marilee:** A priestess of Morgana, Ember's mentor. Possibly human—unknown.
- **Myrna:** An Amazon who had a fling with Herne many years back, which resulted in their daughter Danielle.
- **Rafé Forrester:** Brother to Ulstair, Raven's late fiancé; Angel's boyfriend. Actor/fast-food worker. Dark Fae.
- **Sheila:** Viktor's girlfriend. A kitchen witch; one of the magic-born. Geology teacher who volunteers at the Chapel Hill Homeless Shelter.
- **Unkai:** Leader of the Orhanakai clan in the forest of Y'Bain. Dark Fae—Autumn's Bane.

Raven & the Ante-Fae:

The Ante-Fae are creatures predating the Fae. They are the wellspring from which all Fae descended, unique beings who rule their own realms. All Ante-Fae are dangerous, but some are more deadly than others.

- **Apollo:** The Golden Boy. Vixen's boytoy. Weaver of Wings. Dancer.
- **Arachana:** The Spider Queen. She has almost transformed into one of the Luo'henkah.
- **Blackthorn, the King of Thorns:** Ruler of the blackthorn trees and all thorn-bearing plants. Cunning and wily, he feeds on pain and desire.

- **Curikan, the Black Dog of Hanging Hills:** Raven's father, one of the infamous black dogs. The first time someone meets him, they find good fortune. If they should ever see him again, they meet tragedy.
- **Phasmoria:** Queen of the Bean Sidhe. Raven's mother.
- **Raven, the Daughter of Bones:** (also: Raven BoneTalker) A bone witch, Raven is young, as far as the Ante-Fae go, and she works with the dead. She's also a fortune-teller, and a necromancer.
- **Straff:** Blackthorn's son, who suffers from a wasting disease requiring him to feed off others' life energies and blood.
- **Vixen:** The Mistress/Master of Mayhem. Gender-fluid Ante-Fae who owns the Burlesque A Go-Go nightclub.
- **The Vulture Sisters:** Triplet sisters, predatory.

Raven's Friends:

- **Elise, Gordon, and Templeton:** Raven's ferret-bound spirit friends she rescued years ago and now protects until she can find out the secret to breaking the curse on them.
- **Gunnar:** One of Kipa's SuVahta Elitvartijat—elite guards.
- **Jordan Roberts:** Tiger shifter. Llewellyn's husband. Owns *A Taste of Latte* coffee shop.
- **Llewellyn Roberts:** One of the magic-born, owns the *Sun & Moon Apothecary*.

- **Moira Ness:** Human. One of Raven's regular clients for readings.
- **Neil Johansson:** One of the magic-born. A priest of Thor.
- **Raj:** Gargoyle companion of Raven. Wing-clipped, he's been with Raven for a number of years.
- **Wager Chance:** Half-Dark Fae, half-human PI. Owns a PI firm found in the Catacombs. Has connections with the vampires.
- **Wendy Fierce-Womyn:** An Amazon who works at Ginty's Waystation Bar & Grill.

The Gods, the Luo'henkah, the Elemental Spirits, & Their Courts:

- **Arawn:** Lord of the Dead. Lord of the Underworld.
- **Brighid:** Goddess of Healing, Inspiration, and Smithery. The Lady of the Fiery Arrows, "Exalted One."
- **The Cailleach:** One of the Luo'henkah, the heart and spirit of winter.
- **Cerridwen:** Goddess of the Cauldron of Rebirth. Dark harvest mother goddess.
- **Cernunnos:** Lord of the Hunt, god of the Forest, and King Stag of the Woods. Together with Morgana, Cernunnos originated the Wild Hunt and negotiated the covenant treaty with both the Light and the Dark Fae. Herne's father.
- **Corra:** Ancient Scottish serpent goddess. Oracle to the gods.

- **Coyote, also: Great Coyote:** Native American trickster spirit/god.
- **Danu:** Mother of the Pantheon. Leader of the Tuatha de Dannan.
- **Ferosyn:** Chief healer in Cernunnos's Court.
- **Herne:** (see The Wild Hunt)
- **Isella:** One of the Luo'henkah. The Daughter of Ice (daughter of the Cailleach).
- **Kuippana (also: Kipa):** Lord of the Wolves. Elemental forest spirit; Herne's distant cousin. Trickster. Leader of the SuVahta, a group of divine elemental wolf shifters.
- **Lugh the Long Handed:** Celtic Lord of the Sun.
- **Mielikki:** Lady of Tapiola. Finnish Goddess of the Hunt and the Fae. Mother of the Bear, Mother of Bees, Queen of the Forest.
- **Morgana:** Goddess of the Fae and the Sea, she was originally human but Cernunnos lifted her to deityhood. She agreed to watch over the Fae who did not return across the Great Sea. Torn by her loyalty to her people and her loyalty to Cernunnos, she at times finds herself conflicted about the Wild Hunt. Herne's mother.
- **The Morrígan:** Goddess of Death and Phantoms. Goddess of the battlefield.
- **Tapio:** Lord of Tapiola. Mielikki's Consort. Lord of the Woodlands. Master of Game.

The Fae Courts:

- **Navane:** The court of the Light Fae, both across

the Great Sea and on the eastside of Seattle, the latter ruled by **Névé**.

- **TirNaNog:** The court of the Dark Fae, both across the Great Sea and on the eastside of Seattle, the latter ruled by **Saílle**.

The Force Majeure:

A group of legendary magicians, sorcerers, and witches. They are not human, but magic-born. There are twenty-one at any given time and the only way into the group is to be hand chosen, and the only exit from the group is death.

- **Merlin, The:** Morgana's father. Magician of ancient Celtic fame.
- **Taliesin:** The first Celtic bard. Son of Cerridwen, originally a servant who underwent magical transformation and finally was reborn through Cerridwen as the first bard.
- **Ranna:** Powerful sorceress. Elatha's mistress.
- **Rasputin:** The Russian sorcerer and mystic.
- **Väinämöinen:** The most famous Finnish bard.

TIMELINE OF SERIES

Year 1:

- May/Beltane: **The Silver Stag** (Ember)
- June/Litha: **Oak & Thorns** (Ember)
- August/Lughnasadh: **Iron Bones** (Ember)
- September/Mabon: **A Shadow of Crows** (Ember)
- Mid-October: **Witching Hour** (Raven)
- Late October/Samhain: **The Hallowed Hunt** (Ember)
- December/Yule: **The Silver Mist** (Ember)

Year 2:

- January: **Witching Bones** (Raven)
- Late January–February/Imbolc: **A Sacred Magic** (Ember)
- March/Ostara: **The Eternal Return** (Ember)

PLAYLIST

I often write to music, and THE ETERNAL RETURN was no exception. Here's the playlist I used for this book. You'll notice I've taken a definite turn in my listening for writing.

- **Air:** Moon Fever; Surfing on a Rocket
- **Airstream:** Electra (Religion Cut)
- **Android Lust:** Here and Now
- **Arcade Fire:** Abraham's Daughter
- **Brandon & Dereck Fiechter:** Night Fairies; Troll Bridge; Will-O'-Wisps; Black Wolf's Inn; Naiad River; Mushroom Woods
- **Chip Davis:** Walking in Straw Grass; The Crow Knows; Harvest Dance
- **Colin Foulke:** Emergence
- **Danny Cudd:** Double D; Remind; Once Again (2011); Timelessly Free; To The Mirage
- **Dizzi:** Dizzi Jig; Dance of the Unicorns; Galloping Horse

- **DJ Shah:** Mellomaniac
- **Eastern Sun:** Beautiful Being (Original Edit)
- **Faun:** Hymn to Pan; Punagra; Sieben
- **The Hang Drum Project:** Shaken Oak; St. Chartier
- **Hang Massive:** Omat Odat; Released Upon Inception; Thingless Things; Boat Ride; Transition to Dreams; End of Sky; Warmth of the Sun's Rays; Luminous Emptiness
- **Hedningarna:** Ukkonen; Gorrlaus
- **J Rokka:** Marine Migration
- **Mannheim Steamroller:** Chocolate Fudge; Saras Band; Mist; G Major Toccata; Crystal; Interlude 7; Dancing Flames; Embers; The First Door; The Second Door; The Third Door; The Sixth Door; The Sky; Midnight on a Full Moon; Lumen; Dancin' in the Stars; Z-row Gravity
- **Many Rivers Ensemble:** Blood Moon; Oasis; Upwelling; Emergence
- **Marconi Union:** First Light; Alone Together; Flying (In Crimson Skies); Always Numb; Time Lapse; On Reflection; Broken Colours; We Travel; Weightless; Weightless, Pt 2; Weightless, Pt 3; Weightless, Pt 4; Weightless, Pt 5; Weightless, Pt 6
- **Mythos:** Surrender; Andalucia; Icarus
- **Rue de Soleil:** We Can Fly; Le Francaise; Wake Up Brother; Blues Du Soleil
- **Tamaryn:** While You're Sleeping, I'm Dreaming; Violet's in a Pool
- **Tingstand & Rumbel:** Chaco

- **Tuatha Dea:** Tuatha De Danaan
- **Wendy Rule:** Let the Wind Blow

BIOGRAPHY

New York Times, Publishers Weekly, and USA Today bestselling author Yasmine Galenorn writes urban fantasy and paranormal romance, and is the author of more than sixty-five books, including the Wild Hunt Series, the Fury Unbound Series, the Bewitching Bedlam Series, the Indigo Court Series, and the Otherworld Series, among others. She's also written nonfiction metaphysical books. She is the 2011 Career Achievement Award Winner in Urban Fantasy, given by RT Magazine.

Yasmine has been in the Craft since 1980, is a shamanic witch and High Priestess. She describes her life as a blend of teacups and tattoos. She lives in Kirkland, WA, with her husband Samwise and their cats. Yasmine can be reached via her website at Galenorn.com.

Indie Releases Currently Available:

The Wild Hunt Series:
The Silver Stag

Oak & Thorns
Iron Bones
A Shadow of Crows
The Hallowed Hunt
The Silver Mist
Witching Hour
Witching Bones
A Sacred Magic
The Eternal Return
Sun Broken

Whisper Hollow Series:

Autumn Thorns
Shadow Silence
The Phantom Queen

Bewitching Bedlam Series:

Bewitching Bedlam
Maudlin's Mayhem
Siren's Song
Witches Wild
Casting Curses
Demon's Delight
Bedlam Calling: A Bewitching Bedlam Anthology
The Wish Factor (a prequel short story)
Blood Music (a prequel novella)
Blood Vengeance (a Bewitching Bedlam novella)
Tiger Tails (a Bewitching Bedlam novella)

Fury Unbound Series:

Fury Rising
Fury's Magic

Fury Awakened
Fury Calling
Fury's Mantle

Indigo Court Series:

Night Myst
Night Veil
Night Seeker
Night Vision
Night's End
Night Shivers
Indigo Court Books, 1-3: Night Myst, Night Veil,
Night Seeker (Boxed Set)
Indigo Court Books, 4-6: Night Vision, Night's End,
Night Shivers (Boxed Set)

Otherworld Series:

Moon Shimmers
Harvest Song
Blood Bonds
Otherworld Tales: Volume 1
Otherworld Tales: Volume 2
For the rest of the Otherworld Series, see website at
Galenorn.com.

Chintz 'n China Series:

Ghost of a Chance
Legend of the Jade Dragon
Murder Under a Mystic Moon
A Harvest of Bones
One Hex of a Wedding
Holiday Spirits

Chintz 'n China Books, 1 – 3: Ghost of a Chance, Legend of the Jade Dragon, Murder Under A Mystic Moon

Chintz 'n China Books, 4-6: A Harvest of Bones, One Hex of a Wedding, Holiday Spirits

Bath and Body Series (originally under the name India Ink):
Scent to Her Grave
A Blush With Death
Glossed and Found

Misc. Short Stories/Anthologies:
Once Upon a Kiss (short story: Princess Charming)
Once Upon a Curse (short story: Bones)

Magickal Nonfiction:
Embracing the Moon
Tarot Journeys

CPSIA information can be obtained
at www.ICGtesting.com
Printed in the USA
LVHW012149070120
642793LV00005B/675